To Harry

Teppi:

The Blue Bears Race

Off to Jurby

Diane Batty

Happy Reading

Diane B

Illustrated by Peter Mylchreest

The Blue Bears Race Off to Jurby

Diane Batty

Illustrated by Peter Mylchreest

The Blue Bears Race

Off to Jurby

© Diane Batty

Diane Batty has asserted her rights in accordance with the
Copyright, Designs & and Patents Act 1988 to be
identified to be the author of this work.

Published by:
Wibble Publishing

British Columbia, Canada

Email: info@wibblepublishing.com
Web: www.wibblepublishing.com

First published 2013

Legal Deposit: Library and Archives Canada, Ottawa, Ontario, Canada.

13-digit ISBN: 978-0-9919266-5-7

Printed in Great Britain

DEDICATION

To the kids,
for their inspiring conversations.

TEPPI RUNS AWAY

There was a huge crash. Poppy jumped out of bed and ran into the hallway. Teppi and Tunis were sitting on the floor amongst a pile of cereals. The two little bears crunched at every move and they laughed at each other as they tried to get up.

"What's going on?" A gruff voice made them dive for cover. Poppy hid behind the door post.

"Nothing much," Teppi squeaked, then held his breath. Bigpuss put his head out of the room at the bottom of the stairs. He was quickly followed by Curly.

"Oh no! Look at the mess you two!" Curly said sharply. "You will have to clean it up." The bears nodded, trying not to laugh. "Come on!" Curly said, trying not to laugh too. "What were you trying to do? That was, Bigpuss' breakfast. What is he going to eat now?"

"We were practising," Teppi announced proudly, "…for the TT."

"Oh, not that again, you've got your sidecar thing for that… and not in the house either," Curly explained.

"We couldn't get it around the corner at the bottom of the stairs. It broke, then the cereals spilled out. We used a cereal box for our sidecar last time, so we thought we could use one to practice in!"

"Well it didn't." Bigpuss said from behind Curly. "I am sure that the other one didn't have the cereals still in it!" He gave them a stern look and went into the kitchen.

Teppi and Tunis were two little blue bears who have just moved in to Curly Towers, a big house on the Isle of Man. They used to live in an empty kipper box in a local park before they met Poppy. He is a little blue bear from the Island of Crete. He lives with Bigpuss and Curly too. Teppi and Tunis want to race in the TT, a big race that is held once a year on the island for motorbikes and sidecars. They are not sure what the 'TT' is but they know that they have to practice, a lot, for it.

Poppy went down the stairs to help them clear up. Curly gave them a brush and dustpan, and then disappeared back into the kitchen.

The bears began to sweep up the cereal until Poppy said that they were a bit stupid because they could not get it to go around corners. Tunis threw some cereal at him and he threw some back.

The mess was getting worse by the time Curly realised nothing was getting done. Bigpuss put his head out of the kitchen and shouted at them. Teppi looked scared and ran out of the back door.

"What's happened now?" Curly asked.

"Teppi has run away!" Tunis said tearfully, "He doesn't like to be shouted at. I don't either."

"Well stop doing daft things then!" Curly sighed. "You two had better go and look for him. I will be along in a minute to help. You'll know where to go won't you Tunis?" He nodded, put the dustpan and brush down and the two bears followed Teppi out the door.

Teppi was a bit upset by the shouting but he was more worried about the sidecar. It had been raining so he headed up towards the park. He found the sidecar hidden under the trees where they had left it. He did not know it but the rain had made the cardboard very soft. He pushed it to the top of the hill and jumped into it as it began to roll down the hill. Suddenly the floor of the box gave way and he ended up in the middle of a big puddle, while the sidecar box rolled over the top of him to carry on down the hill. He jumped up and ran after it but could not catch it before it hit the fence at the bottom. It

had a big dent where it had hit the fencepost.
He prodded it sadly.

His eyes filled with big tears as he tried to
pull it back into shape. The box was too soggy
so it just flopped back down again. He did not
know what to do. He turned to go back up to the
box he and Tunis normally slept in. He saw
that a man was already picking it up to put it in
the munching lorry. Now he had nowhere else
to go but back to Curly Towers. He wondered if

Curly would let him go back after the mess they had made in the morning.

Teppi felt very sad as he went back to his sidecar box. He pulled it behind him as he went out of the park gate at the bottom and started to push it down to Curly Towers. Just as he left the park, Poppy and Tunis made it to the top gate. They saw the men putting the kipper box into the munching lorry. They thought Teppi would be in it so they ran towards it to stop the munching men from taking it. Luckily, Tunis caught sight of Teppi heading out of the park. They ran as fast as they could but they were too late to catch up with him. They were please that he was not in the box when it went into the munching lorry.

Teppi pushed his sidecar to the top of the hill that leads down to Curly Towers. It was very steep but he did not know any other way to get there. As the sidecar began to roll down the hill it got faster and faster and faster. Teppi could not keep up with it. Very soon the sidecar got away from him and only stopped when it hit a lamp post at the bottom. Another dent appeared in the other side of the cereal box. He poked at it miserably. Slowly he pushed the sidecar onto the promenade and sat beside it on a bench. While he sat, with even bigger tears in his eyes, his friend the seagull flew down to sit beside him.

"What's the matter Teppi?" he asked. Teppi sniffed but said nothing. "You can tell me."

He put his wing around Teppi. "My sidecar is broken and soft. I don't know what to do. My house is gone and I can't go back to Curly Towers because Bigpuss shouted at me. What do I do?"

"Nothing is ever that bad. I am sure you can go back to Curly Towers. Where is Tunis? He'll know what to do."

"Don't know." Teppi stuck his lip out and began to sniff again. "Anyway, I've got mud on my parka again so Curly will make me get a bath again. I am not taking it off for a bath."

"Why not?"

"Somebody might pinch it. They pinched my other one and it took me ages to get this one. I am not risking it."

"Oh... I tell you what... I will fly around and see if I can find him. He will know what to do."

The seagull took off and flew over the town. It was not long before he spied Tunis and the other bear. He flew down and landed gently beside him. Poppy was scared of the big bird and jumped behind a bin.

"Hello Sidney. What are you up to?" Tunis did a high five with the seagull's wing as he landed.

"I've been talking to Teppi. He's not very happy. I'll take you to him if you like. Hop on… your mate too."

Poppy was not too sure about riding a seagull. Tunis was obviously used to it and hopped lightly onto its back. Poppy made a messy scramble up behind Tunis. He closed his eyes tightly as he felt the bird take off.

Teppi looked very sad. He was sitting on his own looking sadly at his squashed up box. The seagull landed beside him. Tunis climbed off and Poppy sort of fell off into a heap. Teppi hid a giggle behind his hand.

"Oh dear, Teppi, your sidecar does look a bit squashed!" Poppy said as he righted himself. Teppi just nodded with big tears in his eyes. "Why don't we take it home and get Bigpuss to have a look at it?"

Tunis got up onto the bench the other side of Teppi and put his paw around his shoulder.

"Are you sure Curly will let me come back?" Teppi was worried.

"Yes, I am sure she will. You might have to have another bath. You smell a bit again. You look like you've been sat in a puddle; you have haven't you?" Poppy and Tunis both fell about laughing. Even the seagull thought it was funny.

They all walked along the Prom, Teppi and Tunis pushing the sidecar between them.

Bigpuss had gone to work but Curly was just coming out in her coat to look for them all. She was pleased that they had found Teppi. She gave him a big hug.

"You look like you have been sat in a puddle… into the washing machine… again. I guess you will want to keep your parka on?"

P☼PPY MEET'S W☼D☼GER☼

The following morning, Bigpuss and Curly got up before the three bears. Curly rushed in and shook the quilt to get them awake.

"Come on you lot, Bigpuss is taking us to Jurby to see some real racing!" she said happily and then she was gone. The bears looked at each other sleepily and Poppy asked, "Jurby?" None of the bears knew what she was talking about so they all rushed downstairs to the kitchen to see what was happening.

Bigpuss and Curly were filling flasks and putting food into a basket.

"Get your breakfast quickly; we are going up to Jurby for a picnic. And don't forget to clean your teeth!" she shouted cheerfully as she disappeared out the door.

Bigpuss put his head in, "Come on you lot… we will be late! Go and get in the car!" He disappeared as well. The bears went to clean their teeth, then they all ran out of the front door. Where they found Bigpuss and Curly packing the picnic basket into the blue car they called 'Zoe.' They all jumped in and off they went.

It was not long before they arrived at a big park, or that was what Poppy thought it was. A bit like Nobles Park but it had lots of vans and trailers with motorbikes parked beside them strung out along, what looked like a long road.

"This is called the Jurby race track." Curly said as they all got out of the car. "We've come to show you lot what real racing is all about!"

She smiled at the little bears as their faces lit up with pleasure. "We'll have something to eat and then you can have a look around, but you will have to be careful that you don't get run over… okay?" They all nodded furiously.

Curly put down a blanket and some paper plates with sandwiches and cakes on. Then they all sat down with their paper cups and she poured out the drinks. They were all quiet for a while as they ate.

"Who's got my sandwich?" Bigpuss asked looking around at the three bears. Poppy looked up guiltily but he had jam around his mouth.

"Is that mine?" he asked.

"No!" said Curly, "You had ham."

"What? Jam, he's got jam." Bigpuss insisted pointing at Poppy.

"I said 'ham!'... Turn your hearing aid up, silly!" The bears laughed.

"Hey! Who's got my cake?" Tunis asked looking around at his empty plate. "It was here a minute ago!"

"Nobody... you probably ate it," said Teppi. "You always think that somebody has eaten your share of things."

"No I do not!" Tunis began.

"Now, now, don't you start falling out. You can have another cake if you like... wait a minute, there were three there a minute ago! Now there are two! What's going on?" Curly exclaimed looking around to see if one had fallen off onto the grass. Everyone shook their heads and claimed that they had not eaten any of them. It was a bit of a mystery.

When they had all had enough to eat they cleared the picnic away and Bigpuss said that they could go and look around at the race bikes.

There were motorbikes everywhere. All the colours and noise just amazed the three bears; they just did not know where to look. There were red ones, green ones, orange ones and blue ones... the colours were endless.

Teppi saw something and he disappeared. They took the next half hour looking for him and found him staring lovingly at a real 'Sidecar!'

"Look Tunis, a proper one!" His little face lit up with joy. It looked very different to his soggy box. The owner let him sit on it when Bigpuss asked him. Teppi spent ages helping to polish it afterwards before Curly said that they were going to watch them race for real.

The three bears ran to the fencing around the race track to watch. They strained but could not see much of the track. They were leaning over a fence at the first corner.

"How do they know when to start racing?" Poppy asked Bigpuss.

"They sound a big horn to tell the bikes to go to the place over there; it's called the 'holding area.' Then the bikes go up to the start line and wait for the red lights to go off," he said as the bikes all left the holding area.

"How do they know it is finished?" Poppy continued, curious to know everything.

"Well, when the flag person knows that it is the last lap they put out a yellow flag with a black cross on it. The racers know they have one lap to go before the flag person waves the chequered flag. They know the race is finished and come back into the paddock over there," he said pointing. "When the last lap flag is out, the people in the holding area know to sound the horn to get the people in the next race ready."

There was a loud roaring noise and all the motorbikes came charging round in a big group. The bears could not hear themselves speak but Poppy put his paws over his ears and shouted over the noise.

"This is great, but you can't see much!" he shouted at Bigpuss.

"If you grow a bit you will be able to." he laughed. Poppy did not say anything but he looked thoughtfully over his shoulder.

After the first race, Poppy and the other two bears were allowed to wander around the 'Paddock,' as Bigpuss said it was called.

"Look over there Teppi, Tunis." Poppy pointed at a big blue bus parked by the start line. "If we went up to the top we would be able to see the whole race track. What do you think?" Tunis and Teppi nodded. They raced off.

There was nobody around to say that they could not go up to the top deck of the bus so, off they went. Somebody had taken all the seats out of the top deck of the bus and replaced it with shelves. These were covered in papers and there was a microphone with a big fan beside it on the top near the front.

"Wow!..." said Tunis, "… it's a great view from here!" The other two agreed. The next race was lined up to start.

"Those motorbikes only have one person on them? Why don't they have two, like when you were racing?" Poppy asked.

"They only have one person because they are 'solos' not sidecars... silly!" Teppi said as if Poppy should know.

"So you don't have to have two people to race then?"

"No, of course not if you are a solo, but we like to race together. It is better," Teppi said smugly.

"That's because you can't ride a bike on your own. You need stabilisers." Tunis laughed. Teppi did not look happy with his friend.

"I can ride a bike," Poppy said.

"Well you could be a solo rider then." Teppi turned his back on them both.

"Look it's the turn of the sidecars," Teppi almost shouted. The bears climbed up onto the desk. They leaned up against the front windows to watch the sidecars race. As the starter waved a flag the sidecar racers roared off like the motorbikes in the previous race. The little bears were cheering and shouting at them as they raced by the bus.

"'Ere! What's going on?" A furry head appeared out of a box from underneath the desk. "What's all this noise?"

The bears turned and climbed down off the desk.

"Hello, who are you?" Poppy asked.

"Who are you? I'm Wodger. What are you three up to? Looks like you are up to mischief, and you aren't allowed up here!" he said suspiciously.

"I'm Poppy and these are Teppi and Tunis. How come you are up here then?"

"Well… I am Wodger, I am always up here. I live here… well while racing is on. This is my bus," he nodded to himself, happy with the answer. Wodger was a little bluish bear like the other three but just a little bit fatter.

"I'm Wodger the Spanner, and I help around the paddock sometimes when the racers are having trouble. They feed me and I mend the engines."

"So why are you up here then?" Tunis asked.

"Well, this is the marshal's office as well. They keep the marshal's lunches up here and I come up and borrow a sandwich when I get a bit peckish."

"Hang on a minute..." Poppy said leaning closer to look at Wodger's shirt. "You've got pink icing on your t-shirt... we had some pink icing on the cakes that disappeared at the picnic. Are you sure you didn't borrow some of our food as well?" Wodger looked a bit guilty and tried to rub off the tell tale pink stains.

"Well, you did have plenty and I was hungry. I am still a bit hungry now. I think that I better check out the marshal's sandwiches. Just make sure that they are eatable still."

As he stepped back his tail switched on the microphone, then as he bent down Wodger trumped and it was broadcast over the speaker system. The flag person heard it and thought that the race was into its last lap. The flag person waved the chequered flag so all the sidecars pulled in to the paddock.

"Oops!" said Wodger.

"Phew!" said Tunis holding his nose. "What have you been eating? That really stinks!"

"Yeah…" joined in Teppi, "… like cabbage." They all started laughing.

"We better blow that away." Tunis switched on the fan before anyone could stop him. The fan blew all the papers around in a big swirl.

It looked like the bus was a giant snow globe from outside. The bears were jumping around, trying to catch the papers and laughing, having a great time. It did not occur to any of them to switch the fan off to make it easier to catch the papers.

Wodger looked out of the window; there were some people with orange jackets on running towards the bus.

"Now we are in trouble!" Wodger said.

"Who are they?" Poppy asked.

"The marshals… and they don't look very happy!... and a few of the racers!"

"That's Bigpuss with them!" said Teppi, joining them at the window.

"Oh no, we're in trouble again, aren't we?"

Poppy nodded. "I think so."

All that Bigpuss and Curly could see were the four little bears looking down at them from the side window of the bus with the swirling paper behind them. Bigpuss climbed the stairs and turned off the fan. The papers fell down covering everything like a blanket of snow. He looked at the bears and they knew that they were in trouble… again!

"I think that you should pick up all the papers… don't you?" They all nodded and began to collect them all into untidy piles.

"The marshals will have to sort them out. Now I think that you should all go and get into the car… don't you?" he told them when they were finished. They all nodded and scrabbled off down the stairs and back to the paddock.

The car was parked by the burger bar. "Maybe I should get a burger for the journey back?" Wodger said aloud, looking thoughtful.

"No!" chorused the three other bears. "We are in trouble enough!"

Wodger got into the back of the car and squashed in beside Poppy.

"Will Bigpuss and Curly mind me coming home with you?" he asked Poppy a bit scared. "I don't think that I will be able to stay in the bus anymore." Poppy shrugged his shoulders.

"He told you to get in the car so I don't think he minds. Curly never said anything. Don't worry about it. There is plenty of room in Curly Towers; you can stay in our room. It has a lovely big fluffy bed."

"Yeah and you can keep your parka on. Curly doesn't mind that either," Teppi chipped in. Wodger nodded and grinned although he did not have a parka.

"Will I have to get a parka?" The other bears did not know. He put the seat belt on and waited for Curly and Bigpuss to calm the people down and take them home.

It was not long before they were on the way home. The bears were soon rocked off to sleep by the motion of the car. They were nearly home when Tunis started making snoring sounds. Curly looked in the back seat and smiled. Then she looked again!

"How many bears did we bring with us?" she asked Bigpuss.

"Three…why?" he answered without looking round.

"Well there are four in the back seat!"

"Poppy!" Bigpuss shouted.

John Batty Racing

Isle of Man

A BAD WOMAN

by

Elinor Hunter

A Kinord Book

Published by Kinord Books
Edinburgh
www.kinordbooks.com

ISBN: 978-0-9928080-0-6

Printed and bound by Robertson Printers, Forfar, Scotland

For Jim, my love, my life

1
Growing Pains

'At fifteen, beauty and talent do not exist; there can only be promise of the coming woman.' – Honoré de Balzac

GALLOWAY, 1861

NOTHING IS EVER as it seems. Bella looked devoutly towards the pulpit while the echo of his voice bounced off the oak rafters. She watched his ruddy face and neck turn an alarming shade of purple against the black of his robe. His arms flailed like the wings of a monstrous bat till at the climax of his sermon he bellowed as if tormented and roared for God to have mercy on them all, sending a silvery spray of saliva in all directions.

Forgetting the cold clamminess of the church and the hard discomfort of the pew, she found his furious righteousness amusing. Did such unholy rage signify demons writhing within him, ready to come bursting forth in a sickening deluge? She tried to listen to his words, but a sparkle lit up her blue-green eyes and a bubble of illicit laughter rose deep in her chest, though she checked herself for such wickedness. The corners of her mouth had turned up in a smile when, to her horror, her gaze met the minister's.

She glanced away, raising a hand to her cheek.

The slight movement did not pass unobserved. With a fierce sidelong glare, her mother hissed, 'Stop your fidgeting!' and gave Bella a sharp nudge in the ribs which instantly restored her sobriety.

Mrs Pattie tucked in her chin, to resume her pious Sunday pose.

Bella squared her shoulders and stared at the beads of perspiration that glistened on the preacher's brow.

In the painful, threatening stillness that followed his performance, the Reverend Adam Haggerty stood contemptuously surveying his flock: illiterate peasants to whom his erudition meant naught, their ignorance the cross he had to bear. Was it to serve these dullards he'd been educated? They had no concept of the enormity of his task. Week after week he strove to explain to them the Bible and the mysteries of creation, yet all too frequently he suspected his efforts were wasted. In addition to his Sabbath duties, there was the mind-numbing round of pastoral visits, Kirk Session meetings, and the occasional wedding, christening or funeral. However, this was his calling, if not an easy one, and the position did bring certain advantages. Now he could look forward to the stiff dram of whisky that would precede his lunch.

God knows, he deserved it!

Scowling down from the pulpit, his expression softened at the sight of Bella. She must recently have turned fifteen, he reckoned. He itched to reach out and caress that glorious golden hair of hers that gleamed in the watery sunlight filtering through the leaded glass windows. The cherubic innocence she had possessed as a child, once so enchanting, was gone. Puberty had refined her facial features, filled her out nicely in other places and lent a pertness that defied her humble origins. Increasingly she resembled someone he was acquainted with ... but he was damned if he could remember who! For ages, he had wrestled with the problem. Then in a flash, right there in the pulpit, it came to him: of course, why hadn't he realised it sooner? The girl was the living embodiment of Sandro Botticelli's 'Birth of Venus', a painting that never failed to stir him! A delicious tingle of excitement went coursing through his loins. For longer than was proper, he allowed his gaze to linger on her, until a cough disturbed the deathly hush.

Quickly Mr Haggerty shifted his focus and strove to regain his inner calm.

There was a flutter of uneasiness in the pews. Mrs Pattie crossed and uncrossed her neat ankles. Though less vain than most, she was inordinately proud of her small feet which on Sundays were forced into tiny black leather button boots. Others shrank back guiltily inside their best clothes, their disquiet greater with each second that passed as they tried to avoid the minister's beady eye.

Did they imagine *he* could not see into their hearts, did not appreciate the evil of which they were capable? Well might they squirm! This was the moment that made his dedication worthwhile. As if they were whimpering puppies, he could grab them and rub their noses in the mess of their sinfulness, suspending them in misery for an hour, if he chose!

The tension became almost unbearable before he said in a syrupy little voice, 'Let us pray.'

As was his habit, Mr Haggerty stood smugly by the church door to nod and smile as the congregation filed slowly out, a glob of spittle still hovering by one side of his mouth. To a favoured few, he extended a limp, sweaty hand, and Bella always cringed at his touch. With an involuntary shudder, she wiped her fingers down the side of her dress and followed her family out of the churchyard, relieved that she'd not have to see the minister again for a whole week.

* * * * *

Each morning she woke at dawn to the crowing of the rooster in the farmyard. Her two brothers slept on, oblivious to her sharp intake of breath as her bare feet met the icy hardness of the bedroom floor. Never would she be allowed to forget the solitary instance when she had turned over and gone to sleep again; it was a woman's duty to be up and about before the men in the house.

Pulling on her working dress and woollen stockings in the early gloom, Bella shivered her way through to the kitchen. She knelt in front of the hearth to shovel out the cold ashes, took them outside and fetched a handful of dry straw and kindling to light the fire. When it began to crackle and blaze, she laid some small pieces of peat on top, went to draw water from the well outside, and hung the kettle on a hook above the flames. With the clank of the iron pot being placed on the heat to make the porridge, the heavy curtains covering the kitchen recess quietly opened and Mrs Pattie rose from the box bed she shared with her husband. There was nothing like a good bowl of porridge to start the day, Mr Pattie declared over breakfast, but nonetheless Bella knew it would leave her fast as she toiled in the fields.

It was October, when the dry earth got everywhere at the annual potato harvest. She tasted it in her mouth, and felt the familiar crunch of grit between her teeth as she stooped to fill the wire basket on the ground beside her. On no account would she be dismissed for laziness: she worked as well as any man, until she was too tired to speak. Soil lodged under her fingernails, dirt streaked her face, and she would find worms of black muck between her toes when she took her stockings off at night.

From the tiny side window of their cottage, Mrs Pattie stood watching for her daughter to come up the narrow track, clicking her tongue in irritation when the girl veered off towards the trees instead of coming inside.

'You're late ... I thought you'd surely got lost!' she snapped, when Bella finally appeared in the doorway.

'I don't feel right, Ma.' Bella set the precious pennies she'd earned on the mantelpiece.

'Aye, there's many a time I don't feel right, either, but I just have to get on with it.' Impatiently she dumped a tight, glossy green cabbage on the table. 'Are your hands clean? Get that chopped up and into the pan afore your Da gets in.'

Sympathy did not come easily to Mrs Pattie: she too had experienced the rigours of digging potatoes in her youth. Stealing a look from the corner of her eye, she decided maybe Bella *did* seem whiter than usual, but then she was always pale, as if the red of her hair somehow drained the colour from her complexion.

The mother stretched up for five dinner plates from the shelf, placed them at the side of the table and said, 'What's wrong with you anyway?'

'I've no idea,' Bella said, drawing out a kitchen chair that scraped against the flagstone floor. She sat down, glad to take the weight off her feet, and lightly touched her stomach. 'I've a kind of a pain here, and there's blood ...'

'Och, give me strength!' Mrs Pattie recoiled, screwing up her nose in distaste. She bustled across the room to raise the lid of the old wooden chest. 'That's all we need! I forgot you'd be starting. Well, you'd best get used to the monthlies. Now you'll understand what we all go through – one o' the joys o' being a woman.'

'What d'you mean, the *monthlies*?'

'*Wheesht!* You can't sit talking of such a thing, and your father due in any minute – away you go and get freshened up! There's nothing as bad as a dirty woman's smell ... it's a foul, horrible thing, a hundred times worse than rotten fish.' She held out a fistful of cotton rags. 'When you're done, wash them and let them dry beside the mangle where your Da and the boys won't see them.'

She sighed and lifted an arm to her forehead: as if she didn't have enough to cope with!

'But what will ...?' was all Bella managed to say before Ma's determined fingertips were around her wrist, hustling her unceremoniously outside.

'On you go! And hurry!' said Mrs Pattie.

Indignantly jerking out of the vice-like grip, the girl slammed the door behind her. She drew water from the pump, and furiously cleaned herself in the miserable blackness of the privy. Already she hated the shameful redness that stained her underclothes, resented this sudden affliction that was not to be spoken about.

Without realising it, Bella had joined the sisterhood of grown women, which guards its secrets from the uninitiated, and treats its own with a very special unkindness.

* * * * *

WHITBURN, LINLITHGOWSHIRE, 1861–1865

Life was not easy in mining villages like Whitburn, a hundred miles north of Galloway. The Bartholomews were no better and no worse off than anyone else of their acquaintance, which made the deprivations they endured more bearable. Everyone subsisted in equal misery and hardship in the rows. Youngsters seldom had enough food in their bellies and were lucky to have shoes on their feet. By the age of twelve, only a minority attended school. If you want to make something of yourself, fathers told their sons, you should quit the books as fast as possible. You must *be a man*, grow up and get earning. Learning was for idiots and malingerers who were fit for nothing else. *Real men* went down the pit.

Charles Bartholomew was not quite thirty. He had worked underground for more than half of his existence, as witnessed by the tiny coal shards permanently lodged beneath his sallow skin, visible only during the few waking hours when he wasn't black with dust from top to toe. Nearly two decades had passed since he was first taken on at the mine, and it was on that day he grew up. At the tender age of eleven, he had queued with other new fresh-faced recruits, most of them not even past boyhood, and artlessly committing their futures to the darkness. The child had stepped forward smartly, in boots that were much too big, when the call came for him to sign up for a man's job.

'Name?' growled the clerk, with scarcely a glance at the urchin in front of him.

'Charles Bartholomew.' The boy spoke timidly, his voice crackly, unbroken.

Without listening, the clerk had begun to write.

'Excuse me, Sur,' said Charles fearfully, 'but that's no' what I said. I think you've made a mistake. You wrote Barclay but my name's Bartholomew.'

'Is that so?' sneered the official. 'Well you'd better mind that come payday, laddie, because you're down in the ledger as *Charles Barclay*, and that's how it stays! You're the one that made the mistake – you didnae speak up loud enough. Your name's *Barclay* in this office, and that's the end o' it. There's twenty men behind you, so move along,' he ordered peremptorily.

Glowering over the boy's crown, he roared, '*Next!*' and Charles had no choice but to stand aside. The slapdash error of a petty official gave rise to a ripple effect that would surface off and on in the Bartholomew line for a century.

* * * * *

In the same year that Bella Pattie turned fifteen, Charles and Isa Bartholomew celebrated the birth of their fourth baby, a fine-looking lad they named after his father. They lived in a humble row cottage that consisted of a room and kitchen. Despite having two sons and a daughter, Isa believed her new-born was the most adorable creature she'd ever seen, with his dark curls, big brown eyes and the longest lashes in the world. Folk said he was in danger of becoming a spoiled brat, the way she doted on him, but Isa didn't care. Of all her children, she would always have a particular soft spot for Charlie, even after the arrival of his baby sister, Henrietta.

On the morning of February 15, 1865 Charles rose at six as usual, and lit the fire while his wife breast-fed the infant. Having waved her husband off to the pit and her three oldest children off to school, Isa could relax over a cup of tea. She cradled the infant in her arms, revelling in the stillness of the kitchen until Charlie's piping voice cried from the bedroom.

'Mammy! Can I get up now?'

'Come on through, pet, and see what I've got for you this mornin'!' Isa replied, laying Henrietta on the box bed. Charlie's 'treat' would be nothing more than a spoonful of cream rather than milk with his porridge, or a sliver of butter on his bread instead of the lard his siblings got, but it was his mother's way of making him feel special. In just a year, once he was five, she'd have to send her favourite off to school with the rest. Till then, she would make the most of these moments with her little prince.

Around ten o'clock, having cleared away the breakfast dishes, she set off for the grocer's, carrying Henrietta close to her body in the plaid, with wee Charlie trailing alongside her. Suddenly, from nowhere, panic descended with the urgent, discordant clanging of bells, a sound everyone dreaded. The boy yelled out in fright and instinctively made a grab for Isa's skirts. With never a word, she clutched Henrietta more firmly to her, seized hold of Charlie and went running along the street towards the pit head.

A crowd had gathered. In a shivering huddle they stood, young women with pasty complexions etched with lines of anxiety, old before their time. The persistent ringing of the colliery bells meant disaster, an event that could mark the end of life as they knew it. Bereavement was practically guaranteed for some who waited.

After five long hours of digging, Charles Bartholomew's mangled body was carted out of the tunnel where he'd been working. On the accident report was written:

Engineman allowed his engine to go the wrong way and took him over the pulleys.

The death certificate stated that he had died instantly, which brought a small measure of consolation to his distraught relatives. After nine years of marriage, in her late twenties with five children, Isa was a widow.

2
First Love

'We have chains, though no eye beholds them; and are slaves, though men call us free.' – Oscar Wilde

QUEEN VICTORIA COULD HARDLY CONTAIN her overwhelming love for Prince Albert, who was her first cousin. After their marriage, she wrote to her uncle, King Leopold of the Belgians:

> *Oh! my dearest uncle, I am sure if you knew HOW happy, how blessed I feel, and how PROUD I feel in possessing such a perfect being as my husband ...*

Nine months after her marriage in 1840, the Queen gave birth to Princess Victoria, and a son, Bertie, arrived a year later. She wrote of her fervent prayer that the boy would grow up to *'resemble his angelic dearest Father in EVERY, EVERY respect, both in body and mind.'* As the future King Edward VII, much was expected of the Prince of Wales. His childhood was devoted to a gruelling educational regime, and discipline was maintained by physical punishment when deemed necessary by his father. With no regard for the pupil's interests or aptitude, private tutors followed Prince Albert's rigorous instructions to the letter. The boisterous Bertie nevertheless grew up to be a charming, sociable young man, despite a disappointing lack of scholastic accomplishment.

His tour of North America in 1860 – the first by an heir to the British throne – was a resounding personal and diplomatic success. In Canada, he inaugurated Montreal's Victoria Bridge across the St Lawrence River, and laid the cornerstone of

Parliament Hill, Ottawa. With amusement he watched Charles Blondin cross Niagara Falls on a high wire, and went on to spend three days at the White House in Washington D.C. as the guest of President James Buchanan.

Released from the tyranny of his earlier teachers, Bertie's academic record improved during terms at the Universities of Edinburgh and Oxford. Reports of the undergraduate's high jinks unfortunately reached the palace, resulting in a spell with the Grenadier Guards at Curragh Camp in Ireland. But the move intended to teach him greater self-control backfired badly. During the summer of 1861, the irrepressible Prince lost his virginity to Nellie Clifden, described by some as an actress and by others as an Irish whore.

The boy had to be married as quickly as possible, stated his exasperated mother, before any further scandal erupted. Within three weeks, the Prince of Wales was whisked off to Germany for an introductory meeting with Princess Alexandra of Denmark, his parents' choice of bride for him. Subsequently he went to study at Cambridge University, where he was kept under constant surveillance.

Convinced that the lad was not adequately chastened, Prince Albert travelled to Cambridge in December 1861. On a miserably cold afternoon, when it poured with rain, father and son took a walk together during which Bertie was subjected to another vicious tongue-lashing for his misdemeanours.

No sooner had Prince Albert returned to Windsor than he fell ill: he passed away a fortnight later. Queen Victoria would forever blame her wayward son's philandering with Nellie Clifden for hastening his father's death. Her beloved Albert had been *'killed by that dreadful business'*, she declared.

In a letter to her eldest daughter, she wrote that the very sight of Bertie made her shudder. The Prince of Wales would never be forgiven.

* * * * *

Too much learning was not good for girls. It gave them ideas that could not be put into action, and led to discontent – or so the minister frequently declared. All the same, James Pattie believed that sons and daughters merited equal education, and had insisted that Bella went to school until she was fourteen. She was an able student, but needlework class was where she shone.

In the evening her father read aloud to the family from the newspaper. Abraham Lincoln's struggle to abolish slavery in America was underway, while slave labour in Britain had officially been banned thirty years earlier. Still, it seemed to Bella that indentured farm workers like Da led lives of virtual servitude. Just once was she brave enough to actually say so.

'Nonsense!' came the reply. 'There are masters and there are servants because that's the natural order of things. We're aware of our place, but we're *not* slaves. We do an honest day's labour for an honest day's pay, without trying to rise above our station.'

Ma agreed wholeheartedly: Bella should hold her tongue and keep her opinions to herself. Women were frail creatures, born to tend the home, husbands and children. Politics were best left to men. If the girl wasn't careful, no decent man would marry her, the way she questioned things. In the not too distant past, she might have been burned as a witch for less! She'd end up with some wastrel, Ma cautioned, might even land in the hovels or the poorhouse, with only herself to blame.

Bella pretended to listen, but the rebellious glint in her eyes worried her mother. It was a bad sign. Spirit in a woman was undesirable, a fire to be damped down. The lassie would need a tight leash. Fifteen was a dangerous age.

* * * * *

Mrs Pattie could shirk her responsibilities no longer. She prepared herself to broach the facts of life with Bella one afternoon as they stood alone together peeling vegetables in the kitchen.

In mixed company, the mother began, a young woman should speak when spoken to, neither smile too readily nor laugh out loud. She should wear a hat out of doors, as proper ladies did, since over-exposure to the sun would ruin the pale complexion considered attractive. Her hair might be her crowning glory, but it should be pinned up, rather than left around the shoulders. Makeup should be shunned as a mark of immorality, used by actresses and 'loose women'. True beauty was natural, devoid of artifice.

Bella listened dutifully, her interest piqued only when Mrs Pattie touched on the topic of marriage.

Good girls remained chaste until their wedding night. Then they would take the leap from virginity into the unknown. *And all your ridiculous notions of romance will go flying out of the window,* the mother wanted to add.

Instead she said sternly, 'Guard your self-respect. Don't give in to any lad, however tempted you may be, till you've got a ring. You'll go to the altar clean and pure, like I did, and afterwards all will be revealed. Learning to please a husband is part of the bargain of marriage.'

From the set of her mouth it was evident that the subject was closed. She had told Bella what was necessary for her protection and Mrs Pattie would fret no more. Her duty was done, thank God. Female confidences were not for sharing. Her daughter had been launched into womanhood, armed with as much knowledge about the birds and the bees as any girl could possibly aspire to in the early 1860's.

Bella continued with her task, her mind brimming with questions she dared not ask. Experience would be her guide.

* * * * *

The terrain of south-west Scotland is one of contrasts, a mosaic of lush pastures and fields of arable crops, rolling hills, woods, rivers and coastline, swampy peat bogs and dry thorny heath-lands. For centuries the old harbour at Palnackie had been an important destination for barges ferrying commodities to and from the area. James Pattie was full of stories of how Galloway was invaded by the Romans – with her siblings Bella had played in the ruins of a round Roman fort – and by fierce Norsemen, who had ruled the area from the ninth to the twelfth century. With her red hair, he called Bella 'his wee Viking'.

When she first went to school, her older brother's pals had teased her, chanting, 'Gin-ger! Where's Gin-ger?' Cheeks burning with annoyance, she would chase them, raising her arm to hit out at them, but they were forever beyond her reach, laughing. Yet she had no objection to the nickname when it came from the new driver of Keane the grocer's cart.

Twice a week Tam called at the Pattie cottage. He waited on the dirt road, hoping it would be Bella, and not her mother, who would come hurrying along the path. His eyes lit up as he straightened his white cotton apron and said, 'What can we get for you today, Ginger?'

His arrival always brightened her morning. His easy banter never failed to bring a smile to her face, a smile she still would be wearing when she got to the door and laid down her basketful of provisions. Checking that Ma was not by the window, she turned round to wave, since Tam would be seated high up on the wagon with the horse's reins in one hand, ready to wave back to her.

Preparations were made on Saturday for the lunch that followed the church service, because Sunday was a day of rest. In the afternoon, an intimidating silence reigned in the Pattie dwelling, broken by the occasional hushed voice and the doleful tick of the mantel clock. Even a loud sigh brought one of Ma's black looks, and Bella seethed with frustration that her scant leisure hours had to be squandered on reading and quiet reflection. It would have eased the dreariness to knit or sew, to trim her nails or her hair, but only heathens did such things on the Lord's Day. She might even have played a game of cards with wee Jimmy, her brother, but the 'devil's books' were not to be touched on the Sabbath: they stayed in the sideboard drawer. Hardest to stomach was seeing her older sibling, Johnny, leave to meet his friends. It rankled to watch him go off gallivanting while she was imprisoned indoors.

With her sixteenth birthday a miracle happened. Worn down by her pleas and persuasion, Da agreed that she could tag along with Johnny on his Sunday jaunts. Had she been a lady, she would have worn pretty frills and flounces, daintily carrying a lacy parasol to promenade, but such fripperies were not for working-class girls. After tidying the lunch table, washing the plates and scouring the pans, Bella put on her church bonnet and shawl, to go waltzing off with her brother along the winding dirt path to the main road. Conscious of Ma's scowling disapproval, she tried to curb the gleeful spring in her step. Safely out of sight of the house, she tore off her hat to break into a little run, from sheer happiness.

In her delight, she barely noticed their two mile walk into Palnackie. But evidently something had changed with those same boys who had teased her mercilessly about her red hair: bold no more, Johnny's friends were shy, almost tongue-tied when she spoke to them. Tam the delivery boy knew no such awkwardness.

Whether straggling in twos and threes along the banks of the Urr or wandering through the Doach Woods, Tam made a point of walking close to Bella's side, immediately glancing round with a mischievous grin if by chance their hands brushed. Once as they climbed a steep grassy slope, she lost her footing and he saved her from falling. For the rest of that afternoon they strolled with her fingers gently yet firmly laced in his, both oblivious to the sniggering and knowing winks of their companions.

'You'll no' half catch it from Ma and Da if they find out what you were up to with Tam,' Johnny warned her on their way home.

Tartly Bella replied, 'What d'you mean? I wasn't *up to* anything! He's the one that took *my* hand.'

'Aye, and you let him, didn't you?'

'But ... they'll not hear unless you tell them. You wouldn't do that to me, would you?' she said, taking his arm and smiling up at him.

She had yearned for romance. Now it had arrived, and nothing else mattered – or so she was naive enough to imagine.

3
Tea and Sympathy

'That which is loved may pass, but love hath no end.'
– Gilbert Parker

P RINCE ALBERT'S UNTIMELY DEATH in 1861 had sent Victoria into an extended period of mourning. She withdrew into seclusion, avoiding public events and social engagements. To her Uncle Leopold, King of the Belgians, she wrote:

The poor fatherless baby of eight months is now the utterly heartbroken and crushed widow of forty-two! My LIFE as a HAPPY one is ENDED! The world is gone for ME! ... Oh! to be cut off in the prime of life – to see our pure, happy, quiet, domestic life, which ALONE enabled me to bear my MUCH disliked position, CUT OFF at forty-two – when I HAD hoped with such instinctive certainty that God never WOULD part us, and would let us grow old together (though HE always talked of the shortness of life) – is TOO AWFUL, too cruel!

While she wallowed in her misery, even visiting foreign royalty were refused an audience. The Prince of Wales bore the brunt of her impotent rage and depression at Albert's demise; her younger children were abandoned entirely to the care of others. Life as a recluse left Victoria out of touch with her family, her country, and reality. Questions were raised as to her fitness to rule, but she refused to share power with her heir, declaring, *'I am DETERMINED that NO ONE person is to lead or guide or dictate to ME ...'*

By 1864, both Parliament and the public were losing patience with their invisible monarch. In March a protest notice was pinned to the railings of Buckingham Palace that announced:

These commanding premises to be let or sold in consequence of the late occupant's declining business.

On the advice of her uncle Leopold, she took to appearing more often in public. She drove through London in an open carriage, and graced the Royal Horticultural Society at Kensington with her presence. When a rumour circulated that she was about to go out of mourning, the newspapers rejoiced. Queen Victoria responded with a hand-written letter to the Times:

This idea cannot be too explicitly contradicted. The Queen heartily appreciates the desire of her subjects to see her, and whatever she CAN do to gratify them in this loyal and affectionate wish, she WILL do ... But there are other and higher duties than those of mere representation which are now thrown upon the Queen, alone and unassisted – duties which she cannot neglect without injury to the public service, which weigh unceasingly upon her, overwhelming her with work and anxiety.

Her physician recommended she adopt horseback riding as a hobby, and John Brown was summoned from Scotland, arriving at Osborne in 1865. He spoke bluntly with a strong Scottish accent, and treated the Queen no differently from anyone else. With just a look, Victoria might strike terror into the hearts of her ministers of state, but the gillie from Balmoral would not be intimidated by her.

'*I am on a dreary sad pinnacle of solitary grandeur,*' she is reported to have said, but Brown was unimpressed. She might be the most powerful woman on the planet, but to him, she was a sad, lonely wee widow. Members of her household gasped in horror at the arrogance of the uncouth, whisky-drinking Highlander who had infiltrated their elite circle. In his kilt and tweed jacket, he stood head and shoulders above the formal, dark-suited courtiers, like some rare exotic species plucked from its native habitat.

The monarch was charmed.

* * * * *

WHITBURN, 1865

Isa was in shock, sleep her sole refuge. She would dream that Charles lay beside her, till she woke up and the awful truth struck her: he was gone and would never be back. Closing her eyes, she would snuggle down under the blankets hoping to recapture the sweet forgetfulness of the night. She loathed the relentless cheeping of a blackbird in the half-dark outside, announcing the start of a new day. In the bleak gloom of early mornings, she lay cowering as the silhouette of the empty grate emerged from the shadows, its cold black hollowness a bruising reminder of how she felt inside. Gone was the joyful spark that used to get her up. It took all her willpower to drag herself out of bed and dress, light the fire and put on a pot of water to heat before the bairns woke up, when their whining and incessant squabbling would resume.

Apprehensively she opened the door to solicitous friends and relatives who called. However kind their intentions, each one unwittingly reopened the wound of her bereavement. Far from bringing consolation with their worn platitudes over endless cups of tea, they left Isa feeling strangely violated: like an animal in a zoo, a permanent exhibit to be stared at with pity and curiosity. She was a hostage to convention in her own house, forced to listen to words she did not want to hear, and wanted to scream that time was *not* a great healer, it was her enemy. Her husband had been her best friend, and the breadwinner. Yes, she had tenure of her tiny row home, but when the small financial compensation brought by Charles's death had run out, how was she to pay the rent and feed her five bairns? Time would not alleviate the penury that loomed ahead.

Haunted by her loss and the uncertainties of the future, her inner calm was gone. She could not be still, or she would fall apart. As Henrietta napped, she would slip out for water from the pump to resume another round of laundry and ironing, cooking, mending or knitting – it made no difference *what,* as long as there was something, anything, to occupy her. When she went out to buy provisions, carrying the baby, her pace did not slacken for one moment, and wee Charlie had to run to keep up with her. Regular routines bordered on binges of manic activity. Unable to quell her agitation, she'd become like a woman possessed, and feared she was losing her sanity. She hardly dared contemplate the fate of her children if she were carted off to the lunatic asylum.

One Sunday afternoon, Henrietta lay asleep while her four siblings were out playing on the street. Isa stood in the kitchen mixing batter, as was her custom at that hour because Charles had appreciated a fresh pancake on his day off. When the knock came at the door, her first instinct was to ignore it. What if it was Charles's brother again, with that snaggle-toothed wife of his, whose smirk belied the sympathy of her gaze? Isa stood holding her breath, hoping the caller might think no one was at home, yet knowing that was foolish. There was no escape. *Of course* she was in: there was nowhere for her to go. No decent woman would be out a month after her husband's death! In ten seconds came another rap, more insistent.

Inhaling deeply, she wiped her hands on her apron and went to lift the latch, unleashing a chain events no one could have foreseen.

A stranger stood at her door, a man who seemed vaguely familiar. Perhaps she'd noticed him among the sea of faces at the funeral? Isa couldn't be sure.

He smiled, taking it for granted that she would recognise him.

'I was out for a walk. Thought I would swing by and see how you are.'

'Och, I'm all right, thanks. Just takin' everything as it comes ... nothing else for it, is there?' She wished he'd go away, but he continued to stand awkwardly on the doorstep. 'Will you come in?' she said, her tone not overly encouraging.

'Well, I dinnae want to disturb you, Mrs Bartholomew. But I decided I should bring you this.' Almost apologetically, he held out Charles's lunch box.

'Oh!' Isa gasped at the sight of the scratched rectangular tin, its rounded corners rubbed and dented. For a decade, she had dutifully packed it each working morning. In the hurly-burly of the early hours when countless chores cried out to be done, it had been a tyrant, that box, demanding to be filled, no matter what other concerns she had ... but then no man could keep going on an empty stomach. How casually she had thrust it at her husband as he set off for the pit, little dreaming that fateful day was his last on earth. Now she would give anything to have Charles back, would willingly pack his lunch a hundred times a week, if things could be as they once were! An unexpected lump rose in her throat. She swallowed hard and forced herself to look up.

'You'd better come in, Mr ... eh ... I'm sorry. You were at the pit wi' Charles, and I remember your face, but I forget your name. My memory's like a sieve, wi' all the ups and downs we've had recently!'

'Aye, that's understandable. My name's Inglis. Peter Inglis.' He followed Isa into the kitchen, taking off his cap to reveal cropped, spiky hair that was turning grey.

'Take a seat, Mr Inglis.'

It would be polite, she realised, to sit and make conversation, but she stood frozen, staring at the tin lying on the table between them. She could still picture her husband with that box tucked under his arm, as he went to the pit. Ridiculous as it seemed, Charles's grubby prints on the lid disconcerted her. Those oily whorls, never much observed, had come from his strong hands that only touched her with gentleness, cut and callused though his fingertips might be.

The guest cleared his throat and Isa gave a start.

'I'm sorry, I was in the middle o' makin' pancakes when you came to the door.'

Her mouth quivered and he discreetly lowered his eyes.

She drew the mixture towards her and blindly began stirring, her wooden spoon giving a dull, liquidy *thwack* as it hit against the sides of the bowl. Tiny air bubbles formed on top of the thick creamy batter. Determined to regain her composure, she blinked and moved away to ladle some of the mix onto the black cast iron griddle that hung over the fire. With a palette knife she deftly flipped the half-cooked pancakes, leaving them to sizzle and rise for several seconds before serving them, steaming and fragrant, onto a painted china platter of her mother's – one of Isa's few treasures. Then she covered them lightly with a white linen cloth.

He watched approvingly as she bustled around, taking dishes, cups and saucers from the shelf. She was a fine figure of a woman, he was thinking: tall and slender despite five children. Kept a clean enough house, too – poor and maybe a bit untidy – but quite comfortable. He breathed in, absorbing the homeliness of the kitchen, and the sweet, mouth-watering aroma of baking that filled the air.

Accustomed as she was to visits of condolence, Isa was uncertain how to deal with this stocky outsider who remained so quiet, a mere acquaintance about whom she knew virtually nothing. Was it even proper for a widow woman to entertain a man alone? She was full of doubts these days. She poured two cups of tea and sat herself down.

'Help yourself, Mr Inglis.' She pushed the hot cakes nearer him, desperately searching for something to say till she had a flash of inspiration. 'The kids are oot playin'. I'll get them to come in, will I?' Already she was rising up.

'No, sit still. It's really you I came to see.'

Isa perched on the edge of her chair. He was about Charles's age, she was thinking: quite short for a man, barely as tall as she herself was, but fit and muscular.

'It cannae be easy for you and the bairns, this situation ...' The caller spread his arms helplessly. 'I'm no' very good wi' words, I'm sorry ... and I dinnae want to upset ye further after what ye've been through, but ye know what I'm tryin' to say – ye'll have heard it all before.'

All of a sudden, irrationally, she felt sorry for him. The poor wee man meant well. This errand was probably as much of an ordeal for him as it was for her!

'There's always accidents, but somehow I didn't dream anything would happen to Charles, and I'd be left like this,' she said. 'But maybe that's what everybody thinks.' Henrietta gave a whimper and Isa leaned across to the box bed, grateful for the diversion. 'Sshhh, darlin'! Mammy's here, it's all right,' she crooned as she lightly stroked the baby's cheek with one finger.

Peter Inglis spread a spoonful of jam on his pancake, and took a bite so soft and delicious, it positively melted on his tongue. He fought the urge to devour it in one mouthful and reach for a couple more. Some decorum was in order, he reminded himself. 'Ye'd been a fine wife tae Charles, I can see that.'

Unaccustomed to such high praise, Isa struggled to think of a suitable reply.

'Well, I tried. He was a good man to me.'

'Aye, I'm sure he was, Mrs Bartholomew. In fact, he was a good man, full stop.' He nodded in respect, then washed down the remnants of his pancake with a gulp of tea.

Talk of Charles was making it tough for her to keep the tears at bay.

'Can I top you up?' she said, rather too hastily.

'That would be grand. Thank you very much,' he said, extending his cup and saucer.

26

'Have another pancake with it, Mr Inglis, they're best when they're newly made. You might as well take two ... they'll be tougher than the soles of your boots by tomorrow.'

As if food ever lasted any time in her house! If the children weren't out playing, the dish would have been emptied in one fell swoop.

'I'd feel better if you called me Peter. Ye could manage that, could ye not?'

He certainly didn't stand on ceremony! She gave a tight smile, unused to such fast familiarity. Yet where was the harm?

'I'm not ... well, yes, I suppose I could,' she said.

What did the trivial rules of accepted behaviour matter, when her whole life had been turned upside down? No normal person could have any concept of the dazed isolation into which Charles's death had thrown her: and if they did, she doubted they'd care. Her plight was a common one, to be dealt with as best she could. At that very instant, Isa decided that she would be afraid no longer of what other people might think. To hell with them all and their damned etiquette! She would do and say whatever she herself considered appropriate. Even so, when she eventually spoke, his name felt foreign on her lips.

'So, do you and your wife have any kids, *Peter*?' she asked shyly.

'No. No kids ... and no wife naggin' at me either! Just the landlady in Bathgate to answer to, and she's happy provided I pay my rent when it's due. I'm *my ain boss* and that's how I like it!'

He laughed, and sat chewing thoughtfully.

Isa responded with a tentative laugh, and the ice was broken. She began to relax.

'Bathgate did ye say? That's quite a walk ye've had!'

'Aye, but I enjoy the exercise. It's a grand thing, a walk, gies ye an appetite.'

'And your landlady, does she feed you well enough?' Isa enquired.

27

'She's no' a bad cook, I suppose. I eat what she puts in front o' me – it's better than what I could make – but believe me, that's no' sayin' much! Her pancakes are rubbery; never in a million years could she bake anything as light and fluffy as yours.' He licked a dollop of jam from his thumb, and added as a mischievous afterthought, 'Could I give her your recipe?'

Had it seemed she was fishing for compliments? Embarrassment brought a trace of pink to Isa's cheeks. 'Oh, no, I didnae mean it that way! But I wondered ...'

Peter saw her confusion and laughed aloud.

Gently he said, 'Fine I realised what ye meant. I was kiddin' ye on!'

She raised her brows to smile, and gave a quiet chuckle.

Could he be trying to flirt with her? She dismissed the notion. 'Well, I appreciate you goin' to the trouble o' bringin' back the tin. I hadnae minded a thing about it!'

'Nae bother. I didnae know what else to do wi' it ... and it was an excuse to come and see ye.' He drained his cup, and delicately set it on its saucer.

His eyes sought hers.

For several minutes, they looked at one another across the table.

And in that companionable silence an understanding of sorts was born between them.

'Another wee drop?' Isa finally said, lifting the teapot.

'No, I'll get goin' – I honestly didnae want to inconvenience ye, but I did enjoy talkin' to ye.' He stood up and gestured towards their empty plates. 'This was very nice, thank you.'

'It was kind o' ye to come by.' To her astonishment, she wished he didn't have to leave. 'If you're over this way again, come by for a cup o' tea, won't ye?'

Immediately she feared that she'd sounded too forward.

'Ye should be careful what ye say! I'll maybe take ye up on that. Ye're a dab hand wi' a pancake – I could eat them to a band playin'!'

He smiled and picked up his cap.

She closed the door, feeling more cheerful than she'd done in a while. He'd been like a breath of fresh air, this person who materialised from nowhere, who showed compassion without treating her as an object of pity. It was surprising how effortlessly the talk had flowed once they got started. Even more astounding was her appreciation of Peter's droll sense of humour, when she'd thought her ability to laugh had died with Charles.

Glancing at the tin, her smile faded. She tried to count: she must have filled that thing two thousand times. How amazing that she hadn't missed it! It was as if it had returned to reproach her. Foolishly she imagined Charles was observing her from afar, but even if he was, so what? Surely no rational being could claim she was disloyal to her husband for engaging in conversation with Peter Inglis ... or could they?

With Peter she had rediscovered the mystical rapport there could be between male and female, even as strangers. It had been comforting to have a man about the house, if just temporarily, though she would not admit it to a living soul. He'd made her feel human once more.

Hearing the children's voices at the door, she snatched up the box, and crossed the room to climb on to a rough wooden crate that was used as a stool. She stretched up as high as she could, and very deliberately shoved the offending item to the back of the highest shelf, safely out of sight. It had served its purpose, was a relic of her previous existence.

She had to think of the future.

4
The Manse

'How very little can be done under the spirit of fear.'
– Florence Nightingale

GALLOWAY

WHEN JAMES PATTIE ARRIVED HOME one night, it was obvious something was afoot.

'Oh, my!' was his wife's reaction to the news he whispered in her ear.

An announcement was made at the tea table. 'You've got a new job, Bella. Mr Haggerty wants you to go and work at the manse as a scullery maid. You'll begin tomorrow,' said Ma importantly.

As Mr Haggerty's scullery maid, her status would improve immensely, and she would earn more than she could by lifting potatoes or digging peat. Overjoyed at this chance for her daughter to move up in the world, the mother gushed that it might even lead to a full-time position at the minister's house.

The girl's heart sank. It was an offer she could not refuse, Bella agreed, but her voice lacked enthusiasm.

After lighting the fire the following morning, she put on the dark servant's dress that was a hand-me-down from Ma, hastily adjusted to fit her better. She was accustomed to pre-owned garments. Where fashionable society ladies required several different outfits each day, change was a luxury beyond ordinary folk. The poorest often wore the same clothes for months on end. Variety was a prerogative of the rich.

When she reported for duty at seven, the spaciousness of the manse took her breath away. Her family's humble kitchen, with its leaded hearth, small oven and shabby metal side trivets that swung over the flames for cooking, was primitive in comparison. A deal table occupied the middle of the floor: against the back wall was an elegant oak dresser stocked with large blue and white patterned dinner plates that stood to attention like soldiers on parade. She marvelled at the *inside* water pump and metal sink, at the cavernous recessed fireplace with a range huge enough to keep three or four pots simmering, while a loaf, scones or a cake and perhaps a creamy rice pudding might be baking in the oven. Since Mr Haggerty required a cooked breakfast, lunch and dinner, the gardener toiled to produce a vast selection of vegetables and fruits to accompany his master's platters of meat, fish or poultry because every meal was a feast for him.

Bella's early stints at the manse went smoothly. Then it became apparent that Mr Haggerty had other appetites to be satisfied, and her problems began.

* * * * *

Cuil was a big farm three miles distant, where Agnes Pattie, Bella's older sister, had a live-in position as a general servant. On her one day off each month, Agnes traipsed home to visit, anxious for the family's latest news. Scarcely had she removed her hat till she was demanding details of her sibling's work at the manse.

'So what about this grand new job you've got, eh? Does Mr Haggerty come through to the kitchen at all?'

At the mention of the minister's name, Bella flushed pink. 'No ... I don't see much o' him,' she said. She stood up abruptly. 'Let me put on the kettle for the tea.'

Agnes looked at her mother, and winked.

Bella always regarded herself as smarter and prettier than her sister, yet Agnes possessed an uncanny knack of finding her weak spot, could goad her into saying things she'd regret. But on this occasion Bella would not be drawn. Da had often counselled her to think well before she spoke: after words have left your mouth, you can't take them back.

31

'So d'you think he *likes* you?' Agnes teased, when Bella sat down at the table once more, their foreheads so close they were nearly touching. 'Come on, this could be the most excitement we've had since Mr Tait the schoolmaster married Margaret Brydson. That one certainly landed on her feet, nineteen years old, and hooked an educated man with a good income! You might do the same thing if you play your cards right. *I wouldn't say no*, that's for sure!'

Bella winced.

Mrs Pattie scowled at her two daughters. 'Now, now! That's quite enough! You should be ashamed of yourselves for such talk, especially discussing *Mr Haggerty*! If your Da knew, he'd wipe the floor with you!'

Agnes ignored the reprimand. 'I'm only asking whether ...' but got no further, because at that moment Bella sprang up out of her chair.

'*Be quiet*, Agnes! Leave it be, would you?'

Reminded of events from the previous night, Bella ran outside to hide her distress.

* * * * *

It happened when the others had gone. As scullery maid, Bella was the drudge who stayed to clean up after the minister had dined on a meal that could have fed a family of four. She stood alone at the sink, busily scouring the pots and pans, when Adam Haggerty breezed into the kitchen.

'Well, Isabella, how are things? Almost done, are we?'

From her first day in service he had stated that he would not call her Bella. It sounded common.

She turned round. 'Good evening, Mr Haggerty. Yes, just about.'

He moved to stand by her, a concerned expression on his face. 'And you're happy enough working here, I hope?'

'Oh, yes, thank you, Mr Haggerty,' she replied, discreetly trying to inch away from his warm, foul breath, but the arm he had slipped around her shoulder clamped her firmly to his side.

He gazed into her eyes for what seemed an eternity.

Ultimately he spoke. 'You're a nice addition to the kitchen, Isabella. You brighten up the place.'

He lifted his other hand, letting it glide softly down one side of her hair to her cheekbone, down to her jaw and on to her neck, stopping primly at the collar of her dress.

With a peculiar smile, he said, 'It's getting late, I'll let you finish up. Goodnight, my dear.'

The exchange left Bella troubled, alarmed that he held her and stroked her skin. Yet of all people, surely he knew how to behave appropriately, a man with such an important position in the community? It had to be innocent, simply Mr Haggerty's attempt to be friendly, one of his little eccentricities – or so she wanted to believe.

It wouldn't be worth raising it with Ma unless the situation cropped up again. She'd be told she was imagining things.

* * * * *

Her next encounter with him allowed no room for doubt that his intentions were less than honourable. A week had passed, and again she was alone in the kitchen. Mr Haggerty sidled up to her, his complacent smile revealing a scrap of parsley from dinner stuck in his teeth.

'Well, Isabella, how goes it tonight?' he asked breezily. 'Nearly all cleared up?'

'Yes, Mr Haggerty.' She smelled whisky on him.

His warm clammy fingers reached round to the nape of her neck, then slid down past her shoulder blade to her waist, grasping her tightly to him, and pinning her to the sink. His eyelids were heavy, and suddenly his mouth was on hers, his tongue forcing its way between her lips. Horrified, Bella jerked to one side and gave a muffled cry as she strove to fight him off, but his bulk had her covered. There was no escaping his body that ground ever harder against hers until she feared she would suffocate.

33

'Isabella ... for months ... you've been torturing me ... so demure, an angel smiling at me ... in church ... as if butter ... wouldn't melt ... in your mouth,' he breathlessly moaned during the ghastly embrace. With a concluding shudder he was done, and turned away to go slinking out of the back door.

The predicament was worse than any the girl could have envisaged. She wanted to tell him to stop, but her courage had failed her when the crunch came: how could a lowly scullery maid challenge her employer? Brought up to respect the minister's wisdom, in secret she had viewed him as a grotesque figure of fun, but recently he'd become fodder for her worst nightmares. She would definitely have to speak to Ma when she got home.

Unfortunately a crisis of a different sort had already struck the Pattie household that evening. No sooner had Bella entered the kitchen than she recognised the overpowering, sour stench of illness that filled the air, a stench that not even the sweet smokiness of the peat fire could mask. For days, Wee Jimmy had been complaining of a sore throat, and now he lay in the box bed, wheezing. Ma sat weeping while Da stood by, unable to console either one of them. The boy had been sickly from birth: unable to run as fast as the others at school, always the weakling most prone to vomit or bruise, to have a cough or a runny nose.

When he began to thrash and whimper through his delirium, Mrs Pattie delicately wiped the child's brow with a cool damp cloth. The hours dragged on, and Jimmy's condition continued to deteriorate. In desperation, the father borrowed a horse and rode to Castle Douglas. Late though it was, James Pattie banged on the door of the doctor's dwelling till the poor man agreed to get dressed and come to Torglass with him.

After examining the patient, the doctor backed away and quietly whispered, 'Diphtheria, I'm afraid. There's nothing I can do. Keep him calm and as comfortable as possible, that's all. I'm sorry.'

Bella watched him solemnly touch Ma's forearm and shake Da's hand prior to his departure, his downcast eyes betraying his utter impotence.

Jimmy died within hours, and it seemed his mother's howling would never end.

* * * * *

For the poor, gin was the drug of choice and alcoholism was prevalent. The purchase of opium, cannabis and cocaine was legal: drug addiction was a widespread problem among the better-off. Queen Victoria herself called frequently on her physician to administer a draught when sleep would not come. It has been reported that she also was prescribed cannabis leaves, which were made into a tea, for menstrual pain.

To ease Mrs Pattie's grief at the loss of her youngest child, the doctor prescribed regular doses of laudanum, a tincture of opium. Not one to talk much previously, she became unreachable, as if encased in glass. On bad mornings the effort of getting out of bed to dress was more than she could manage. Though physically there, the drug sent her into a twilight world of her own, rendering her incapable of her wifely tasks of cooking, cleaning and laundry.

These duties all fell to Bella, doubling her load. Her job at the manse provided respite from the bleakness at home, but filled her with dread. As a scullery maid, in the daytime she had to scrub floors, light fires, wipe down walls, windows and woodwork, polish silver and empty chamber pots – all of it preferable to the evening shift, when the image of Mr Haggerty eating his meal through in the dining room brought a tight knot of anxiety to her stomach. When the cook had gone for the night, the housekeeper retired to her room. Clearing up was not their concern. They were above such menial chores.

Alone in the kitchen, Bella was alert to every noise from the next room. As she toiled she listened for the creak of the minister's chair as he rose from the table, and the low groan of the floorboards as he shambled across to the door and into the hall. His ponderous footfall on the stairs meant that he was going up to bed, but she suspected he had something else in mind when the dull, menacing clump of his shoes echoed in the corridor, and the brass door handle slowly turned.

'Good evening, my dear,' he said.

Bella moved towards him. 'Good evening, Mr Haggerty.'

'No, please, carry on,' he said. 'I wanted to tell you I've thought a lot about you recently. I'm *so sorry* for the loss of your brother.'

Standing behind her, he slid his arms around her waist. Seconds later, he was nuzzling her neck as he pressed himself upon her.

But she was ready for him. Grunting with the exertion, she braced against the sink to push him back. 'Mr Haggerty, please *stop this!*' she said, whipping round angrily.

He laughed. 'Isabella, stop what?' he said, playfully holding up both hands.

'Please stop ...' she pleaded, her cheeks scarlet, '... stop coming so close to me. I don't think it's ... it's ... appropriate.'

The minister pouted coyly. '*I beg your pardon*? Playing hard to get, are you? Well, I've met your kind before, with your "Stop it, I like it". You're not always so particular ... I've heard what you get up to with that grocer's lad, so you needn't act the innocent with me!'

His hint that she might accept his advances was intolerable: worse was the implication of impropriety in her relationship with Tam.

'I don't know what you're talking about!' she protested.

'*Well I think you do,*' he drawled, pulling her roughly towards him. 'And how's this for closeness?' he mocked, clasping her firmly to him while she tried to avoid his breath. 'You have two options. We have some fun together, you retain your job, and I'll be quiet about your trysts with your young buck. Or you can get the hell out of here, right now.'

Smoothly he unpinned Bella's hair, stroking it as it tumbled, long and silky, down her back. She stood frozen in horror, fear and revulsion mounting inside her.

'If you choose to leave,' he continued, 'people will learn that your work at the manse had to end abruptly, after what came to my ears regarding you and young Thomas. I'd have to inform your parents exactly what kind of *little whore* they've bred and you'll never again find employment in this parish, with such a reputation.'

Holding up a tress of her hair to sniff, he leered at her. 'By the same token, if you were nice to me, you could keep your good name intact, and we'd both be happy. Get it?'

She gave a nod, and forced her mouth into a hint of a smile, raising one brow as she stared, deep and unblinking, into his bloodshot eyes. He fumbled with the buttons of her dress, so near that she could have counted the open pores that dotted his shiny nose.

And all the while he remained blissfully unaware of her one free arm reaching tentatively behind her, ever so slowly advancing towards her goal.

Taking her benign expression as acquiescence, perhaps even encouragement, the minister's arousal increased. It was his due, he believed, to take the first taste of any local girl who caught his fancy, and Bella – she was special! He'd watched and waited for her to mature. He *would* have her, unspoiled, before she was nabbed by some of the village yokels. They could pick up his leavings, after he'd asserted his *droit du seigneur*.

Intoxicated that victory was almost his, he failed to notice her fingers spidering gingerly across to the drying-rack ... failed to notice as she surreptitiously stretched and strained towards the cutlery from which he had eaten dinner less than an hour ago.

He basked in the soft peachiness of her cheek and inhaled her sublime, virginal sweetness, delighted that he owned her at last. She was like a perfectly ripened plum, juicy and unblemished, waiting to be plucked from the branch! His lecherous eyelids drooped for a few heavenly moments and triumphantly he leaned in to place his mouth on hers ... moments in which Bella's mind raced. Cornered, unable to move an inch, it would be futile to scream because no one would hear, but as he closed his eyes ... at that exact instant, she seized her chance. Grabbing a silver fork, with one violent thrust she rammed its sharp tines right through the skin to the bone on the back of his hand. Mr Haggerty yelped and went reeling sideways in pained confusion.

'*You bloody bitch of hell!* What have you done to me?' he yowled, cradling his bleeding fist against his body. 'You'll pay for this!'

His warning was ignored.

Bella was half way out of the door, fleeing blindly into the darkness. Her heart pounded as she ran and ran, sobbing from sheer terror, feet barely touching the ground to put as much distance as she could between herself and the manse. At the Doach Burn, gasping for air, she bent down to splash icy droplets from the stream onto her face and neck, then dried herself as best she could with her apron: rinsed her mouth with some of the cold clear waters, spat and rinsed time and again, frantic to eliminate all trace of him. Sitting on a boulder, she straightened up her clothes and hair. Gradually her breathing steadied and her calm returned.

It was all very well to flee but she had to think of the repercussions. Mr Haggerty had promised she'd pay for what she'd done, and it was no idle threat.

She'd done?

That was the maddening part! As her panic subsided, fury took its place. She had performed the duties she was paid for, but he imagined he could bully her into doing anything else he desired. She'd refused to submit to his assault, but it would be his word versus hers.

If only she'd had the sense to speak up about it at home when he began making advances! Ma would doubtless have defended the minister, but Da would have listened. Bella had been too timid, had allowed things to escalate, frightened that somehow she was to blame. Was she brave or reckless enough to accuse someone with so much power when she had none? Mr Haggerty claimed she'd sat smiling at him in church, after all. Could any girl overcome the shame of recounting how a grown man had stroked and fondled and pushed himself so lewdly against her?

She was convinced that she was not the sole object of the preacher's attentions. He had been too presumptuous, too confident of success for this to be an isolated incident. Angered by her resistance to his advances, he could easily destroy her family's reputation, her future employment and even her marriage prospects. Such was the influence of a man of the cloth.

Though it would have been easy to dissolve into tearful helplessness or uncontrollable hysteria, Bella steeled herself to confide in Da once she got home. There was no other choice if justice was to be done. Chalk-white and trembling, she slipped like a ghost into her parents' kitchen.

James Pattie glanced up from his newspaper, startled to see her so early.

Before her courage left her, Bella immediately launched into her account of what had transpired that same evening. The whole story of recent events came pouring out. In the most steady voice she could summon up, she described her walks with Tam, and how they'd laughed and held hands. The father listened and gritted his teeth, while Mrs Pattie lay doped with laudanum in the box bed, with her back to the room.

Having revealed all, Bella fell silent, suspended in misery and humiliation.

Mr Pattie rose wearily from his seat. 'You've had some night of it, lassie, and it was correct to tell me what's been going on. Is there anything else?'

She shook her head.

'Well, you stood up for yourself, and I'm proud o' ye.'

39

In one of the rare tender gestures of affection he'd ever shown, he put an arm round his daughter. That and his soft tone brought her nearer to crying than any reproach could have done. 'Go off to your bed, Viking, and I'll bring you a cup o' tea in a minute or two. Try and forget Haggerty – I'll deal with him. He's not getting away with this.'

Bella was sure it would be impossible to sleep after such shenanigans, but the drink Da made, laced with a few drops of Ma's medicine, sent her drifting off into a welcoming blackness. Memories of the escapade were swatted away like flies. Yet somewhere in her unconscious nagged the certainty that the minister was out for revenge.

5
Payback

'Men never do evil so completely and cheerfully as when they do it from religious conviction.' – Blaise Pascal

U P AT THE MANSE, Adam Haggerty found that rage was not at all conducive to a decent night's sleep. Far from content with the way things had turned out, he consumed a late breakfast. His aching hand was a constant reminder of the previous evening's events, and in addition his best silk waistcoat had been ruined, stained with blood. His feeble efforts to explain away the injury appeared to stretch the credulity even of his servants, let alone of the doctor they called in. The man actually had the audacity to smirk as he dressed the wound! The whole episode was unforgivable, the minister reflected, touching the bandage. He'd been placed in an intolerable situation by that slut, and her vicious handiwork with the fork most definitely could not go unpunished. He planned to walk over to her family's house after the father was home from his day's toil. In the meantime, he would pray for guidance on the matter.

* * * * *

The rap at the cottage door at seven sharp came as a shock, if not entirely as a surprise to Bella. The blood drained from her cheeks at the notion of confronting Mr Haggerty again, but her father was ready, and sent her through to the bedroom. James Pattie's countenance was grim as he showed in the visitor and sat down opposite him at the table.

41

'I'm afraid I've come to execute an unpleasant duty,' the minister began, 'though it grieves me immeasurably to bring more trouble to your door, following your bereavement.'

Mr Pattie looked him squarely in the eye. 'Aye, well, you'd better get to the point. Tell me what you have to say, if it concerns me or mine.'

With his stubby fat fingers steepled in front of his chest, Adam Haggerty inhaled deeply.

'It's *à propos* of your daughter, Isabella. She's been misbehaving rather badly of late with that grocer's lad. When I attempted to counsel her on mending her ways, she turned on me, screeching like a madwoman! I needn't tell you how distressing I found it, after all my kindness to her. Her hysteria upon hearing that I no longer wished her to work at the manse was such that she *attacked* me. As a God-fearing man, you presumably will not condone such conduct. The girl sorely lacks guidance and self-discipline – her actions cannot go unpunished. She must be chastised for bringing shame and disgrace upon herself and her relatives, not to mention inflicting a considerable wound upon me, without any provocation. As you can see, I required medical attention as a result.' He held up his bandaged hand. 'Let us not forget that most useful of sayings, "Spare the rod and spoil the child".'

Having said his piece, he leaned back, his chest puffed out and his mouth set in a bitter line. How he relished the power that surged through his veins at such moments, to so easily destroy a father's illusions about his offspring! The pleasure almost compensated for the humiliation he had endured.

Mr Pattie was very still, and cleared his throat. 'I'm an ordinary man, Mr Haggerty, and I don't have your grand education – but I can tell the difference between truth and lies. Bella arrived home in a terrible state. For your information, she admitted to walking out with Tam, and furthermore I know what she's been subjected to at the manse in the last few weeks. You have a damned nerve to cross my threshold, let alone sit there and speak ill of her, when *she* is not the guilty party!'

The minister snorted. 'Your allusion is a mystery to me ... but hearing your attitude, sir, I regret this sorry tale must be reported to the Kirk Session. Your superior, who owns this very cottage you live in, will also be notified and at the very least a stern reprimand to *you and your family* will be in order. It's feasible you'll find yourself out of a house and a job, as a consequence!'

'Is that so? Well, I'm happy to put your story to the test. Make it public, if you dare, and let's see how much faith there is in the word of a lying charlatan like yourself!'

'You foolish, foolish man!' scoffed Mr Haggerty.

In a flash, James Pattie had got to his feet and was round at the other side of the table. Clutching him by the coat collar, he hauled the minister up out of his seat, knocking over a chair in the process. Then they were in the hall, and Mr Pattie was holding open the front door, saying, 'Get the hell out of here, and don't ever come back!'

The indignant Mr Haggerty scuttled out into the night, baring his dirty little teeth in fury. 'You'll be sorry for this, Pattie!' he spluttered, glaring round and shaking his good fist.

Mr Pattie was not one to gloat, but he knew he'd come out best when the preacher's departure was announced very soon after that. Adam Haggerty was neither seen nor heard of in Galloway again.

* * * * *

The showdown with the minister was fortuitous, spurring James Pattie to act upon a long-held ambition. Aged fifty, he decided to take the leap to independence and announced that the family was moving. He'd scraped together just enough to buy a horse and wagon, and would set up in business for himself, as a carrier. No longer would he remain beholden to a landowner who could evict or reprimand him at will. They would leave this place where Jimmy had died, and would live in Kelton parish.

'So there's no undoing it. I've given notice that we're moving. Are you all right with that, Missus?' he asked his wife at supper.

Mrs Pattie's face betrayed no emotion. 'Whatever. It's all the same to me.'

Her apathy made things easier. With no arguments against relinquishing the security of the home and the small income they'd had for over two decades, the Patties moved to Gelston village, two miles from Castle Douglas. Johnny took lodgings in Palnackie close to the smiddy where he was a journeyman, and Bella found herself living alone with her parents.

Their growing affluence inspired a new confidence. With their own vehicle, and sufficient money in her pocket to shop where she chose, Bella accompanied her father weekly to the Castle Douglas market, eagerly absorbing its different sounds and smells.

And she was given permission to step out with Tam.

'But anybody you're meeting will come here for you,' Mr Pattie told her. 'No sneaking around. Things are to be open and above board. A lad that wants to walk with you should be prepared to present himself at our door, and shake my hand.'

On Sundays, she and Tam invariably strolled past Carswell the coal merchant's dwelling. Bella would declare that in the future she too might live in a detached stone villa with six rooms.

'And what would you use for money?' Tam would laugh, though at eighteen, anything seems possible.

James Pattie threw himself into his new work with astounding enthusiasm. By the end of the first year, he had established a regular clientele, driving long distances to pick up produce from local farms – potatoes, turnips, milk, butter, cream, eggs and livestock – for delivery to markets in Castle Douglas, Dalbeattie or Kirkcudbright. During the sheep-shearing season he took huge mounds of raw, smelly wool to the mills, ferried supplies back to village shops and carried tons of iron from Dumfries for the local blacksmiths. The orders kept coming in, nearly becoming too much for one man.

When necessary, Tam was there to lend a hand with heavy lifting. He was like one of the family, and by all appearances, soon would be: already he'd confessed to Bella that he loved her.

* * * * *

The construction of the railway from Dalbeattie to Castle Douglas brought a squad of able-bodied men to Galloway, many of them from Ireland, with the task of digging out tunnels and cutting through mounds of clay or rock. They caused a stir among the local lasses, but of greater interest were those who actually manned the steam locomotives that followed. Their dashing accounts of travelling at a rate of forty or more miles an hour smacked of worldly wisdom and glamour. Imagine hurtling along at such speed! To operate one of these trains would take such skill and courage, young women simpered, as they stared in amazement at the mammoth iron horses that were about to make history. Ordinary people could now undertake previously inconceivable journeys. Faraway places provided fresh opportunities for amorous liaisons and the unanticipated mingling of blood lines.

But Bella had eyes only for Tam.

When he said, 'I've been thinking ...' her spirits soared.

This was it at last. He was about to propose!

'Oh? Thinking about what?' she answered breathlessly.

'Emigrating. To Nova Scotia.'

Her stomach lurched. In what she hoped was a normal voice, she said, 'Nova Scotia? That's on the other side of the ocean!'

'Aye, but you can get there in less than a fortnight, from Liverpool – they go at such a speed, the new steamers! It's a land of opportunity, so the papers say. I've read a lot, and I've talked to folk with connections there.'

'But ... why now?'

Tam paused. 'I have to do something different, I need some adventure. Honestly, did you want me to drive a grocer's cart all my days?'

'No, but there's the railway, or you'd easily get a better-paying job in Glasgow.'

'Aye, Glasgow's the place, if you're willing to slave in a rotten factory and live in a rat-infested tenement! It would be torture, no more what I want than this is. Once I've got established, we'll get married, Bella ... we could make a grand life for ourselves there.'

Trembling with indignation, she nearly choked on her words. 'D'you call this a proposal?'

He shrugged. 'Yes, since you put it that way. I'm sorry, I've wanted to discuss it with you for weeks, but I was always waiting for the right moment.'

'Could there ever be a right moment for such nonsense? Come on, don't throw up your job and leave all you've ever known, Tam. Let's get married *here*, the same as ordinary folk.' Lamely she added, 'Talk to Da ... he'd be glad to have you come and work for him! You could ask him while Ma and I make the tea.'

'You have to allow me some pride!' Tam retorted. 'You couldn't respect me if I'd been just a delivery boy till your father took pity on me. Let me see how things go in Nova Scotia, will you not? This is the best chance I might have, to make something o' myself. Then we'll get married.'

'So I've to put everything on hold, and you'll go off on your great adventure? You've got *some nerve!*'

'I'm sorry, it's asking a lot, but I'll save up for your ticket, and I'll send for you when I can.'

'You've no idea what it would be like over there – this scheme could be disastrous!'

'Yes, or it might be the making of me! That's why I have to go – to know if there's something better, before I settle for what our folks ...'

She'd heard enough. Scarcely had he finished when she turned to step into the house, and slammed the door. Too bad if he was counting on coming in as usual. With such scant regard for all that was familiar, he'd have to learn to seek hospitality elsewhere.

* * * * *

On their final walk, they went round by the Patties' former home at Torglass.

'I want to keep a picture of you here in my head, Bella,' he said. 'D'you remember how you used to come out, carrying your basket? I thought you were the most beautiful creature ever to walk on this earth!'

'If that was true, you'd not be so keen to leave me,' she said, giving him a playful push while a sob welled up inside her, that this might be their last outing.

'I'm serious, Bella. I've always wanted to marry you. Trust me.'

He grabbed her hand, his eyes looking into hers, deadly earnest. Then she was in his arms, and it was as if their bodies had caught fire. When passion threatened to overrule reason, they drew back from the brink.

'I wish you'd stay,' she whispered, shamefacedly tidying her hair.

'We'll be together again, Bella, I swear, and things will be done properly. We'll get married as soon as we can. Just wait for me, and take care o' yourself.'

She kissed him softly on the lips, sure that her heart would break to see him go.

Tam promised he would write to her as he took off for Liverpool.

And Bella was left high and dry, to endure a winter that seemed colder and wetter than any she could recall. When six months went by with no word from him, her hopes began to fade, replaced by anger at having squandered precious years.

Perhaps he'd simply been toying with her, suggested her sister Agnes. Rubbing salt in the wound, she added, 'Where are his letters to you, eh? He'll be spinning yarns to the lassies in

47

Nova Scotia about all the great things he's going to achieve, and no doubt they'll fall for his charms exactly as you did!'

Bella found the taunt unnerving. She deserved better than a wretch who would let months go by without contacting her, she told herself. Why pin all her faith on someone who apparently had already forgotten her? Where was her self-respect? If he had moved on, so could she. She'd been happy prior to their meeting, and she would learn to be happy once more.

Tam wasn't the only pebble on the beach.

6

Fresh Pastures

'Keep your face always toward the sunshine – and shadows will fall behind you.' – Walt Whitman

JOHN BROWN WAS APPOINTED 'Queen's Highland Servant', answerable exclusively to Victoria, with a salary of £120 per annum. Daily he led her out on her favourite pony, Lochnagar. Bereft of Prince Albert – her best friend, lover and confidant – she had despaired of rescue from her grand isolation. But her hours alone with the ruggedly handsome Scot fostered a unique bond of trust between them. As neither politician nor family member, Brown could safely be made party to her innermost thoughts. The distance between him and her uppity household staff guaranteed his absolute discretion. His allegiance was to her and no other. Gradually her depression lifted, and rumours of romance circulated.

Few understood their mutual attraction, but during an upbringing circumscribed by pomp and protocol, Victoria had been denied the company of other children. Never had she learned to play or stretch her imagination. Little girls dream of being princesses, but the Queen was fascinated by Brown's sheer ordinariness. With him, she was gently brought down to earth, introduced to a new world outside her gilded cage. As with Marie Antoinette and her rustic fantasies at Versailles, Victoria learned the art of adopting a different persona. Shocked bystanders often heard Brown reprimand her, and address her as 'woman', a feat accomplished by no other living soul, but it was part of their game. She found it great fun to be treated as unexceptional – *when* she so desired.

Communications were developing fast with the electric telegraph. By 1865, messages could reliably be transmitted from Britain to America, and a reply received by nightfall. Newspaper reports from all over the globe now reached Britain's rural areas, aided by the vast state-of-the-art network of railways that was steadily crisscrossing the land, offering speedy transportation at reasonable prices. By law, a minimum of one train had to run once per day in each direction on every route, at a cost to passengers of one penny per mile.

Queen Victoria and her household could travel north by train as far as Ballater in Aberdeenshire. Previously an annual destination for her and her consort, it became a twice yearly port of call. The Queen and her servant were inseparable, and she was whisperingly referred to as 'Mrs Brown'. Edward Stanley, 15th Earl of Derby, wrote in his diary that she and John Brown slept in adjoining rooms at Balmoral Castle, *contrary to etiquette and even decency*.

* * * * *

The arrival of the gypsies for the annual Castle Douglas Gala Day sent an excited shiver of anticipation through the town. Though scorned as ne'er-do-wells by some, their colourful outfits, the pungent, foreign aromas of their cooking and the gaudy glamour of their painted caravans lent an enticing air of mystery. Children were sternly warned by their parents to keep their distance from 'the tinkies', yet none but the worst skinflint could stay away. Lively fiddle music or skirling pipes drew young and old to stalls selling everything from toys, ribbons, hat trim, buttons and baubles of all kinds, to savoury or sweet pies, tablet, toffee apples and other sugary delicacies. Freak shows displayed unfortunates as the 'ugliest' or 'fattest' on earth, while jugglers and acrobats performed amazing tricks. Potions, pills and ointments were offered for any medical condition. Psychics 'read the minds' of the gullible, and fortunes were told. Illusion abounded, all part of the Romany magic.

The Gala Day also presented opportunities for the public demonstration of local skills and talents. Blacksmiths competed in horse-shoeing and tool-making contests, local strongmen joined in a tug-o'-war, and merchants held a procession of decorated wagons. Farmers proudly exhibited their best animals and their wives produced cakes, preserves and craftwork. Local youngsters marched in a fancy dress parade, to be rewarded with a 'lucky bag' containing a paper hat, a biscuit, a piece of cake and some candy, donated from the parish fund.

This social highlight of the season offered something for everyone. The big marquee provided welcome shade from the sun or shelter from the rain. Men stood to drink at the bar, and their wives happily lingered over afternoon tea, glad of a rare chance to exchange news with friends and family. Children drank up their lemonade fast, eager to chase one another round the trestle tables, and go crawling on the grass under the benches, mischievously weaving between unsuspecting legs before ultimately exhausting the patience of their elders. But it was hard to scold on such a day of leisure and good humour, one of the few occasions in the year when little tykes could hope to be indulged.

Bella had made herself a new cotton dress with a matching ribbon on her straw hat. For all her finery, she felt a twinge of disappointment as she strolled round the fairground with Ruby, who lived next door. She should have been there with Tam, leaning on *his* arm, listening to *his* voice!

'*Roll up! Roll up!* Fortunes told, a penny a time!'

The raucous call of a barker interrupted her thoughts. Catching Bella's attention, he exclaimed, 'Ah, here are two pretty lasses! Come along, m'dears, let Madame Rosa tell your fortunes.'

Dodging between her and Ruby, he cheekily clasped an arm round each girl. 'Want to hear about the handsome men who'll sweep you off your feet, eh?'

'Should we?' asked Bella, smiling dubiously.

'Why not?' Ruby replied, gamely fishing out a coin. 'It might be a laugh!'

Hunched over a table in the dimly-lit, smoky caravan, Madame Rosa sat waiting. Her greasy hair was held back under a grubby red scarf tied at the nape of her neck, her gold hoop earrings glinting in the half-darkness. Advancing age had not dulled her piercing brown eyes. She nodded, unsmiling, as the girls clambered up the rickety steps to enter her domain.

'Sit yourselves down,' she said, indicating two stools opposite her.

She pointed at Bella. 'You first. Lay down your hands.'

Casting an apprehensive smile at Ruby, Bella obeyed. How ridiculously white and freckly her fingers were against the olive-skinned talons that gripped her!

For what seemed like ages, the gypsy studied Bella's palms.

'You're impatient, but your life is about to be transformed. I see two lovers ... and lots of babies for you.'

Without thinking, Bella giggled out loud.

'What? You think this is *some kind of joke?* Eh?' said Madame Rosa, baring discoloured teeth.

The frightening intensity of her glare wiped the smile from Bella's face.

'There's another thing ... a late child, sorrow,' she breathed, 'and a woman who is your enemy.'

With that, she stretched down for a grimy glass that sat on the floor, and lifted it to her lips. Greedily she gulped some mouthfuls of amber liquid, then straightened up and wiped her mouth with the back of her wrist.

She took Ruby's extended forearms, raising her palms for a closer inspection. When she abruptly let go, Bella saw her shudder, despite the warmth of the air. The gypsy fumbled in her apron pocket and produced a copper.

'No more today,' she mumbled, pushing the coin over the table. 'Here's your money.'

Her eyes, apparently with the power to foresee so much just minutes previously, had become guarded, unwilling to meet Ruby's.

'But what about my fortune?' the girl gasped.

Madame Rosa said nothing. From her dismissive wave it was clear that the session was at an end.

* * * * *

Unaccustomed to the sudden brightness, the two girls blinked as they rejoined the seething throng outside, unaware of a couple of well-dressed lads not far behind. Within seconds, Bella felt a tap on her shoulder.

'Fancy seeing you here!'

When she glanced round, a lanky youth drew away in feigned embarrassment. 'Oh, I'm sorry. I could have sworn you were somebody I'd met before!'

'No, I don't think so.'

He persevered, 'Anyhow, I'm Jock, this is Will. We're both from Glasgow. We work on the trains.'

The quiet one, Will, seemed nice. There was something about him that reminded her of Tam, Bella thought to herself. She nudged Ruby, a look passed between them, and with a cautious smile the girls introduced themselves.

'We were going to the tent for a scone and a cup of tea,' said Jock. 'Would you care to join us?'

* * * * *

'I'm seeing Will again tomorrow,' Bella announced as they made their way home.

Her friend was scandalised. 'You can't go out with someone you met a couple of hours ago!'

'Says who? I'm only going out for a walk round the village with him in broad daylight.'

'What'll your Ma and Da say?'

'They'll meet him when he comes to the house for me.'

'You're a bold one, Bella Pattie!'

'Just don't let on that we went to a fortune-teller, will you? You know how straight-laced my mother is – doesn't approve of that kind of thing.'

'Your secret's safe with me. I'll say nothing,' Ruby replied.

Bella shrugged and gave a little smile. Of course it was all absurd, the predictions Madame Rosa had made ... and yet, if they'd not entered the gypsy's caravan and exited at the precise moment they did, she and Ruby would not have become acquainted with Will and Jock. A tune began in her head and everything seemed a shade brighter.

She loved Tam, but she was done with hanging around like a knotless thread. She had to confront reality. Either he'd got lost at sea, or he'd met somebody else. It was his choice to go three thousand miles away across the Atlantic Ocean. She'd be crazy to sit at home pining, hoping for a letter that might not come.

Will appeared regularly at the Patties' door each Sunday after that, till early in 1866 his job took him north. When a postcard arrived saying he'd soon be back and couldn't wait to be with her again, Bella was flattered.

In her innermost heart, though, she wished the card had been sent from Nova Scotia.

7
The Slippery Slope

'It is only through labor and painful effort, by grim energy and resolute courage, that we move on to better things.'
– Theodore Roosevelt

WHITBURN, 1866

THE COMPANIONSHIP OF a loyal, sympathetic man would prove an effective antidote to the grief of widowhood or abandonment. Isa took comfort in Peter's arms and Bella dated Will in an effort to forget Tam. Both discreetly – or so each woman wanted to believe. Queen Victoria, however, made no secret of her affection for John Brown.

The vacancy left at the pit by the death of Charles Bartholomew had been easily filled. There was no shortage of men glad to take his place underground, regardless of the risks involved. Not for twenty more years would unskilled workers finally dare to form trade unions and petition for better terms of employment. Isa would forever harbour a grudge against the mine owners who were too profit-driven to consider the safety of their hirelings. The accident report had absolved them of any responsibility for the loss of her husband. And as with many others in her situation, she was powerless to challenge the judgment.

In the months following Charles's demise, the Bartholomew relatives had grown increasingly concerned for the welfare of their brother's children. Particularly disturbing to them was the frequent presence of Peter Inglis at the widow's home. The delusion that her romance would go unnoticed was shattered when Isa found herself pregnant. With her condition apparent for all to see, Charles's siblings were outraged at her brazen abuse of their goodwill. Though it might be argued that her activities were none of their business, Charles's oldest brother and his wife arrived uninvited at Isa's door one night, and trouble was in the air.

'We have to talk to you, Isa. You're a disgrace, the state you're in!' the brother-in-law said, without preamble, as he took a seat at the kitchen table. 'Take a look at yourself! It's not so long since you'd have been tarred and feathered for such conduct. You've fallen into the gutter, and you're draggin' the Bartholomew name down wi' you!'

No fonder of her in-laws than they were of her, Isa's hackles were raised. 'Who do you think you are, comin' here to criticise me?' she demanded. 'What I do is my own affair! You've been kind to me, I'll admit, deliverin' the occasional basket of stuff to help me feed my five bairns, but I don't have to account to you for every move I make!'

'Excuse me, but did you just say *occasional* basket?' interrupted the sister-in-law. 'Well, I thought once a week wasn't bad. It was out o' the goodness o' our hearts, we didnae have to do it – oor ain family went hungry so we could help yours!'

'I'm sorry to hear that, but in fact *mine* would've died o' starvation if they were relying on *your* charity!' Isa scoffed ungraciously.

Afraid a catfight was brewing, the brother-in-law interjected, 'Enough! The point is, it's not right, you havin' an illegitimate baby and our Charles hardly cold yet. He's barely gone a year, and already you've reduced our name to a laughin' stock in Whitburn.'

Isa knew better than waste her breath attempting to explain herself. Blinded by their own complacency and loyalty to Charles, her in-laws would not see things from her point of view. She could not describe how the death of her husband had practically unhinged her, leaving her adrift in a sea of lonely helplessness. Only Peter's intervention had rescued her from these dire straits. He had provided a modicum of financial support, and most important of all, had drawn her back from the brink of mad despair. For that, pregnancy seemed a small penalty. She would not tolerate a word spoken against him. She would be eternally in his debt.

Easing herself up from her chair, Isa bent menacingly over the table. 'So is it really the Bartholomew *name* you're concerned about? Well, let me tell you something, I never liked it anyway! When Charles was first taken on at the pit they put his name down as *Barclay*, so from today onwards that's what we'll call ourselves. Then you'll not have to worry about anything I do, because we'll no longer be associated wi' you, nor any of the other Bartholomews!'

With that, she went lumbering across to the front door, threw it wide open, and ushered her astonished ex-relatives out of her house and out of her life forever.

The disapproval of her in-laws was of scant significance; what shocked Isa was an envelope that arrived shortly afterwards. It was with regret, stated the letter from the mine owners, that they had to ask her to vacate her dwelling the following month, since it had been brought to their attention that she was not now living as a widow.

* * * * *

'Come on, get up out o' there!' she cried, prodding her sleeping children. 'This is the mornin' we flit, there's no time for you to lie sleepin'. There's a pile o' work to get done!' She went storming through to the kitchen.

'Have I to get up as well, Maw?' Charlie coyly called out.

'And why wouldn't you? You're the same as all the rest! Peter's comin' wi' the carter in an hour, and our stuff's to be out on the street by then, ready for loading. So you'd better get movin' this minute!' Isa shouted back at him.

'*Have I to get up as well, Maw?*' squeaked one of his older brothers, mimicking him and making the others giggle.

57

Charlie scowled. He hated when they mocked him, but worse was having Maw yell at him. Things had changed and it was all Peter Inglis's fault. Since *his* arrival on the scene, Maw was different. She kept growing fatter and fatter. Often she got angry without cause, and had stopped laying aside tasty titbits for him. In truth, Charlie didn't feel very privileged at all any more.

He wasn't sure he liked this upheaval, regardless of Maw's assurances that it would be great fun to move to Durhamtown near Bathgate. It was far bigger than Whitburn, she said, and they were going to play a game where everything would be new: new home, new school, new friends, new town, and a new name. They would turn into new people, and their family would even have a new baby as well!

It perplexed Charlie and his siblings that they might also get a new Paw. Mercifully there had been no mention of that, but they had grown sick of the sight of Peter Inglis. Maw would bundle them out to play or through to the bedroom when he showed up, and they would all crouch down behind the door, holding their breaths to listen to the strange panting and grunting that emanated from the kitchen. Charlie would wonder what could be happening while the older ones sniggered knowingly at each other. How much worse would it be if Peter actually lived with them? They might end up being kicked out onto the streets altogether!

They'd lost their father, and suddenly had to share their mother's affection with an unwelcome interloper. They all wished they could have Maw to themselves again, but the chances of that were remote.

* * * * *

The relationship between Queen Victoria and John Brown, meanwhile, grew ever more intense. Nicknamed 'the Queen's stallion' by her household staff, Victoria's daughters joked that Brown was 'Mama's lover'. The Prince of Wales, however, developed such a hatred of Brown he refused to utter his name, simply alluding to him as 'that brute'. With greater access to her than anyone else, John Brown was granted the rare privilege of entering the Queen's apartments without knocking first. Rumours that the pair were secretly married in 1866 remain controversial, but their exploits increasingly incurred the disapproval of her family and household.

Victoria found her double role exhilarating. In private she could defy convention as a royal 'enfant terrible', and in public she posed as the epitome of morality and prudishness. The Queen of the United Kingdom of Great Britain and Northern Ireland, and Empress of India was above reproach. She would do exactly as she pleased!

Rules of behaviour were for the little people, her subjects.

* * * * *

BATHGATE, 1866

Only those on the verge of destitution willingly settled in Durhamtown. Its shoddy houses were built from rubble, their two small rooms with stone floors and unplastered interior walls oozing dampness. The reck of garbage rose from the ash pits behind the rows to mingle with the stench of open sewers. Each privy and communal standpipe was used by a minimum of eight families. For many, this was the final refuge before the ultimate degradation of the workhouse.

Reaching the end of their new street, Isa already smelled its desperate misery. Despite her brave face, her heart sank. Still, there was no going back, and it wouldn't be permanent – or so she hoped. Peter's refusal to move in with them was a further disappointment, but he insisted on staying in his lodgings nearby, and Isa was in no position to argue. He was putting a roof over their heads and this was a bright new beginning, she kept saying to herself. Now they were the *Barclay* family.

'Tell me your new name again, son,' she said in feigned cheerfulness, as Charlie helped her unpack their meagre possessions.

'Charlie Barclay!' he replied stoutly. *'B-A-R-C-L-A-Y.'*

'That's a clever boy. And what'll you say to the teacher when you start the school?'

'I'm Charlie Barclay, I'm five, and I live in Durhamtown. Is that right?'

'That's the stuff,' Isa said, stroking his beautiful curls. What would she do without Charlie? Unfailingly eager to please, he could instantly make her feel better.

By September, Christina and her three younger brothers all were in school, giving Isa a brief respite with just two year old Henrietta at home till the arrival of Alexander, her new baby. Thus far, the move to Bathgate had gone smoothly, and no one had questioned Isa's use of the name Barclay. Peter had correctly predicted that once she was more than a half hour's walk from Whitburn, no one would give a damn who she was or what she'd done in the past. It was as if she was in a foreign country, her history erased.

Then an unforeseen problem cropped up.

'Will you come wi' me to the registrar's one o' these days, Peter?' Isa inquired during one of his visits.

'What for? Why would you want *me* to come wi' ye?' he snorted.

His insolent tone alarmed her, but she was sure he meant nothing by it ... that was his manner.

'We have to register the bairn, that's what for! You *are* his father.'

Peter grimaced. 'I don't think so, Isa. Y'see, you're a stranger here. Nobody's going to look twice at you when you go in and say you're a widow and you've had this ... brat. But I *work* in this area, they know me! It's givin' them somethin' to gossip about if I go and say it's mine.'

'Och, come on, Peter, will you not come wi' me? It wouldnae take long. Please, eh? Go on, say you will!' Isa leaned over the back of his chair, her cheek next to his, and planted a kiss on his brow. He was tired and needed humouring. But he would not be persuaded.

'No, I've told you I'm not goin' with you and *that's final*.' He edged away from her to yawn, stretching his arms out to either side of him. 'Time for all good folks to be in their bed, Isa! I'd best get down that road before they lock me out.' With that he got up and left for his lodgings.

And so seven weeks after Alexander's birth, Isa put her daughter, Christina, in charge of her siblings, while she herself reluctantly suffered the disgrace of going to the Registrar's Office alone. Like many petty officials of his kind, David Rankine used his position to punish those women who had 'fallen by the wayside'. His assistant, Mr Napier, admiringly observed the disdain with which he executed his duties.

'You do realise I could impose a fine for late registration?' was his opening salvo.

Isa made no response. Asked about the baby's paternity, she was obliged to divulge that she was not actually married to Peter. In the father's absence, announced Mr Rankine jubilantly, Alexander could not be given the Inglis name.

Her request to register her son as Alexander Barclay was met with a blank stare. Did she have papers legalising her use of that name? The registrar sniffed when she admitted she had none. But she was damned if she would call the child Alexander Bartholomew! All she could do was register him under her own maiden surname. With a flourish Mr Rankine wrote *'Illegitimate'* below the name of Alexander Graham.

Isa remained impassive. When he held out the required document, she grasped it with a curt 'Thank you', ignoring the sneer that was intended to further humiliate her. It wasn't much, but she still retained a shred of dignity.

Not even the registrar could take that from her.

61

8
The Green Beads

'Dancing is a vertical expression of a horizontal desire'
– Robert Frost

GELSTON, 1867–1870

ABSENCE DOES NOT NECESSARILY make the heart grow fonder.

It had been eighteen months – which at Bella's age felt like an eternity – with never a word from Nova Scotia. Though her sweetest dreams at night were of Tam, he was her Prince Charming only till she woke up, when foolish anger pushed her closer to Will. His caresses were as smooth as silk, so difficult to resist that one stolen kiss on a Sunday afternoon became two, then maybe three, and Bella hungered for more. He might not measure up to Tam in some ways, but Will was *there* – and Tam was gone, possibly forever.

In 1867, Will was in lodgings near Buittle station. It was his ambition to obtain a permanent post, which would entitle him to a railway house, he explained: perhaps one of the new cottages they'd built in the country, or a tenement flat in one of the big towns. He just had to be patient.

Their walks took them past the edge of the wood and the hovels that provided temporary shelter for seasonal workers who arrived each year to help with the harvest. Often the men's paltry earnings were squandered on ale at the Gordon Arms Inn before their womenfolk got any money to buy food or clothing, but any child from the hovels who dared show up at the school with bare feet would be shunned. No shoes, no education, that was the parish rule, religiously enforced. Ragamuffins were not welcome. The less you had, the less you got.

Munshes, by contrast, was a huge stately home that could be glimpsed from a distance through the trees. It had been the ancestral seat of Wellwood Herries Johnstone Maxwell's forebears since the 1600's, when they displaced the Douglas clan. Like Queen Victoria, the lady of the manor was disgusted by the idea of breast-feeding her own offspring. In any case, it was widely believed to inhibit conception, and a large number of heirs was paramount. Instead, the Maxwells employed a healthy, clean-looking young local girl whose own illegitimate child had died, to tend and feed the latest addition to their brood. By the time that one was weaned, Milady would probably have given birth again. While the wet nurse kept feeding, her supply of milk kept flowing. A number of crooked carers swapped their own progeny for those they'd been paid to nurture, or made their job easier by doping their charges up with Godfrey's Cordial, but this nurse took a pride in her work.

As she wheeled the big expensive baby carriage from Munshes through the village, she stopped to chat with Bella and Will.

'Have a look at Baby Jessie,' she said. 'Did you ever see such a lovely wee thing?'

Bella bent over to peep into the pram where Jessie Maxwell's golden head rested on a pillow of snowy white lace. Wrapped in a pale ivory shawl of unimaginable delicacy, the infant was a picture of privileged contentment. Even as she suspected that a perambulator would always be beyond her means, it was then that Bella first began to fancy having a bonny bairn of her own.

* * * * *

Summer drew near, and with it the Castle Douglas Gala Day in June.

'What about coming with me to the marquee dance next weekend?' asked Will.

Unable to conceal her excitement, Bella replied, 'I'd love to, but I'd need to ask Da's permission.'

As was proper, she had gone out alone with Will – and Tam before that – in daylight. Never after dark.

She washed her hair and scrubbed herself down in the privacy of the bedroom. As she fastened up the dance dress she'd made, her mother appeared.

'Do you want to try these on?'

Bella glanced at the pool of emerald-green beads in Ma's outstretched palm. 'I didn't realise you possessed such a thing! Where did they come from?'

'From your Granny Hyslop. You can wear them tonight, if you want. They're one o' the few things o' hers that I have, so don't lose them.'

Bella went to the mirror and clasped the beads round her neck. 'They go with my frock, do you not think? Why don't you ever wear them yourself, Ma?'

Ma tsked her disapproval of such a notion. 'I'm not one for jewellery. But they suited your Granny, because she had the same colouring as you. I enjoy having them all the same, they're like part of her.'

It was a revelation that Ma would still actually miss her own mother. Equally surprising was Mrs Pattie's interest in what was going on around her.

'I'll look after them, Ma. I promise.'

Will's knock on the door came exactly at seven. As they walked briskly to the town, he commented, 'You're a smasher in that dress, Bella!'

This was a compliment indeed. 'If I didn't know you better, Will Turner, I'd think you were Irish! You must have kissed the Blarney Stone!'

'No blarney, I just want to kiss you,' he replied earnestly.

She blushed.

* * * * *

No Gala Day would have been complete without Big Andy. A stalwart of the cattle judging events, he fearlessly led prize bulls round the ring; any that grew obstreperous during the parade received a sharp smack over the snout from Andy's shovel-sized hand. In the evening, the marquee was his domain. Tables were removed and in their place a wooden dance floor was laid, with benches round the sides, and Andy had a different role, as upholder of the law. Occasional drunken fights broke out, or youngsters would try to infiltrate the forbidden territory of the dance by crawling under the side panels of the tent. No sooner would a few fingers, then an arm come snaking under the canvas in a bid for illegal entry, than the perpetrator was subjected to Andy's summary justice. With his piggy eyes screwed up vindictively, and a grim set to his lantern jaw, he took a deep breath and uttered a string of nearly unintelligible oaths before bringing his size twelve work boot stamping down on the unfortunate offender's hand, which was withdrawn to a loud yelp of pain. Each little success earned Andy a shot of whisky, and the more he knocked back, the more florid his complexion became. In a good year, his three-mile hike would take longer than usual, but he always made it home for breakfast the following morning.

* * * * *

The dance was already in full swing when they reached Castle Douglas. Coming from the puritanical reserve of the Pattie household, Bella gazed in wonder at the scene before her, an alien planet where music, laughter and alcohol flowed freely. Will swept her into the crowd, to take her gliding and whirling into her first ever waltz. An eightsome reel was followed by the 'Gay Gordons' and some strenuous rounds of the 'Dashing White Sergeant'. Left breathless and laughing, they went to stand by the door, where it was cooler. He bought two glasses of something clear and tangy that reminded her of lemonade, except for its strangely bitter aftertaste, and Bella sipped delicately. She relished the calming glow that spread inside her with each drop, a real taste of the grown-up pleasures that lay outside the sober confines of home. A delightful dizziness made her giggle. Things shifted slightly in and out of focus, as if she were on a merry-go-round, and she took Will's arm to steady herself.

When he suggested they step outdoors for some fresh air, she readily agreed. A few paces from the entrance to the tent, they huddled close in the twilight. His kisses were more passionate than any they'd shared, his black stubble rough on her pale skin. They held one another tightly, her body curving into his till she heard the sound of voices nearby.

Abruptly she moved away, face burning, and raised her hankie to her cheek. 'Let's go in.'

Afraid she could not trust herself, she dared not linger.

But Will caught her wrist and brought it to his lips. His breath was fast and hot, his white smile irresistible, the urgency in his voice overwhelming when he pleaded, 'Not yet, Bella, just stay a wee while out here, eh? *Please, my love!*'

For a moment she hesitated, knowing she should not ... but again her feet carried her towards him and she allowed herself to be drawn back into his embrace. Hypnotised by the intensity of his dark eyes and the hardness of him against her, she offered no protest when he steered her to a secluded spot. He nibbled at her ear and kissed her throat then his mouth found hers once more, and their tongues touched. She did not object when he reached one hand down towards the hem of her dress and lifted up the folds of her skirts, when his fingers crept among the flounces and frills of her petticoats, when they probed ever so gently above her garters and stocking tops to the soft silky warmth of her thighs and beyond.

They should stop, she knew, but she grasped him closer to her.

It was too late, impossible to switch off the current that had their bodies moving to and fro as one in a persistent unison that grew increasingly desperate as they tore at each other's clothes.

Slowly they sank down onto the grass. With one searingly sharp stab of pain that made her gasp out loud, he was inside her and she wanted to drink him in, deeper and deeper into the surging, moist ecstasy that overwhelmed them.

On the lonely road to Gelston, Will said he loved her and for a few short hours, Bella imagined she had found true happiness.

* * * * *

The house was dark when she silently opened the front door at eleven o'clock to creep through to the bedroom. Intoxicated and exhausted with the emotions of that fateful night, she heedlessly threw off her things to tumble into bed and fall asleep, unaware that her virginity was not the only thing lost in the shadow of the marquee.

At dawn she woke to a tune from the previous evening playing in her head. As she sleepily adjusted to the morning light, she peered at the garment draped over a chair. But wasn't the pattern wrong? It seemed darker than she remembered ... then to her alarm, the reason for her confusion became horribly clear, for what she spied was no pattern, but a huge grass stain on the back of her dance dress. She sprang up in dismay.

Her immediate instinct was to bundle it away, to keep it out of sight until she could cram it into the wash tub. Horrified, she snatched up the frock, stuffed it far under her bed, and quickly hauled on her working attire, frantic to get the fire lit and the porridge on, before Ma came to check if she'd overslept.

But a worse thought hit her. The necklace! What had she done with it when she got home? She scanned the windowsill and the mantelpiece. Nothing. In her agitation, she scooped up the blankets and shook them, willing the beads to fall to the floor. Please let them be here! Will had complimented her on them as they danced, she vaguely recalled, but she had no memory of seeing them afterwards. Wildly she flapped the bedding around yet again, but to no avail, because Ma's green beads lay scattered on the grass behind the marquee.

It was time to face a different kind of music.

Had Mrs Pattie shown some reaction, it wouldn't have been half as bad. If she had shouted and screamed on hearing that the necklace was lost, slapped or given a thorough scolding, Bella would have felt better. Hardest to endure was the mute hurt in her mother's eyes.

'I'll retrace our steps this minute,' the girl said, aware that a search would be futile. 'Maybe the beads are still lying where I dropped them.'

'Aye, that'll be right! You needn't bother yourself, the tinkies will have scoured the park ages ago. They'll have my beads in their pockets by now, not that they'll be worth much to *them*!' Mrs Pattie glanced away in disappointment.

'I'm sorry, Ma. I'll try and make it up to you somehow.'

The older woman would speak no more, and the three of them ate breakfast in pained silence.

* * * * *

Just days after the dance, Will announced that he had to leave.

'So when will I see you again?' Bella asked.

'I won't lie to you – I really don't know. But I'll be back in a month or two. Take care o' yourself, won't you?'

In bed that night, she lay staring into the darkness for hours. When at last she slept, she dreamed of standing naked and alone, among a crowd of strangers. Her efforts to cover herself up were met with loud jeers and whistles that grew increasingly strident. Unable to bear it any longer, she woke up in a cold sweat.

Weeks passed till it occurred to her that Will's parting words had been an uncanny echo of Tam's.

9
If Only …

'It takes two flints to make a fire.' – Louisa May Alcott

I T WAS AT THE END of September 1867, three months after Will's departure, that Bella went hurrying outdoors to fetch kindling for the fire, and to her surprise, she was sick. At that same hour of the morning, it became a ritual for her to vomit in the undergrowth by the trees. In addition, her senses seemed to have sharpened overnight. Previously unremarkable for its flavour or odour, tea suddenly was horribly unpalatable. Even as she spooned dry leaves into the pot, the smell that wafted up from the open caddy left her nauseous.

Her mother watched, and her suspicions grew.

'Is there something ailing you?' Mrs Pattie inquired, when Bella yet again declined the offer of a cup of tea.

'It's the taste, I just can't go it these days.'

'Is that so?' Mother and daughter surveyed each other for a second or two. Mrs Pattie drew her mouth in, and continued eating.

That evening, Bella was alone in the bedroom when Ma appeared.

'Well now.' Mrs Pattie sat herself on the bed, smoothed her skirt and folded her hands primly in her lap to show she meant business. 'I think there's a matter you and I have to discuss, is there not?'

'I don't know, Ma. Is there?' Bella laid down her sewing.

'Did you think I wouldn't notice how you've stopped having tea? That's not normal for you. What's wrong?'

'Nothing … honest!' Bella smiled, all innocence.

'Aye, honest, you say, *but I don't think you are being honest.*
You're fooling yourself, but you won't fool me. Something
happened with that Will Turner, didn't it?'

There was no escaping Mrs Pattie's penetrating stare. Bella
moved to stand up, blushing to the very roots of her hair. She
wished she could die at that very instant. 'No, what would have
happened?' she said, but her voice shook.

The older woman let out an exasperated sigh. 'Fine you
know what I'm talking about. D'you think I can't guess what
you've been up to? I've not been myself recently, but I'm not
blind, Isabella!' she said. 'When did you have your monthlies?'

'I can't remember exactly ... I suppose it's a while.' Despite
her apparent nonchalance, the colour drained from her face, and
her knees went weak. She turned away in confusion.

'So you can't recall when you last saw blood?' Mrs Pattie
exclaimed, jumping up from the bed to grab hold of her daughter
by the wrist. They stood frozen together like statues. 'Look at
me when I talk to you!'

But Bella refused, instead staring straight ahead over her
mother's shoulder.

'You went and let Will Turner have his way with you, didn't
you? *Didn't you?* You might as well tell me, it'll come out
whatever!' Her iron grip was tightening with each second that
passed, her mouth distorted with the effort.

The girl cried out in futile denial, 'No! You're hurting me,
Ma! Let me go!' and a tear trickled down her cheek.

'I'll hurt you worse if you don't tell me the truth. Tell me,
then I'll let you go!' Mrs Pattie shrieked. 'You gave into him,
didn't you?'

'*Yes!*' Bella yelped. 'Yes ... but it was just once, the night of
the Gala Day dance. *We couldn't help it*! I'm sorry! I'm sorry,
Ma!' she groaned, falling to her knees, as if being sorry would
make everything right again.

'Aye, and not half as sorry as you'll be afore you're done, my
lady. You *couldn't help it?* Well, you'll be lucky ever to cast eyes

on that rascal, since he's had the best of you. No wonder he made off! Your Da's going to hit the roof when he hears.' Mrs Pattie bit her lower lip in disbelief. 'You're a silly lassie, not even an engagement ring on your finger, and you land yourself with a *bairn*.'

What?

Had she misheard, in the panic of confession? *What was it that Ma said?*

The word 'bairn' struck Bella like a thunderbolt, left her feeling faint.

A bairn! No, surely not, she couldn't be having a baby: it wasn't as easy as that, was it? Inside her a voice shrilled, '*No! No! No!* God, please help me! Let me wake up and find this is all a bad dream!'

But it was no dream. She wanted to curl up and die.

Poorly versed in biology, Bella had been blind to the symptoms of her pregnancy, never linking the activities of that evening with Will to her morning sickness and her unexpected aversion to tea.

Only married women were supposed to know such things.

* * * * *

She answered Ma's call to come through to the kitchen.

'I gather you have something to tell me, Isabella,' said her father, his brows drawn. He sat straight, his palms flat on the table, waiting.

She wanted to run and hide herself in shame. Taking a deep breath, she blurted out, 'Da, I'm sorry to let you and Ma down, to disgrace our family ...' She was close to tears. 'It was at the dance, one thing led to another ... it got out o' hand. But I didn't think it would come to this! I'm sorry!' She hung her head.

Like a rotten smell, silence filled the room.

'Aye. Your mother and I are sorry, too,' the father eventually said. 'And Turner? When's he coming back?'

71

'He didn't say ... he mentioned a month or two, but it depends on the job,' Bella wailed.

'Leaving you well and truly in the lurch, eh?' Mr Pattie cleared his throat. 'Is there to be a wedding? Or was there no talk about that before things reached such a pitch between you?'

'When Will gets a permanent post, he'll qualify for a railway house. And he'll be here in no time – he said he would.'

'We'll believe that when we see it!' said the mother sourly.

Will had also said he loved her, Bella wanted to confess, but thought better of it, conscious of the disdain with which such an admission would be met. Love was the preserve of poets, romantics and dreamers, or of ministers describing God's love. Its mention would be practically obscene at that moment.

James Pattie exhaled heavily. 'You must have lost your reason!' Gravely his eyes shifted from Bella to his wife and back again.

The girl squirmed.

'What are you going to do about this?' he inquired, glancing at her stomach. (The word 'pregnancy' was not one that would pass his lips.)

'I don't know ... if I'm to be banished to have this bairn, then I'll go. I'll do as you say.'

'Aye, and if you'd minded to do that a few months ago, you'd not be in this mess!' Mrs Pattie muttered.

'I won't pretend I'm not disappointed – it's hard to believe you'd be so stupid. There'll be fingers pointing at us, and you'll forever carry the stigma of having an illegitimate bairn,' continued the father.

In her self-loathing, Bella wanted to crawl under her seat, away from the awful intensity of his stare. But there was no escape.

Finally he spoke again. 'You'll stay here where you belong. Just remember this is a new being *you've* created. An extra mouth to feed means we'll need extra income which you'll have to provide.'

Receiving no answer, he said more loudly, 'Isabella! Are you listening to me?'

'Yes, Da,' she mumbled, not daring to look at him.

He struck the table with the flat of his hand, making the teacups rattle, and startling both his wife and daughter. 'Well for God's sake, lassie, *hold your head up*! Take responsibility for your actions, and don't be afraid. You made a mistake but it's not the end of the world! Now it's time we all got off to our beds.'

* * * * *

A year earlier, a cholera epidemic had swept the country, claiming the lives of thousands. When an outbreak of scarlet fever hit the village, it was decreed that Bella should stay indoors, safe from possible sources of infection. Given her predicament, she could not argue till she heard that Ruby had fallen ill.

'I have to go and see her, Ma.'

'You'll do no such thing.'

Nothing else was said, and Ruby's condition grew steadily worse. News of her friend's death arrived, and Bella was seized with a terrible guilt that drove her almost to distraction. In the cold darkness of her bedroom each night, jitters crept down her spine to recall the visit to Madame Rosa.

It had seemed such harmless fun, for her and Ruby to have their fortunes told, not doubting their futures were anything but bright! Could such a foolish entertainment bear any relation to the recent string of events? It was illogical to credit a dirty old woman with the power of prophecy. And yet ... it was on that same fateful afternoon that Will Turner, father of the child she was carrying, came on the scene ... and unless the gypsy really *could* foresee a life about to be cut short, why did she return Ruby's penny and refuse her a palm reading?

Bella shivered, and decided to dabble no more in the supernatural.

* * * * *

73

Mail arrived for her, and her spirits soared. Will was coming back, and things would be all right! So much for the way Ma and Da had spoken ill of him, saying he'd used her. She *knew* he'd get in touch, had been sure of it. The letter she held proved her faith in him was justified. Rushing through to the bedroom, Bella tore open the envelope with trembling fingers.

But her colour changed as she read.

> *134 Granville St,*
> *Halifax,*
> *Nova Scotia.*
> *September 20, 1867*

My Dearest Bella,

> *I don't know how to begin, but first, I'm sorry for being so slow to write. I hope you'll find it in your heart to forgive me when you hear what's been happening, because not a single day has passed when I've not thought of you.*

> *We had barely left Liverpool when typhoid broke out on the ship. I was fine for a wee while, believed I'd be one of the lucky ones, till I got so ill I was convinced that would be the end of me. Miraculously I made it to Halifax, but it took nearly two months for me to recover my strength.*

> *Business was booming in the dockyards, and I found a job with Mr Elliot, a ship's chandler. The town was growing so fast that he saw an opportunity to branch out with a general store, selling foodstuffs, clothing and dry goods. I begged him to let me run the new shop – I vowed to work all the hours God sent – and he agreed to give me a try.*

> *Now I've saved a bit of money. I want you to join me in Nova Scotia, and become my wife. We'll not be living in the nice wee cottage I promised, but in the*

apartment above the shop, which has five rooms.
You'll have a live-in servant to help you.

Don't worry about the journey here – whatever the
cost, I'll ensure that you travel in safety and comfort.
This is a magnificent country, Bella, so bonnie you'll
believe you're in Scotland!   I'm sorry for the delay, but
I had to wait until I had something worthwhile to offer
you.

Please give my warm regards and best wishes to
all your family.

I look forward to hearing from you.
Affectionately,

Tam.

Scarcely had she reached the bottom of the page when water gathered in her mouth and a wave of nausea washed over her. Out! She had to get out! Going to open the front door, she stood fanning herself as she rested against the doorpost, taking deep breaths of cool air. What a fool she was, not to immediately have recognised that flowing script, nor even to have glanced at the stamp or postmark as she ripped open the envelope! Fancy imagining for an instant that this fine letter could be from that useless numbskull, Will Turner!

But she was the biggest numbskull of all, for getting into this mess. A concrete proposal had been sent from halfway round the globe from Tam, her darling, clever Tam. Unable to accept, she was stuck forever in Gelston, an object of public derision, bearing the child of someone who couldn't make off fast enough after the intimacy they had shared. Someone who wouldn't write to her when he might be less than a hundred miles away!

She went into the kitchen and sat by the window. If Mrs Pattie noticed her pallor, she made no comment. Averting her eyes, she kept on with her ironing.

'What do you think of this, Ma? It's from Tam,' said Bella, holding out the envelope.

'From *Tam*? Are you sure you want to show me it?'

'Just read it.' Bella gulped, in an attempt to ignore the bile that was rising in her throat. 'I'll be back in a minute.'

She ran outside, and made it to the foetid darkness of the privy before the violent retching began. Solitude was what she needed, a place where she could be on her own, unobserved and unheard, to cope with the recriminations rampaging through her brain.

If only this baby were Tam's! But there was the rub: Tam had the self-discipline to plan ahead, would not have allowed this situation to arise. What folly, to surrender to someone as gullible as herself, someone too caught up in the pleasure of the moment to think of tomorrow. Five rooms and a servant, the letter said. She'd thrown up the chance of a lifetime! She had doubted the word of a man who would stand by her, while trusting a galoot that had his fun then fled.

But she'd got what she deserved, and no good would come of beating herself up over what might have been. She had chores to get done.

Straightening herself up, she opened the outhouse door, and struggled towards the midden, carrying the stinking privy pail. With each tottering pace she took, urine, vomit and excrement lapped against the sides of the bucket, threatening to spill over the edge on to her skirts. It occurred to her that this might be her fate, an existence of performing the dirtiest of jobs, at the beck and call of others.

Exactly like Agnes.

But wasn't she was better than that? She wanted to think so. She was prettier than her sister, certainly, but that counted for naught. Her unique advantage lay in sewing, where she'd always demonstrated natural ability and flair. Might that be her saving grace? Whether she was skilled enough with a needle to earn a living from it remained to be seen. There was one way to find out.

Desperate measures were required.

10
Double Trouble

'I like trying to get pregnant. I'm not so sure about childbirth.'
– George Eliot

T HE BEDROOM THE FOUR PATTIES had occupied as children was a haven of luxury in comparison to the loft where Agnes slept at Cuil. In winter, the bare wood rafters above her were white with frost, and she shivered the whole night through, alongside the other housemaid with whom she had to share a bed. When summer came, she wearily climbed the steep attic stairway at the end of her day's toil to lie sweating under the oppressive heat of the slates, till dawn arrived and she had to get back on duty again. For her keep and a pittance in pay, Agnes had relinquished her freedom. Like thousands in service, she was kept constantly busy, with just a few hours off once a month. Even her evenings were given over to mending clothes for the master and his family, or to remaking worn sheets by splitting them down the middle and joining the hemmed edges. No economy was too petty if domestics would otherwise have idle hands. Not for fifty years, with the changes brought by the First World War, would working women revolt against the life of bondage inflicted on domestic servants.

As the first-born of the family, Agnes had resented the many responsibilities that fell to her with the arrival of her three younger siblings. Her childhood had been sacrificed for the others, she frequently claimed when jealousy got the better of her. Bella had long since learned to ignore her sister's spiteful barbs.

'You're lucky you're getting to stay here, and have it at home,' Agnes whispered viciously, pointing at Bella's midriff. 'If you go to the poorhouse, you'll need a ring. Let on that you're not married, and they'll press a mattress over your face and that'll be the death o' you – or so they say!'

'Be quiet,' Bella retorted.

* * * * *

Around the fifth month of her pregnancy, the morning sickness faded, and Bella positively glowed. Her usually pale cheeks were rosy, her red hair shone, and she was filled with energy. Along with the daily cup of raspberry leaf tea foisted on her by Mrs Pattie, Bella was assured that physical activity – scrubbing, sweeping and digging – would speed the delivery process, making for an easy birth. In the evenings she sat sewing.

Almost at term, when her stomach resembled a big, hard football, Bella felt real terror. How on earth would she get the creature out of there? Neither explanation nor reassurance was forthcoming when she tried to ask about her mother's experiences. Mrs Pattie delighted in painting the birthing process as a terrifying ritual of womanhood, its awfulness beyond the worst imaginings of the uninitiated.

'You'll know all about it soon enough,' Ma told her. 'Remember you're the one that got yourself into this! We'll get Wee Teenie when you're due, and she'll get you through it. Keep your fingers crossed she's sober.'

Wee Teenie was a venerable local character. Short and fat, with dishevelled hair and permanently rumpled clothes that suggested she wore them night and day, her midwifery skills nonetheless commanded a huge degree of respect.

On February 25, 1868, Bella went into labour. The fire was built up, with a huge pot of hot water at the ready. When the midwife arrived, she said, 'We might as well settle ourselves down for a wait ... I've seen lassies take two rounds o' the clock to get the first one out o' there!' Nonchalantly she took up her knitting.

But two hours later, the birth was near. At the final, agonising contraction, there was a last exhortation from Teenie, 'Come on now, Bella, PUSH! PUSH! Come on, lassie, you've had a stiffer shite many a time! PUSH! PUSH!'

All of a sudden in one slimy whoosh, the baby was there, and the midwife announced, 'Oh, you've got a lovely wee girl, look at her!' She placed a wrinkly red creature in Bella's arms. 'Did you think of a name for her, yet?'

'Yes.'

Mrs Pattie raised an eyebrow, for no such thing had been discussed.

'She's going to be called Thomasina Hyslop Pattie,' Bella stated.

Then she sat up in bed to sip at a cup of hot tea, better than any she'd tasted in her life, and thought of Tam.

* * * * *

Dear Bella,

I'm missing you and working hard. See you before long.

Will.

It bore an Edinburgh postmark, no return address and no indication of when he would come back to Galloway, but Will said he was missing her. He hadn't forgotten her, for what that was worth, though his poor penmanship made Bella ashamed.

Mrs Pattie read the postcard, and remarked disdainfully, 'Don't hold your breath. He maybe mails notes to lassies all over the country.'

But Will would not send more cards or letters than strictly necessary, because writing was not one of his strong points. Of that Bella was sure.

James Pattie had made no reference to Bella's pregnancy after that night months earlier when the truth had come out. He did, however, astound her with a gift for the baby. During odd moments he had crafted a wooden cradle and could scarcely conceal his pride when Thomasina was laid in it. The old chest drawer that Agnes, Bella, and the two boys had slept in as infants was not good enough for his grandchild.

If she'd been presented with the crown jewels, they would not have seemed as beautiful to Bella than that cradle her father had lovingly created with his own hands.

* * * * *

'You need to think about going to the registrar,' Mr Pattie said. 'You can come with me when I'm next taking the cart round by Rhonehouse, and I'll drop you off. Take your birth certificate, and tell Mr Johnstone you want to register Thomasina, that's all.'

But it was not quite all.

Bella was shown into the kitchen by Mrs Johnstone, who said, 'I'll tell him you're here. He'll be through in a minute. Have a seat.'

The one minute turned into twenty, and at last the registrar appeared. He entered the kitchen, busily fastening up his collar stud since this was official business. Taking a seat opposite Bella, he studiously ignored her. First he fussed with his pen, then he signalled to his wife that his ink pot needed refilling, and dug deep into his waistcoat pocket for his monocle.

'So, what brings you here?' he demanded, looking down his thin nose.

'I came to register a birth.'

'I see. Very well,' he said, fumbling with some papers. 'What's the name?'

'Isabella Pattie.'

'Yes, yes, but the child will be called ...?'

'Oh, I'm sorry. No, the baby's Thomasina Hyslop Pattie.'

Date and place of birth were noted, before Mr Johnstone's favourite question.

'Name of the father?'

Pointedly he glanced at Bella's hand on which there was no ring.

She was nervous, but would not be bullied. With a toss of her head and a shrug of her shoulders, she stared the registrar in the eye and said nothing.

'I'm curious ... is the father one of the Hyslops?'

'Indeed he is not. Hyslop is my mother's maiden name,' Bella snapped.

As if it were any of his concern!

'Well, you'd better give me *your* name and your occupation, if you have one.'

'My name is Isabella Pattie. I'm the carrier's daughter,' she said haughtily.

He wrote for a few seconds. 'We're nearly finished. If you'll just sign there, I'll fill in the remaining details.'

Bella watched him smugly complete the birth certificate.

'Almost there,' he announced. 'One small item to enter.'

With a flourish of the pen, he wrote 'Illegitimate' immediately below Thomasina's name, pressed a square of blotting paper over his signature, and thrust the slip of paper across the table.

With an infant in the house again, Mrs Pattie's addiction to laudanum dwindled. Outsiders mistook her for the child's mother, so strong was the bond between them, and Bella felt excluded. The two of them nurtured each other. When she could talk, Thomasina stubbornly addressed her grandmother as 'Mamma' rather than 'Nana'. It was as if the gaping wound left by Jimmy's death had been healed.

Sewing occupied most of Bella's waking hours since she'd found employment as a 'piece worker', putting shirts together at home for a Dumfries manufacturer. Each week, Mr Pattie ferried her completed articles to town, and brought another pile of cut fabric back to Gelston for assembly. A calm routine was established till a bombshell shattered their peace.

11
Humiliation

*'Oh! if those selfish men ... who are the cause of all one's
misery, only knew what their poor slaves go through!'*
– Queen Victoria

BATHGATE, 1870

ISA WAS PREGNANT AGAIN. It had never been easy, with so
many mouths to feed. Some days there was bread and
dripping, and little else to eat at the Barclays' table. Peter
continued to do what he could to help the family, and with the
birth of his second son, William, in March of 1870, Isa began to
entertain hopes of remarrying. It was, after all, five years since
she'd been widowed, and so far Peter had stood by her. Maybe a
hint or two would not go amiss ...

One fine May evening, with the older children out playing on
the street and the infant William at her breast, she and Peter had
a rare moment alone. To Isa, it seemed perfectly reasonable to
broach the subject of matrimony, but Peter's response was not
what she anticipated. He was adamant that he wouldn't marry
her or anyone else.

'I'm just no' the marryin' kind, Isa! I've told you that fae the
start. You picked the wrong man if it's a ring you want, hen.'

'Will you at least come with me to register William? It was
supposed to be done before the wean's three weeks old, and now
he's nearly two months! I hated havin' to go there on my own,
the way that Mr Rankine squints at you. Makes you feel like a
criminal or a piece o' dirt!'

Peter shook his head dismissively. 'Sorry, darlin'. No can
do.' He got to his feet.

'But can we not even talk about it?' she pleaded.

'Nothin' to talk about. I fancy a drink. I'm away down to the pub for a glass o' beer. See you the morn!' With that, Peter put on his jacket and cap, and was off out the door, leaving Isa and the baby alone.

It must be great to be a man, she thought. He could get up and go anywhere, any time he felt like it, and all she could do was wait at home and cross her fingers that he'd return. She'd have to quit nagging him to get married, or he'd find somebody else, and where would that leave her? The possibility that he might already have a wife somewhere was something she would not – *could not* – entertain. And if he did, then what? It was best not to ask. He always paid her rent and gave her just enough to put food on the table. For that she had to be thankful.

With no option but to get herself down to the registrar's office, Isa went alone, in this instance bearing her marriage certificate. In the corner of the room, Mr Napier sat writing, and Mr Rankine glared up from his desk as she entered.

'Can I help you?' he enquired in feigned bewilderment, fully aware of why she'd come, since she carried the new baby, wrapped snugly in the plaid against her chest.

'I've come to register a birth,' said Isa, taking a seat at the other side of the desk.

'Hmm.' Mr Rankine put on his pince-nez, known in Scotland as 'nose nippers'. They helped him see better and added to his gravitas, a distinct advantage in dealing with the type of woman sitting before him. Mr Napier had decided to acquire a similar pair when ultimately he filled his superior's shoes.

'And the child's name would be?'

Isa hesitated. 'Bartholomew. William Bartholomew.'

The registrar leaned back in his chair to scowl sternly across at her over the top of his spectacles. 'Do you have documentation to verify the use of that name? I seem to recall your previously registering an infant here, but *not* as Bartholomew.'

'Bartholomew was my husband's name,' said Isa, bristling.

Mr Rankine took a desultory look at the marriage certificate she thrust under his nose.

'Yes. Quite ... and is that also the name of the father?'

'No it isn't. I'm a widow, but the law says I have to register the birth of my bairn.'

'So, no father,' said Mr Rankine, as he wrote, casting a meaningful nod in the direction of Mr Napier, who listened attentively. 'And what might be appropriate for *mother's* name and occupation?'

'I didn't have to give all this information in the past, so why does it matter now?' Isa was in danger of losing her temper.

'It matters, dear lady, since it is my duty to ensure that a birth certificate provides all the pertinent details. I'm literally following the letter of the law, as you claim to be doing.'

That should silence the hussy!

He paused. 'I'm waiting for an answer. *What* shall we say you do for a living? Do you *have* any source of income that you care to mention?'

She was close to tears, but determined not to cry in the presence of this officious bully. 'No, I don't.'

The registrar pounced on this admission. 'So you have no husband and no visible means of support? Yet you somehow manage to pay your rent and continue having more children!'

Isa made no response.

Mr Rankine filled in the required data, registering the baby as William Bartholomew, and inserting 'or Graham' beneath, with the word 'Illegitimate'. With malicious satisfaction he mouthed 'pauper' as he wrote it where the father's occupation would normally be noted.

The truth will out, thought Mr Napier, barely suppressing a smile at his mentor's truly masterful performance.

'Sign your name here, Mistress!' ordered Mr Rankine in his most peremptory tone.

Furious at what he'd written, Isa seized the pen from him and as boldly as she could, scrawled 'Isabella Bartholomew'.

But even there, Mr Rankine had the final say. Under her signature, he meticulously added 'Or Graham'. He thrust the completed certificate at Isa with a curt nod and said mockingly, 'Good day to you, *Mistress Bartholomew*.'

'Aye, and the same to *you*, Mr Rankine.'

Isa was pink with anger. She struggled to collect herself and William started to wail. Holding him tightly to her with one arm, she went striding out of the office with the two documents in her other fist, and her head high.

A conspiratorial smirk passed between the registrar and his assistant.

* * * * *

'We're goin' out to play, Maw. See you later!'

'Right, mind and be in afore it gets dark, because you've to be up early in the morning!' Isa called to her two oldest boys as they stepped out to the street. It did them good to get out and kick a ball around. They were really still bairns at ten and eleven years of age, and it was healthy for them to get the fresh air. It was amazing, the difference James made with the shillings earned. He was the older of the two, had recently left school to take a job at the mine, and John would join him in a few months.

Christina had gone out, allegedly for a walk with a neighbour's daughter. They seemed to be taking an awful lot of walks together, these two, and Isa suspected some young men were keeping them company.

Curled up in a corner of the kitchen, Charlie was drawing pictures of locomotives. He was daft about trains, nearly to the point of obsession, his mother would say. He spent hours alone on the railway embankment watching them go by, absorbing every detail of the engines, their motion, the noise, the smoke and the steam that made the whistle blow. Any scraps of paper he got his hands on were lovingly smoothed and preserved for sketches.

When he got home from school, he'd gathered from Isa's bedraggled appearance that she'd been crying. 'Is there something up, Maw?' he had asked solicitously.

Isa immediately put on a smile for him, red eyes and all. 'Of course not, son, I'm fine. I'm always fine, you know that!'

But Charlie wasn't so sure. He'd not actually witnessed Maw crying. On the contrary, she contrived to wear a smile, however she was feeling.

The boy's ears pricked up at the sound of Peter Inglis coming in. There was no mistaking his approach. The front door would open suddenly and slam shut very fast, followed by the thud of his boots on the stone floor as he tramped across the kitchen. Taking a seat, he plunked his filthy cap down on the table top.

'And what's doin' wi' ye the night, Isa?'

She placed a bowl of soup in front of him, and cut a chunk of bread. 'I went and registered William, and you've no idea what I had to put up with! I never want to see that Mr Rankine again.'

'Och, come on, ye're far too sensitive.' Peter dipped his bread into the soup. 'Good soup! I was ready for it. Hard labour and a glass or two o' beer can fairly gie a man an appetite!'

Isa was about to speak when she noticed Charlie, ostensibly drawing, but all ears to hear what was distressing his Maw. 'Charlie! You should be out playing wi' the rest o' the bairns. Go on, away you go. I forgot you were still there. This is private, son.'

The boy got up reluctantly. 'Och, Maw! I don't want to play, I'd rather draw. I'll go through to the room, and I'll not wake Alexander and William, I promise,' he whined, hoping to pick up snippets of the conversation from behind the door.

Allowing Isa no chance to speak, Peter barked, 'Hey! You! *Out now before I kick your arse!* You heard your Maw. Go on, dae whit she tells ye, get oot and play. Skedaddle, Charlie Barlie!'

Charlie slammed the door as he went out. He hated it when Peter called him Charlie Barlie. Just who did he think he was, anyway, coming swaggering in as if he owned the place, with his rotten beery breath? Paw didn't stink *and* he'd known better than sit hunched over his food, with his elbows resting on the table, let alone slurp and leave droplets of soup hanging like icicles from his whiskers. But nobody could deny that his Paw had been twice the man Peter Inglis was!

Though he would not admit it, Charlie was finding it tricky to remember anything much at all of his Paw, except that he was everything Peter was not.

* * * * *

'He insisted on puttin' "or Graham" under the bairn's name and mine. Then he wrote "*pauper*"! Take a look for yourself – *that's* what I had to put up with, and not a thing I could do about it!' Isa cried in fury as she brandished William's birth certificate in front of Peter's nose.

She was aware he didn't want to hear the details – didn't want any part of the whole sorry business, including the brat he'd spawned – yet she needed to vent her frustration to someone, had to get it out of her system. It was high time Peter understood some of the indignities she had to tolerate! Bad enough was her annoyance at the registrar's cruel high-handedness, not to mention her own powerlessness. She should have had the wit to state that she was a housekeeper, which was the truth! Instead, poor William would eternally bear the shame of the word 'pauper' beside his mother's name, doubling the stigma of his illegitimacy. It was there for all the world to see, on the certificate that would define him at each important milestone of his life.

'Well, I'm sorry you got put through all that, hen,' said Peter. 'Rankine's a twat, thinks some book learnin' makes him superior to ordinary workin' folk. Such upstarts should be ignored. Forget it.'

Isa would not be consoled. If anything, being brushed aside increased her irritation. 'Maybe so, but I wouldnae get treated like that if I was married.'

Seeing the ominous direction the conversation was taking, Peter said, 'Aye, but you know where I stand on that. Is there ony mair o' that soup?'

Isa wasn't done. She would make him wait till she'd had her say. Since Peter was no longer the sole provider of revenue in the Barclay abode, she could risk asserting herself for once.

'All I'm saying is that it's *twice* I've had to confront him on my own and it's no' fair. It's no' a problem for you, you're a man, he wouldnae dare insult you like that. I'm a soft target and he gets away wi' murder!' she cried, her voice rising.

Still mellow from the beer, Peter offered a grand concession.

'Well, all right, here's what we'll do. If you have to go near that office again – and wi' ony luck you'll not – I'll come wi' ye. I can't say fairer than that. Now are you bringin' me more soup, or do I have to do *everythin'* round here myself?'

A man's magnanimity could be stretched only so far.

* * * * *

Although theoretically against their oppression, Queen Victoria firmly believed that women should be kept in their place. After hearing of peaceful petitions for female suffrage, she wrote in 1870:

> *The Queen is most anxious to enlist everyone who can speak or write to join in checking this mad, wicked folly of 'Women's Rights', with all its attendant horrors, on which her poor feeble sex is bent, forgetting every sense of womanly feeling and propriety.*

Such an unethical deviation from the accepted role of women could not be tolerated! The Queen saw it as her duty to uphold society's norms of behaviour. She was, after all, the moral compass of the nation and the empire.

Her private life was her own concern. What happened in the palace was to stay in the palace – that went without saying.

12
Highs and Lows

'Our deeds determine us, as much as we determine our deeds.'
– George Eliot

GELSTON, 1869–1871

AT THE AGE OF TWENTY-NINE, Agnes Pattie finally found a sweetheart, a stockman who also worked at Cuil. Too late she discovered that her lover was married, because by then she was pregnant. In her fourth month, her expanding waistline led to dismissal in disgrace from her job.

It was in December 1869, that her father came to collect her. Agnes barely acknowledged his arrival. Without a word of greeting, she tossed her bundle into the back of the cart, and climbed up to sit beside him.

As they jolted along the potholed track, she huffed and puffed audibly.

Just a mile into their journey, James Pattie pulled into the side of the road.

'What's this? Why have we stopped?' Agnes demanded.

'We're going to have a talk.'

'I'm cold, Da. Whatever it is can keep till we're home.'

'I'll be the judge of that. There are things we must settle today.'

He launched into the same stern lecture he'd given Bella. The new baby would be Agnes's responsibility, and she had to devise a way of contributing to the household expenses.

'So what do you propose?'

Agnes sighed and pouted. 'I'd need to think about it for a while.'

'Decide now, or you're not coming to Gelston.'

She flushed with indignation. 'We'll see about that!' she retorted, and made to jump down to the ground.

'Sit where you are!' he commanded.

'I'll walk the rest o' the road!'

'You'll behave yourself, and give me an answer. *How are you going to earn your keep?*'

It was pointless to argue further. Da was so stubborn, he'd make her sit there till dark unless she came up with something. With great reluctance, she suggested that she could make a shilling or two a week by taking in laundry.

'But only if there was a proper place for me to work,' she said.

'That could be arranged, I'm sure.'

With a sly smile, Agnes replied, 'Fine.'

She would be safe for a few months, she hoped, because constructing a shed would be a lengthy process. Her father might not get round to it at all.

Agnes relished the idea of intruding on her sister's domain, making her room home to three people – four once her child arrived. It was tough luck that Bella's cosy routine would be disrupted. She might think she was queen of the castle, but that was about to change!

Faster than expected, a lean-to was added behind the stable, and the wash house was completed. James Pattie collected basket-loads of soiled apparel and bedding on his rounds, and dumped them at the side of the building for laundering. Agnes seethed with resentment. Why should she slave out there on her own on a winter's day? She'd to light the fire in the boiler, pump water and ferry bucket loads in to heat. The heavy wet laundry had to be lugged back and forth to the mangle – all as Bella sat smugly sewing by the hearth! It was the story of Agnes's life – again she was a victim. Since isolation was foisted on her, she would turn it to her own advantage.

A plan took shape in her mind. All she'd to do was summon the courage to act upon it, and dislodge the unwelcome being that was growing inside her. It was the logical thing ... she didn't want a baby anyhow. Unceremoniously dropping a pile of wet sheets on the floor, she lifted one foot, then the other, and heaved her bulk up on to a rickety old stool to stand looking around her. Taking a deep breath, she stepped down cannily at first. She clambered up to make a second, less cautious descent. Increasingly daring, she braced herself to take a flying leap forward and landed heavily on the flagstone floor, when Bella appeared.

'What happened, are you all right?'

Sullenly Agnes picked herself up, and moved to climb on to the stool once more. 'Aye, I'm fine. Away you go, get on with your sewing and let me finish what I've started.'

'Stop it! You'll hurt yourself and the bairn with that carry-on!'

'Don't *you* tell me what I can or can't do!'

Gently Bella took her hand. 'Come on, I'll make us a cup of tea, and you'll feel better.'

'Tea? It's a bottle o' gin I want to get hold of, something to pull the plug on the bugger in here!' Agnes cried, pointing at her stomach, before bursting into tears.

Then she allowed herself to be led outside and into the kitchen.

* * * * *

As the birth drew near, her ill humour grew. Like a caged beast, Agnes padded up and down, as if ready to spring at the least provocation.

Mr Pattie's next trip to bring Wee Teenie to the house was in May of 1870.

Having yowled constantly throughout her hours of labour, Agnes cried, 'I can't bear it any more! You'll have to give me something for this pain!'

'Come on, you're goin' to have a beautiful baby in your arms very soon, just think o' that!' soothed the midwife.

'What about the chloroform the Queen got when she gave birth to Prince Leopold? I could do with some of that!'

'Aye, and when you're queen wi' your own royal physician to attend to you, you'll get chloroform too!'

The moans continued, rising in volume till eventually Agnes shrieked, 'I want to die ... I can't stand this! Let me die and be done with it!'

At the end of her tether, Wee Teenie seized her wrist. '*You listen to me*, my lady! I've had enough. You've done nothin' but shout the odds since I got here, and I'm fed up wi' it! You burned your arse nine months ago and now you'll sit on the blisters. And don't dare think o' dyin', because your wean needs you.'

Shortly afterwards, Mary Jane Pattie made her entrance to the world. Bella and her parents heaved a sigh of relief as the new mother slept.

Agnes remained in such poor spirits that her sole desire was to lie alone in a darkened room. She wept and wept. At Mrs Pattie's insistence she got out of bed to sit in the kitchen, huddled in a chair with a shawl round her, but her refusal to feed Mary Jane at her breast meant the little mite had to survive on warm milk from a spoon until James Pattie brought home a feeding bottle from Dumfries.

Mrs Pattie was sorry for Agnes, but on occasion she would scold, saying, 'Come on, get up out of there and get yourself washed. You can't sit like a dirty clart. Your clothes stink, and so do you!'

Agnes paid no heed. She was unhappy, and would ensure everyone else was, too.

* * * * *

The arrival of a postcard raised Bella's spirits.

Sunnyside Road,
Coatbridge,
Lanarkshire.
September 1, 1870

Dear Bella,

I have to come to Galloway for two weeks. It's been a while, but can I see you if you are free?

Will.

She found it difficult to contain her excitement.

Her mother's reaction was ominous. 'The bad penny turns up again, eh? From your smile, I gather you want to talk to him?'

'Of course I do, to tell him what's been going on since he left – including the birth of his bairn!'

Mrs Pattie frowned slightly. 'Ye should think well about this. Mind what you put in writing.'

That same evening Bella sat down and penned her first letter to Will.

14 Gelston Village,
By Castle Douglas.
September 8, 1870

Dear Will,

Thank you for your postcard. I look forward to seeing you. I'll be here at the house and we'll catch up on all the news then. I might even have a little surprise for you!

Bella.

She adopted a beauty regimen of sorts, taking a spoonful of treacle with some powdered flowers of sulphur, to purify her blood and clear her complexion. To wash her hair she used soap and powdered borax, leaving it so clean it squeaked, then rinsed it with vinegar to make it shine. Mornings filled her with elation, to think that might be the day he would arrive.

Learning of Will's impending visit, Agnes quipped, 'I hadn't twigged what was behind all this sudden interest in your appearance, primping in front of the mirror like some love-struck young idiot! Well, I'm warning you, it's not worth the effort. When you tell him you've got a bairn, you'll not see his heels for dust. I'm amazed he's even bothering to look you up again.'

Ignoring her sister, Bella continued with her sewing.

'He should keep away, the trouble he's caused you!' Agnes muttered.

Their mother chipped in. 'Aye, Will Turner needn't imagine he can whistle and you'll come running! Not after what happened the last time.'

Irritation got the better of Bella. 'Have the pair of you quite finished? Don't harp on about "what happened the last time" as if he intentionally ran out on me, Ma!'

'And don't you get ratty with me, my girl! All I'm saying is you've to take care. There's to be no more *funny business* with him or anybody else, till you're wearing a wedding ring and things are signed and sealed. The same goes for you, Agnes!' Wagging her index finger perilously close to Bella, she added, 'Are you listening to me?'

'Yes, Ma.' Bella's reply came through clenched teeth.

She concentrated on rethreading her needle. It took all the restraint she could muster not to slap at Ma's hand. How dared they all think the worst of Will, and presume to ram their unsolicited advice down her throat?

* * * * *

They saw him coming before he knocked at the front door. Immediately Mrs Pattie whisked Thomasina and Mary Jane out to the rear of the house. Bella lifted her chin, smoothed her hair, and went to let him in. He had changed – still had a head of dark hair – but he had filled out during the transition from youthful gangliness to the heavier set of manhood.

'Hello, Bella,' was all he said.

She smiled. 'Come on in.'

Will followed awkwardly into the kitchen, and they sat opposite each other, the room so quiet that she was convinced he would hear the beating of her heart. It was hard to believe he was actually there, this person who had occupied her thoughts for the previous three years.

He sat motionless, staring disconcertingly across at her till she said, 'Let me get you a cup of tea. I baked scones a wee while ago ...'

'No, thanks ... just stay there. I'm so relieved to see you – I was worried you'd be different, or that you'd have married somebody else! And you've not changed a bit, unless you're even bonnier than you used to be. Your hair still shimmers like gold, your skin's still as pale – you're exactly as I've pictured you since I left ...'

He was in mid-sentence when the kitchen door burst open. Thomasina came running in and stopped dead in her tracks at the sight of the stranger sitting at the table.

Will glanced quizzically at Bella, then at Thomasina with her black tousled curls, and back at Bella once more. 'Whose is the wean?'

'Well,' Bella began, trying not to smile, 'I told you there might be a surprise for you, didn't I? This is Thomasina, my ... *our* daughter.'

Will was struck dumb. He gazed at the child, moved his lips, and no sound emerged. Although her entrance was unplanned, Thomasina's timing had been perfect.

'My God, Bella, I'd no idea! I wish I'd known. If you'd written to me, I would have ...' he stammered.

'You'd have *what*? And how could I write to you?' Bella interrupted, scooping Thomasina up to sit on her lap. 'You provided no address, said you'd see me in a few months and disappeared into thin air!' She kept her tone even, tried not to appear angry.

'I just didn't foresee this. I mean, it was only the once that we ... it's a shock, to be honest.'

'Aye, it was quite a shock to me as well. And to Ma and Da.'

Will stretched over the table to hold her hand. 'I'm sorry. I can't imagine what you must have been through ... but I'll do my best to make this up to you, Bella. Trust me, I'm always going to be there when you need me. I won't leave you again.'

* * * * *

Thomasina was quickly won over by the pink sugar mice and lemon drops Will took to bringing her from the village sweetie shop. Mr and Mrs Pattie presented a bigger challenge but even they found themselves warming to him once more. On the night before he was due to depart, he stood with Bella at the side of the house as dusk fell.

'I think we should get married, if you'll have me.'

She drew away from him, overjoyed, but unwilling to seem too eager.

'I might,' she replied playfully. 'It would depend ...'

'Depend on what?'

'On whether your proposal is genuine or not! How am I to believe you, when you might vanish again?'

She had to say it.

He appeared offended, till she smiled.

'I do mean it, Bella! You have my word – it's going to be you, me and Thomasina in Coatbridge. In the spring I'll bring you an engagement ring, that's a promise.'

* * * * *

It was at the end of March 1871, when her child was ten months old, that Agnes ultimately exhausted her father's patience. Despite having regained her strength, she lazed around in the mornings, refusing to get up unless forced to. Her attitude grated on James Pattie until he could contain himself no further. She might think she could sit idle, sulking and neglecting her baby, but he wouldn't tolerate such behaviour any more, he declared.

Agnes made no response. Instead she gathered her shawl more tightly about her shoulders, and bent forward to poke the fire.

'You're not pulling your weight. The shed was built for you, but it sits empty half the week.'

'I'm done with guddling among other folk's mucky, smelly clothes,' she retorted.

'You'd better find some other employment, then, because you can't continue this way.'

'I don't see why not!' Agnes let the poker fall onto the hearth with a clatter.

Mildly Mr Pattie said, 'What about piece work?'

'You know fine I can't sew like Bella. But if I'm not welcome here, I'll clear out.'

'Be reasonable, Agnes. Where else would you go?'

'England, if you'll lend me the train fare. Carr's of Carlisle are advertising in the paper for workers. They make biscuits eaten by Queen Victoria herself.'

Her father harrumphed. 'And Mary Jane? Who'll take care of her while you're in a factory?'

The girl scowled. 'She has a home here with you, hasn't she?'

Exchanging a look with her husband, Mrs Pattie said, 'You're taking a lot for granted. She's *yours,* in case you forgot!'

'If you're flinging us both out, I'll find somebody else to watch her.'

'No!' gasped her mother.

'I'd have no choice.'

'With the horror stories you read about baby farms, it would be a terrible risk.'

'She'll survive,' Agnes responded nonchalantly.

'No grandchild o' mine will be thrown on the mercy of an outsider,' declared Mrs Pattie. 'Go south if that's what you want, and leave the bairn here.'

'Suits me!' The agreement came with indecent haste, so ecstatic was Agnes to be casting off the shackles of parenthood.

In due course, her father drove her to Castle Douglas for the train to Carlisle. When he returned to Gelston, it was to a changed atmosphere, not exactly peaceful with an infant and a toddler around, yet a harmony of sorts had been restored.

* * * * *

As promised, Will reappeared in Galloway to present Bella with a gold band, on which were set three pinhead diamonds.

Mrs Pattie sniffed, 'I hope he'll not *want* some day, wasting his hard-earned cash on a bauble for your finger!'

Bella held her hand this way and that, admiring the sparkle of the most extravagant piece of jewellery she'd known. She would not dignify her mother's remark with a reply. Will obviously was not short of a pound or two! Whatever the engagement ring had cost, he thought she was worth it.

In any case, what business was it of Ma's?

13
The Census

'Do not presume, well-housed, well-warmed, and well-fed, to criticize the poor.' – Herman Melville

BATHGATE, 1871

HAD SHE SUSPECTED who was at the door, Isa would not have opened it. She'd been baking at the kitchen table, with a stack of unwashed dishes at one side. Nappies were steeping in the zinc bath that occupied the middle of the floor, and a pile of laundry was strewn over a chair. Baby William lay in the box bed as Alexander, aged four, played busily with a spinning top in front of the fire. Isa's fingers were covered in flour, some of it smeared on her brow where she'd brushed away a strand of dark brown hair that had worked loose.

It would be one of the neighbours, she thought when the knock came, because it was like that when you lived in the rows. At any hour of the day or night, a neighbour could come to borrow a cup of sugar or flour, and Isa could do the same when necessary, till she had time (or money) to go to the cooperative store. Shopping at the co-op was one of the few advantages of Bathgate: nearly everything there was cheaper than at the mine company's store. She had her own account number and all her purchases were noted. At the end of the quarter, she lined up at the office to receive a dividend based on the amount she'd spent. It was welcome wee windfall, the 'divvy'.

Hearing another peremptory knock at the door, she went to answer it. A young man stood on the doorstep, holding a briefcase.

'Ah, so you *are* at home, I see! Good morning, Mistress!' he said cheerily.

Isa stood on the threshold, one hand on her hip, the other on the doorpost, blocking the entry. 'What can I do for you?' She wore her habitual little smile, trying to recall where she'd previously met him.

'I'm collecting details of each house and its occupants for the census. May I come in? It shouldn't take long.'

The word 'census' immediately jogged her memory. Napier, that was his name, Rankine's sidekick from the registrar's office.

Mr Napier stepped inside, wearing an expression of distaste, as if a bad smell assailed his nostrils. God! The hovels some people kept, they lived no better than animals!

Had she invited visitors, Isa would have tidied up, but anything was good enough for this wee nyaff. She moved the dirty dishes and the dough she'd been kneading for scones, to make room for his papers.

Mr Napier eyed the grubby child playing on the floor, brushed the crumbs from the seat she offered him and gingerly sat down. Had to watch – his new pinstriped trousers had cost a pretty penny!

'Let's proceed, shall we?' he said, producing his pen and fastidiously placing his pot of ink on the table. 'May I have the name of the head of the household?'

'That would be me. My name is Isabella Barclay.'

'And how big is your home?'

'It's a room and kitchen, same as all the rest in the street,' Isa replied dryly. As if he didn't know how big the row houses in Durhamtown were!

Mr Napier dipped the nib of his pen in the ink, and wrote with painstaking slowness. Isa sat straight-backed, her arms folded in front of her. Alexander was still and quiet, gazing up at the intruder, then at his mother, before giving his full attention once more to his spinning top.

'Let's deal with the other members of the family now. Starting with the eldest, if you please.'

Isa enumerated her seven offspring, providing age and place of birth, as the law required.

'Are all seven called Barclay, did you say?'

'I didn't say. But yes, they are.'

Mr Napier squinted at her, his pen in mid-air and a supercilious smile playing around his mouth. 'Hmm … Barclay, you say? But isn't there a *tiny inconsistency* somewhere? I rarely forget a face, and I distinctly recollect being present in Mr Rankine's office when you registered the births of your last two sons. The names Graham and Bartholomew were mentioned, were they not?'

He laid down the pen triumphantly, waiting for her reaction, but when it came it was not what he expected.

Isa rose to her feet, and stood by her chair. It was like a bad dream, to have this upstart from Rankine's office come to her house, and try to interrogate her in her own kitchen! Well, he needn't think he could come here and intimidate her. This was *her* territory, and she would stay in control.

'It may be the case that Alexander and William are registered as Graham, Mr Napier, but our family is called Barclay!' she stated, her brown eyes nearly popping out of their sockets in defiance.

Mr Napier remained in his seat. 'As you will, *Mistress Barclay*, but since I happen to be in possession of the facts, I really must list your sons Alexander and William under their legal surnames. It's my duty to make the census accurate.'

Drawing herself up to her full height, Isa glared at the ridiculous little man as he finished writing. 'It makes not one whit of difference to me, what you write on your silly wee census sheets. I've got more important things to think about. But this is *my home*, and I'll name myself and my offspring anything I please, without having to answer to you! So you can just get out of here – go on, scram! *Bugger off*!' she said, surprising herself. She marched across to the door and held it wide open.

Mr Napier turned bright red. Flustered, he could think of no response to such blatant rudeness. Hurriedly he gathered up his papers and bundled them into his bag with his pen and pot of ink. Never had he been exposed to such unwarranted insolence!

In a final act of disobedience, Isa lifted one foot, narrowly missing his behind as he scurried past her and bolted out onto the street without a backward glance. She was damned if she'd be bullied by a pompous squirt such as him!

Mr Napier had regained his cool by the time he reached the office later that day, though he still smarted from the indignity of being dismissed. To be ejected from a property was tantamount to failure. He had failed to command the respect his position deserved. Heaven forbid that Mr Rankine should hear how he'd been humiliated by a woman in Durhamtown of all places, a repository for the lowest of the low! Mistress Barclay might have thrown him out, but he'd make sure that the census record for her dwelling included a full account of the shenanigans that went on there. Yes, it would all be noted down for posterity.

He would make Mr Rankine proud of him.

14
Wedding Bells

'Never say that marriage has more of joy than pain.'
– Euripides

GELSTON, 1871

PLANS WERE IN PLACE for Bella and Will to get married in December of 1871. It would be a small affair, since the bridegroom's parents were deceased, and he had no other relatives.

Bella rode into Dumfries on the cart with her father to buy a length of brown silk, the best she could afford. She would make her wedding gown using a dress pattern from a magazine. Silk was expensive, but she was determined to wed in style. The minute they arrived back, she rushed into the kitchen, keen to show her mother her purchase, only to be instantly deflated.

Glancing at the fabric Mrs Pattie said, 'Where do you get such big ideas? You need to *save* what money you have, not squander it on fripperies. First you flaunt that engagement ring, and now it's this!' She fingered a corner of the material then let it fall disdainfully from her hand. 'Silk, indeed! Diamonds and silk aren't for the likes of us, you know. And when will you ever wear such a thing again, eh?'

'I'll just be getting married once, Ma, so why not?'

The mother pursed her lips. 'It would be more appropriate to make do with your Sunday frock for the wedding and avoid drawing attention to yourself. It's shameless to parade about, dressed up to the nines, and you already with a bairn.'

It was not the response Bella had anticipated. An exasperated flush came to her cheeks.

'I will *not* get married in that horrible old dress! I want to look my best. What's wrong with that?'

'Delusions o' grandeur make folk talk. Anybody would think you're marrying one o' the Maxwells from Munshes, instead o' Will Turner!'

'Clacking tongues don't matter to me. Let them talk – they're leaving someone else alone.'

'You're so preoccupied with all this nonsense, you show no consideration for anybody else, not even for Thomasina. It vexes me no end. How will she cope with living in a big town with you and Will, when she scarcely even knows him? It's a big shock for her.'

Bella shrugged. 'She'll get used to it, won't she? And Will's not a total stranger – he's her father!'

'Aye, but if she's with us, she'll have Mary Jane and they'll grow up as sisters. It's cruel to suddenly uproot her, to take her from us. She's closer to me than she is to you, anyway!'

'I *am* her mother.'

'Maybe so, but *in name only*,' was Mrs Pattie's icy response.

It dawned on Bella that it was not her engagement ring or the silk that caused Ma's pique. It was the thought of losing Thomasina.

Yet wasn't the girl's place with her *real* parents? It was meant to be the three of them, Bella, Will and their child, starting afresh together in Coatbridge, a proper little family, making up for lost time. But could they in good conscience remove the girl, and risk driving Mrs Pattie back to her daily doses of laudanum?

There was no easy solution.

* * * * *

One month prior to their marriage, Will signed a lease on a two-roomed railway company flat.

'It's very modern,' he said, describing it to Bella and her mother during a visit to Gelston in November. 'There'll be no more running outside for buckets o' water – it's piped into the building, to a shared sink on the landing.'

Mrs Pattie could not believe her ears. 'A sink with piped water in your first house – I never heard of such luxury!'

Bella couldn't wait to leave for the grandeur of Coatbridge.

On the eve of her wedding, as she knelt in front of the fire to dry her hair, her father laid an envelope on the floor beside her,

'Here's a wee something for you, Viking.'

'What is it?' she asked, raising her head.

'It's strictly for emergencies.'

Bella mouthed a 'Thank you,' but James Pattie had turned away. Da was a man of few words, averse to displays of affection. Carefully she placed his gift beside the pile of things she would take with her to Coatbridge.

That night she could hardly sleep for excitement.

On Thursday, December 15, 1871, she got up at six. In the freezing cold she lit the fire, ready for her mother to rise and make the porridge. How weird that this would be her last meal as Isabella Pattie, at home with her own folk! She was about to become Isabella Turner, yet was Will *really* the right one for her? When problems arose, who could she talk to, alone in a strange town, with no parents to turn to? Without Da, her staunchest ally, would she be able to hold her own in Coatbridge? Already she knew she would miss her father more than she was willing to admit.

Challenges lay in front of them, but she'd have Will by her side. Whatever happened, she'd have to survive, because getting wed was a serious business. You made that commitment and you had to stick to it. If you got married, you stayed married. Divorce was virtually unheard of.

It would have been different with Tam, Bella mused as she sipped her tea. If she'd been able to join him in Nova Scotia, her nails wouldn't have got black from taking out the ashes on the morning of her wedding! A maid would have done that, and the wife of a prosperous store manager would live like a lady ...

Her idle imaginings were rudely interrupted.

'You'll not be able to sit and daydream once you've got your own house to keep!' scolded Mrs Pattie.

'No, and I'll not have *you* nagging at me either,' Bella retorted, and instantly regretted her outburst. She laid her hand on Ma's shoulder. 'I'm sorry, I didn't mean that. How will I manage without you all?'

Her mother shook her off, embarrassed. 'Come on, you'll be late. We'd better get going.'

It all seemed surreal, as if someone else stepped into the brown silk dress, with its full skirt, frill round the bottom, fitted bodice and puffy sleeves that gathered tight at the wrists. As she helped Bella fasten the many button loops, Mrs Pattie grudgingly conceded that it was a lovely gown.

Will and their few guests were at Kelton Kirk when the bride and her family arrived. The ceremony itself was so perfunctory, it was over almost before it had begun, and they were riding home, with Bella huddled in a thick wool shawl against the falling sleet, and her new husband by her side.

After a quick bite to eat and a tiny glass of whisky in the kitchen, they were back on the cart, bound for the railway station at Castle Douglas. No one had anything left to say. As the iron monster came chugging towards them, Bella grabbed Thomasina and Mary Jane to give them each a kiss, then gave unaccustomed, panic-stricken hugs to her parents and her brother, Johnny, with a promise to write soon.

Clutching at her skirts, she climbed aboard behind Will, to leave everything and everyone she knew. In a furious slamming of doors, clanking of metal and blowing of whistles the train slowly pulled away. Blinking, she waved until the receding figures on the station platform faded from view. Warily she moved from the shutter to sit down on the hard wooden seat beside the person who was now her husband.

Will smiled. 'Well, Mrs Turner, how do you feel?'

'Fine,' Bella mumbled, dabbing tears from her eyes as the train clackety-clacked along the tracks, carrying them far off for their splendid new life together.

* * * * *

COATBRIDGE, 1871

With the revolution of Britain's trade and industry, steel mills, iron foundries, woollen and cotton mills had sprung up where green fields recently had been. Cheap new housing accommodated the workforce required by the brand new manufacturing plants. Rural hamlets were transformed into sprawling slums.

The parish of Old Monkland was formerly a vast estate, among the wealthiest in Lanarkshire, with its gently undulating terrain rich in mineral reserves. For centuries, friars had farmed the area to produce flax, oats, wheat, turnips and potatoes, in addition to extracting surface coal to give to the poor. Often described as an immense garden with lush pastures and rivers filled with trout, the idyllic tranquillity of the property was marred by the growth of a town whose population increased eleven-fold between 1831 and 1871.

Abandoning their low-paid jobs in agriculture, herds of workers descended on Coatbridge, lured by offers of quick money and accommodation in newly-built row houses or flats. The earth vibrated with pounding steam hammers. New-fangled contraptions roared and rattled and belched acrid smoke into the atmosphere. Blast furnaces operated round the clock, their flames casting a polluting red glow in the night sky, all in the name of progress. Trains rumbled in and out of the railway station at all hours, because Coatbridge helped supply a world gone mad for iron and steel to build bridges, locomotives and ships. As a vital part of Scotland's industrial heartland, the town hummed in perpetual motion. Its energy and dynamism knew no bounds.

It was pitch dark when Bella and Will reached their destination. The smell of stale beer and the foul reek of putrid water in the gutters filled the air as they trudged from the station towards their flat in Sunnyside Road. Dodging drunks who came stumbling out of a tavern, they entered a close, then a dimly lit hall to make their way up the stairs. Will unlocked a door on the second floor landing.

'This is it, Bella, we're home. What do you think?' He flashed her a smile as he lit the lamp.

She remained silent, shivering. This was not the Coatbridge she'd imagined, where it would all be different, better than Galloway. Different it might be, but better it was not.

Will had gone to stand by the window. 'Come over here, till you see what I bought.'

'What is it?'

'It's my wedding present to you – a sewing machine, top of the line. They're all the rage in America. Do you like it?'

She'd risen at dawn and her excitement had given way to cold, hunger and exhaustion. 'I'll check it out in the morning,' was her ungracious reply.

Turning her back on him she removed her wedding hat to lay it on the table by her bundle, kept her things together like a visitor anticipating an early departure.

Tenderly he put his arm round her shoulder. 'Aye, all right. You make yourself comfortable and I'll get the fire going to make us a cup o' tea.'

Later, they lay side by side in their box bed in the kitchen. While he slumbered peacefully beside her, his energy spent, she stared wide-eyed into the darkness, wondering what she had let herself in for.

15
Brass Tacks

*'Financial demands, of all the rough winds that blow upon our
love, (are) quite the coldest and most biting.'*
– Gustave Flaubert

'Y OU PAID *HOW MUCH*?' she exclaimed in horror as she
examined the sewing machine next morning.

'It's not as bad as it sounds,' Will replied
sheepishly. 'I'm sorry, I couldn't pay it all at once: I made what
they call a *down payment*, and each week a man comes to collect
instalments.'

'And what if we don't have the money?'

'I suppose they'd repossess it ... but that's not going to
happen. Of course we'll have enough, no bother! I'm making a
good wage now.'

'I've no idea how to work such a thing.' Tentatively she
touched the cold shiny black lacquered finish, embellished with
the word 'Singer' in gold lettering.

He drank down the last of his tea. 'How difficult can it be?
You're an expert at sewing, and you're not stupid!' He threw on
his jacket and cap, and tied a muffler round his neck. 'You'll
never have to sit making anything the old-fashioned way again.
It's time I wasn't here – see you at night!'

Bella was left on her own in the bare kitchen. Just her and a
table with two scuffed chairs, the range, the box bed – and Will's
gift to her. She hated it already, this liability she could well do
without. Didn't he know she *liked* sewing by hand? She had no
need of some contemporary gimmick. His motive was kind, but

she'd have preferred not to be run into debt and enforced gratitude for something she didn't want.

How simple it would have been to stay on in Galloway! In the silence, she tried to imagine what would be going on in Gelston. She pictured Thomasina and Mary Jane in the kitchen with Ma, and she could have cried from loneliness. But what was she doing, married less than a day, and harking back to her previous existence? She was Bella Turner, a foreigner in this place where her future would unfold. She had to get a grip, take charge of her own destiny and make a success of her marriage. She jumped up, put her hat squarely on her head, and pocketed some change off the mantelpiece, to venture down the stairs and out to an alien street where her path was unmapped. Provisions for that evening's meal had to be bought ... her man would require some dinner when he got home.

That afternoon, she was making her way up the stairs with a bucket of coal, when she encountered two of her new neighbours. One was approximately her own age, the other grey and portly. As Bella approached the landing, they immediately went quiet, eyeing the newcomer with hostility as she struggled up the steps.

'Hello,' Bella said guardedly.

The two women stood sizing her up.

'And who might you be?' demanded the older woman, folding her arms under her mountainous bosom.

'My name's Bella Turner.'

'Oh, fancy that! You're the one that managed to hook Will down south, are ye? The lassies round here weren't good enough for him, apparently.'

Bella moved to pass, but her path was blocked.

'You'll have heard about the cleanin' rota?' asked the younger one slyly.

'No, I just got here last night.'

'Well, *Mrs Turner*, for your information, you've to scrub down the stairs next Monday.'

With that, they pushed rudely past her. The older one said, 'Och, you're terrible, Annie, so ye are!' and they giggled.

Bella was stoking up the kitchen fire when a knock came at her door. Imagining it would be the two harridans from earlier, she ignored it.

With the second knock, a gentle voice said, 'Mrs Turner, are you in?'

The caller was a motherly woman who stood smiling, holding out a newly baked cake. 'Here's a wee thing to welcome you, hen,' she said. 'I'm Mrs Fraser, from the flat directly above ye.'

Over a cup of tea, Bella was introduced to the basic rules of the tenement. She learned when she could use the patch of drying green in the back to hang out her laundry, how the wash house boiler worked, and where the ash pit was, for emptying their chamber pot and garbage. The pair on the landing were Annie McColl and Betty Miller, wife of Archie Miller who was a superintendent with the railway company.

'Betty thinks she rules the roost, tried her best to fix Will up wi' her niece, till she heard he was engaged ... and she took the huff. Annie sooks up tae her, as if that'll get her man a promotion!' sniffed Mrs Fraser. 'Watch what you say to that two.'

Her new-found friend expressed astonishment when Bella raised the issue of stair-cleaning. 'No, no, it's Annie's job on Monday. She must have been haverin', sayin' it was your turn!'

'Havering or having me on, more like.'

At the earliest opportunity, Annie was tersely advised that she would have to scrub the stairs herself the following week. Becoming versed in the art of survival in her new environment was part of Bella's education. Seldom had she felt so alone. She wrote the first of many letters to her parents, to that other universe where all was safe and familiar.

Soon afterwards, she was accosted by Mrs Miller at the front door of the building.

'Mornin', Mrs Turner. We were disappointed not to see you and Will at church on Sunday. I couldn't understand why you weren't there!'

'We've been busy,' Bella answered, resenting her neighbour's accusatory tone.

Mrs Miller laced her fingers piously over her chest. 'Aye, I'm sure. However, Mr Miller and I go *every week without fail* to Gartsherrie Kirk. It's five minutes away, round the corner and up the hill there, you can't miss it. It's not really asking much, to devote two hours to the good Lord, after all he's given us. You should have settled in by *this Sunday*. Come and sit with us in our pew, and we'll introduce you to the minister and some o' the congregation. The service begins at ten sharp. Unless ... you don't kick with the left foot, do you?'

The audacity of the woman was breathtaking, but Bella kept her cool. 'Thank you for the invitation. We're not Catholic, nor will we be joining you at Gartsherrie. We don't go to church. Religion to us is a personal matter,' she said with a sweet smile.

In stunned disbelief Mrs Miller opened her mouth, then thought better of speaking further, and walked off, her ample rear stiff with righteous indignation. It might take years, but she'd see to it that Mrs Turner paid for the rebuff. No one got off with such behaviour towards the superintendent's wife.

Bella had made her first enemy.

* * * * *

The sewing machine sat gathering dust in the corner. During that early phase, it raised an indescribable terror in her. Its alien modernity frightened her, and again Bella wished Will hadn't been so rash as to buy it without consulting her. How could she be expected to operate this very latest invention from America, when her experience of appliances was limited to a mangle and a butter churn? The sight of it brought her out in an anxious sweat. When the tallyman came to collect the payments, she longed to give him back the Singer and be done with it. That cash could have gone on essentials, or on furniture for the other room that lay absolutely empty.

It wouldn't have been so bad if Will's weakness for spending had stopped there, but each payday he arrived home with some trifle, perhaps a pretty plate, ribbons, the occasional magazine or some cakes from the baker's. 'Here's a wee treat for you, Bella,' he always said.

It was on a raw Tuesday at the start of February 1872, with sleet and a biting cold wind, that finally his extravagance was curbed. Going down that afternoon to fill the coal scuttle, Bella heard the shovel hit the bottom of the bunker. Only black dust remained and the fire had dwindled to a few pitiful embers when Will got in from work.

Scarcely had he got his cap off, when she announced accusingly, 'There's just sixpence left in the jar, and the coal's done!'

'Why didn't you tell me before? Did you not see how low it had got?'

'So it's my fault, is it? Even though it's perishing cold out there, and it's pitch dark in the bunker! If you'd once lugged the buckets up the stair, *you* might have noticed!'

He took a seat. 'We don't need to fall out over this. I'll borrow some coal from the Frasers, or I'll ask Archie Miller for an advance on my pay.'

Bella jumped up from her chair. 'You'll do no such thing! We're not borrowing from neighbours – and I won't give that bitch Miller the satisfaction of knowing we can't manage our money!'

'Who cares what folk think?'

'*I care* about getting a red face. I'm short on Wednesdays because I've to pay the rent and the tallyman for a stupid machine I don't want. *You* can't get cash in your hand without frittering it away!'

He looked as if she'd slapped him. 'I don't fritter my wages! I buy the odd wee thing to show you I love you, Bella. It's not as if I gamble or drink on the road home!'

'But the jar's nearly empty and there's still three days to go! *Ma was right*, money runs through your fingers like water.'

The moment the words escaped her lips, she realised she should have kept them to herself.

Will's expression changed. 'Your mother? You and your mother think I'm an idiot when it comes to cash, do ye? Well, at least I do my job! I go out and earn it – and it's up to *you* to manage it!'

With that, he snatched his jacket from the hook on the door, and went clattering down the stairs before Bella could respond.

She stood alone in the dark, silent room. How could she have been so stupid? She should have budgeted more efficiently for their basic needs, had no business blaming him. Even worse, she'd brought Ma's name into an argument. What on earth had she been thinking? The fire had gone out, and the soup she'd prepared for their meal was at best lukewarm. Already it had a thin film of grease floating on top. She cut herself some bread and stood staring at the snow falling outdoors while the room grew colder. Unable to even boil water for a cup of tea, all she could do was go to bed and wait for Will to return.

That night they lay aloof from one another, side by side in hungry silence, both too miserable to sleep. Their chilly avoidance of physical contact, the distant apologies for any accidental touch continued for barely an hour.

'Are you cold?' he whispered.

'Yes,' she replied in a small voice.

'Well, move over here a fraction, and maybe you'd get warmer ...'

Since he had given in first, Bella inched closer, her pride salvaged. Making up was the best part of any argument.

* * * * *

The minute Will left for the station next morning she reached under the straw pallet on the box bed, to draw out Da's envelope. Pocketing the two pound notes it contained she headed up the street to the coal merchant's to place her order, which would be delivered around noon.

The second thing on her agenda would not be so easy to organise. She *would* secure paid employment that very day. If necessary, she'd take mill work, but only as a last resort, after she had tried the dressmaker's two streets away.

'Can you use a sewing machine?'

It was the question Bella most dreaded.

'I have one,' she replied, 'but I don't use it – I'm old-fashioned, I suppose.'

'Aye, you're out o' date! Handmade is too slow, too expensive,' the dressmaker said curtly. She pointed to a Singer. '*That's* the way o' the future. If you're serious about sewing, you'll get up to speed wi' your machine ... unless you want to try the mill down the road. There's always some kind o' job goin' there.'

'I see. Thank you.'

Bella swallowed her disappointment. Reluctantly she began trudging through the slush towards the hulking monstrosity that dominated the far end of the street, its forbidding brick walls so high, barred windows so tiny that it was more like a prison than a mill. With a heavy heart, she stopped by its spiked railings to glance upwards, then shivered.

As Tam had said, there had to be something better than the slow torture of a factory. But she needed money, and perhaps the key to solving her dilemma lay right here, a few paces away – if she could make herself enter by those tall iron gates. It wouldn't be forever, didn't have to be a life sentence ... yet still she made no move. Instead she stood teetering on the edge of the abyss, suspended in cold grey nothingness as she visualised the cloudless skies and green pastures of Galloway. Had she abandoned all that to pass six days a week where no sunlight could pierce the gloom?

A line of the 23rd psalm came to her: 'Yea, though I walk through the valley of the shadow of death ...'

'*I cannae leave it open indefinitely!* Stop ditherin', and make up yer mind, wummin. Are ye comin' in or are ye no'?' roared a coarse voice from the gatehouse.

Unaware of being observed, Bella jumped at the sudden noise. Without thinking, she immediately called out, 'No! No, I'm not coming in.'

The die was cast. With astounding clarity, she saw what had to be done. No longer could she cling to the old methods that were fine in Gelston. If adapting to her new situation meant mastering the modern techniques of sewing, so be it. Far from scolding Will for buying the Singer, she should have praised his foresight. He was smarter than she'd given him credit for. She bought an end of boiling beef and vegetables. Next she invested in some fabric to make a dress.

Before he even opened their door that night, Will could smell the pot of soup that bubbled merrily on the fire, and he heard the hum of the sewing machine. It took hours of practice with botched seams, bleeding fingers, and sheer frustration at her own ineptness, for Bella to sit down and sew with confidence. At last she made friends with the Singer.

Her second trip to the dressmaker's was more fruitful. Bella's first machine-sewn garment met with approval, and her career as a seamstress was launched. She aspired never again to rely exclusively on Will's pay packet. She sewed and sewed, gradually squirreling away a shilling here, and a florin there. Not content with replacing the two pounds in Da's envelope, she continued to save, accumulating a tidy cash reserve under the pallet.

* * * * *

When a letter arrived for her, she read and reread it till she knew it by heart.

Gelston.
March 11, 1872.

Dear Bella,

We're all going on as normal, except I've had bronchitis and I can't seem to shake it off at all. Da and Johnny are fine, also the bairns. Would you believe we still haven't heard from Agnes? It's almost a year since she left, but we can only assume she's all right. No news is probably good news.

Hope you're both well.

Ma.

Never much of a conversationalist, Mrs Pattie had even less to say when putting pen to paper, and she could not bring herself to write the word 'love'. All the same, just to touch the paper her mother had sent from home, so many miles distant, was a comfort to Bella in Coatbridge, the parallel universe she currently inhabited.

16
Progress

'Being pregnant is an occupational hazard of being a wife.'
– Queen Victoria

BATHGATE, 1872

AGED EIGHT, HENRIETTA had seen enough to guess from her mother's size that the birth was imminent. This would be Isa's third child by Peter Inglis in seven years.

'Will I make a cup o' tea for you, Maw?' the girl said apprehensively. 'That and a wee bite o' something might help you feel better.'

'No thanks, darlin',' said Isa, rising from her chair to pace up and down the room, but that left her equally uncomfortable. 'I don't know where to put mysel', but it'll not be long now.'

Footsteps sounded outside. 'That's Charlie,' Henrietta cried, relieved that her brother was home from his work at the railway station.

Isa's face brightened as the boy came in. 'How did you get on the day?'

He placed his week's pay on the mantelpiece. 'Not bad, Maw. I got you a doughnut at the baker's,' he said, holding out a paper bag to his mother.

'A doughnut? That would just hit the spot!'

What a nice laddie he'd turned out to be, Isa thought as she ate. There was nothing wrong with James and John, but somehow Charlie understood her as no one else could. From early on, he had displayed amazing compassion for her. He was only eleven, but she could see he'd make a fine man to some lucky lassie in the future.

As the sugar from the doughnut entered her bloodstream, she found the energy to start peeling the potatoes for that night's meal, before her waters broke. Hours later, her son Peter was born.

* * * * *

The registrar nodded politely as the middle-aged couple took their seats opposite him. Though Peter was dressed in his rough, dirty overalls, Isa was safe from the condescension she'd previously had to tolerate in that office. As with all bullies, Mr Rankine picked exclusively on the weak and defenceless. On this occasion, his conduct was exemplary. To Mr Napier's disappointment, he performed his duties with neither sneer nor snide remark. The arrival of young Peter Inglis was duly recorded, as was his illegitimacy, and both parents signed their names on his birth certificate.

Carrying the baby in one arm, Isa linked her other through Peter's as they stepped out on to the street. This was more like it! He'd promised to accompany her if she had to register another bairn after William's birth, and he'd been true to his word. Wasn't that an indication of long-term commitment? She certainly wanted to believe so. Everyone could see they were a couple, and maybe he'd even change his opinion on marriage, since she'd given him a son who bore his name.

'I don't understand what all your fuss was about, Isa. He seemed a civil enough wee man, that registrar,' said Peter on their way back to the house.

'He wisnae as bad the day as sometimes. Things are just *better* when you're there. I'm glad you came wi' me.'

'Aye, well, I don't do this for all my lady friends, mind!' He winked and gave one of his rare smiles.

Isa found it unnerving. She hoped it was one of his little jokes, but she never quite knew with him, that was the trouble – Peter delighted in keeping her off balance. But he had come round to legally acknowledging paternity of one of their children, which was progress. She'd have to be content with that.

* * * * *

That same year, Queen Victoria was alighting from her carriage at Buckingham Palace when an Irish teenager, Arthur O'Connor, went rushing towards her, bearing a pistol in one hand and a petition to free Irish prisoners in the other. Before she even noticed the pistol, John Brown had knocked the boy to the ground. The gun was not loaded, but Brown was credited with saving Victoria from assassination – the sixth such attempt on her life. O'Connor was prosecuted and jailed. John Brown was awarded a gold medal for his bravery, and an annuity of twenty pounds.

17
Confrontation

'Always forgive your enemies; nothing annoys them so much.'
– Oscar Wilde

THE NEXT RUN-IN with Mrs Miller took place out on the back green. Lugging a basket laden with wet laundry, Bella emerged from the washhouse ready to pin her clothes up to dry, when to her irritation she found someone had beaten her to it.

Pegging up her last item, Mrs Miller turned round at the sound of footsteps.

'Oh, it's yourself, is it?' she said nonchalantly. 'These things o' mine won't take much dryin'. Give them a couple of hours, then I'll get them out o' your road.'

'You had the rope yesterday!' Bella protested, but she was brushed aside.

'I did, but the rain came on ... I'd to bring my stuff in afore it was dry. Not to worry, that's a fine breeze that's got up!'

'I'm not worried, Mrs Miller, because my things are going on the line this instant. You'll be welcome to use it once I'm finished.'

Placing her hands on her ample hips, Mrs Miller squared up to play her trump card. Her voice oozed smug superiority as she said, 'You're still new here. Perhaps you haven't realised it, Mrs Turner, but I have *certain privileges* on account of my husband's position at the station.'

Unimpressed, Bella replied, 'Is that right? Well, your privileges don't include using the green on *my day*. Either you get that stuff down this minute, or I will! I don't care whether you're married to the *owner* of the railway company himself.'

'Don't care, do you? Well, you will when *Mr Miller* hears of this!'

Mr Miller, indeed, who stood barely five feet tall! Bella looked on as her neighbour unpegged her own massive underpants, then reached for a pair of her husband's long johns that fluttered limply in the wind.

'He'll be the one that wears these *fingerstalls* for drawers, is he?'

Mrs Miller's face flushed red at such impertinence. Quickly she took down her washing, swept up her basket and flounced off.

When Bella recounted the happenings on the drying green to Will, he said, 'You didn't, did you? Well, I'd best not count on getting a promotion from him!'

'Just because he's a superintendent doesn't mean Fatty Miller gets to lord it over *me*!'

'Sshhh! Watch what you're saying … walls have ears!'

'I'll say what I like in my own house,' Bella retorted. 'I'm not scared of her!' But she was conscious that the incident hadn't been forgotten.

Mrs Miller refused to speak to either one of them from then on. She was simply biding her time.

* * * * *

Coatbridge.
March 26, 1872.

Dear Ma,

I hope you've recovered from your bronchitis. Good news! I've started to earn my keep since Will bought me a sewing machine – I got a job with a dressmaker round the corner.

On Saturday we went by train into Glasgow. What a place of smoke and dirt, even worse than Coatbridge! The gutters stink to high heaven, but the markets sell everything you could imagine. When toffs come to town in their carriages, they go to the glass-fronted stores in Jamaica Street, Argyle Street and Buchanan Street – shops so big that they have about fifteen different departments.

At Stobcross Road we saw the new Lipton's that opened recently. They stock all kinds of foodstuffs from bacon, eggs, cheese and butter to exotic fruits I'd never seen before, like bananas and pineapples. We finished at a temperance cafe and had afternoon tea with wee sandwiches, scones and a plate of cakes. Will says it's as well we don't live in Glasgow or I'd want to do this regularly!

I trust all is well with you.
Kiss Thomasina and Mary Jane for me.

Love, Bella.

She chose to recount an edited version of events to Ma. Pride kept Bella from admitting how hard it was for a country girl to hold her own amid the rough-and-tumble of tenement living. Rarely had she encountered such rude brashness as in Coatbridge, but she was learning to give as good as she got.

Gelston.
July 3, 1872.

Dear Bella,

You had a grand outing and I'm glad you had Will to protect you because there are reports in the paper about Glasgow's pickpockets. It sounds like a right haven for rogues and vagabonds.

Things are the same as usual here, with the bairns both growing and keeping me occupied. Your Da's kept very busy, does too much for his own good sometimes. Johnny was round on Sunday, and said to tell you he's asking for you. He's decided to emigrate to America, plans to go next spring.

Ma.

When she suddenly went off tea, Bella knew she was pregnant. Untroubled by morning sickness, she toiled harder than ever at her sewing machine. Will began carrying up the coal for the fire, and the neighbours quickly put two and two together. Behind her back, they nicknamed Bella 'Lady Turner'.

Baby Agnes was born in 1873, named not for Bella's sister, but for Will's mother and Bella's grandmother Hyslop, whose green beads were lost at the dance five years earlier. Within a few weeks, the infant was sleeping through the whole night, which allowed Bella to resume sewing. Each evening after work, Will came bounding up the stairs by twos and threes, eager to sit dandling wee Aggie on his knee. Often he'd to take off running to the station, so reluctant was he to drag himself away from his child. Bella's biggest regret was leaving the cradle Da had crafted for Thomasina in Galloway, so wee Aggie had to sleep in a dresser drawer.

Other than that, the three of them were as happy as could be.

18
Quicksand

'Never allow someone to be your priority while allowing yourself to be their option.' – Mark Twain

BATHGATE, 1873

S HE'D BEEN DREADING THE DAY when she'd have to break the news to him, but she couldn't put it off any further.

He was glad she hadn't spoiled his meal by dropping this bombshell before he'd finished up his dinner.

'For any sakes, Isa, ye're an awful woman! How the hell can ye have *another* bun in the oven?'

Her mouth drooped. 'I can't help it! D'you think I do it on purpose? Havin' a bairn is no picnic, ye know! Ye needn't blame me.'

'Nobody's blamin' ye … but it seems I just have to look at ye and ye're away again!'

If all he did was *look* at her, she wouldn't have got pregnant, she could say. But she would not risk uttering anything of the kind, or he might walk out and not come back, then they'd all find themselves out on the street.

'I couldnae believe it mysel', no' when I was still feedin' wee Peter. They say it can't happen when you're nursin', but so much for that story. I'm sorry, honest.'

Against her inclination, she had to placate him.

'Come on, wummin, I'm kiddin' ye!' Peter sighed. 'But it'll be one more mouth to feed, I suppose.' In disgust he shoved his empty plate aside.

'I'll get ye a cup o' tea, will I?' Isa was keen to change the direction of the conversation.

'No, I'm no' feelin' like it … I need somethin' stronger than tea after what ye've told me.' Slowly he rose from the table, as if weighed down with the cares of the world. 'I'll have a daunder along the road tae the pub for this news to sink in. I might come round at the weekend – we'll see how it goes.'

His expression was surly as he put on his jacket and cap and made for the door. A toy lying in his path received a vicious kick that sent it clattering across the floor till it hit off the fender. Then the door banged shut and he was gone.

Isa lifted the kettle from the hearth, poured some hot water into a basin, and started to wash the dinner dishes.

James, her eldest, came to stand beside her. 'You shouldn't have to take that from him, Maw. He's got some cheek, making on it's your fault there's another wean coming!'

'You weren't supposed to be listenin' to what we were sayin'! He'll get used to the idea. That's just how Peter is, son,' she said.

'But it's not right, the way he comes and goes whenever he wants. You've always to dance to *his* tune! You should stick up for yourself more.'

Isa was filled with indignation at this attack on Peter.

'What business is it o' yours, anyway? You may not see eye to eye with him, but he means a lot to me. There's worse can come to your door than a bairn. You'll not hear me complain. You're fourteen, you don't understand how things are between a man and a woman.'

'I'm not too young to know that it's *all about him*, not you! If he respected you he'd treat you better. Every night, you've got a meal waiting for him, and half the time he doesn't even show up! It annoys us.' He nodded encouragingly at his brother. 'Doesn't it, Charlie?'

Charlie agreed.

'That's enough o' your lip! I'm not goin' to argue … but don't think bringin' in a wage entitles the two o' ye to miscall Peter!'

Both boys shrugged. It was futile to try and make Maw see sense regarding Peter Inglis.

Isa went on with her clearing up. She dried the cutlery, set it noisily on the shelf, and fumed inwardly. Her boys were on her side, she knew, but James and Charlie failed to appreciate the harsh realities she'd had to face. As for most women of her generation, her adolescence had been a training ground in domesticity. Left a widow, she had no income, skills or education and the brood of five clinging to her skirts put paid to any prospect of paid employment.

Without Peter, they'd all have landed in the poorhouse. Thanks to him they'd been fed, and had a home of sorts. Granted, her dependency on him grew each year as she gave birth to more of his children. She was being sucked further and further into a quicksand, but that was the price of her family's survival, and they shouldn't forget it. When Peter came to her door, she'd been clutching at straws and found a lifeboat.

Now he'd stumped off to the pub in a bad mood because she was pregnant, and James was getting at her again! It was so unfair. She could handle the disapproval of her eldest son, but the criticism from Charlie stung her.

No matter what she said or did, Isa was everybody's whipping boy.

* * * * *

Hugh Inglis arrived in May of 1873 and fully eight weeks went by until his father would be persuaded to go along and register the birth.

With nine people plus a squalling baby in two rooms at the Barclay residence, Peter was keen to make an early escape after he'd eaten supper at night. There was no peace – too many bloody kids about the place for his liking! Sometimes he queried whether he was missing out on something better. When they first got together, Isa had been not bad-looking. He'd always liked the sway of her hips, but this last birth had knocked the stuffing out of her. She'd changed, seemed older than thirty six.

A staleness had crept up on them, a familiar prickle of discontent that made him question why he bothered going back.

She was definitely past her best. He wouldn't mind somebody younger and fresher, but age was catching up with him, too. Sure, he might get lucky and find a floozy that offered more excitement: but he'd be jumping out of the frying pan into the fire if he landed some bitch that couldn't cook and provide such comforts as he currently enjoyed. There was a lot to be said for Isa, though she kept getting pregnant – God knows how the hell she managed it, still popping out bairns at her age – and it wasn't even as if he was at her every day, not by any means!

It was a shame, how affairs had a habit of souring when the initial novelty and feverish excitement wore off. Intimacy had tarnished all his involvements with women. At the mention of marriage, he would normally show a clean pair of heels. He was his *own man* and needed no one. Isa had been an exception. Was this love? Nah, that kind o' shite was for suckers! He must be getting soft in his old age to contemplate such a thing. That she'd produced four brats of his was a mere inconvenience. Isa's greatest virtue was that she was less demanding than most. She put up with his quirky ways, seldom commenting when he disappeared for days on end. Perversely, it irritated the hell out of him that she *was* so long-suffering. If she'd even once lose the rag with him and stand up for herself, he could respect her more, but unfailingly she had to be a bloody martyr! No wonder he amused himself by testing the limits of her tolerance when the mood took him.

It was fine to have a mile between her house and his lodgings, but how much better might it be to live even further off? That was worth investigating. A good shake-up would add some spice to his life. Meanwhile, he mused, there was nothing that soothed a man's soul like a spell of quiet reflection in the peace of a fine summer's evening.

* * * * *

Widowhood had changed Isa's life, and that of Queen Victoria. Some royal routines, however, were not allowed to die.

In his book *Queen Victoria*, Lytton Strachey writes:

> *At Frogmore, the great mausoleum, perpetually enriched, was visited almost daily by the Queen when the court was at Windsor. But there was another, a more secret and hardly less holy shrine. The suite of rooms which Albert had occupied in the Castle was kept for ever shut away from the eyes of any save the most privileged. Within those precincts everything remained as it had been at the Prince's death; but the mysterious preoccupation of Victoria had commanded that her husband's clothing should be laid afresh, each evening, upon the bed, and that, each evening, the water should be set ready in the basin, as if he were still alive; and this incredible rite was performed with scrupulous regularity for nearly forty years.*

19
Despair

*'What you say of the pride of giving life to an immortal soul is
very fine, dear, but I own I cannot enter into that; I think
much more of our being like a cow or a dog at such moments.'*
— Queen Victoria

Gelston.
May 17, 1873.

Dear Bella,

*You'll find it strange that it's me and not Ma doing
the writing this time. The fact is, we've received some
terrible news and your mother's too distraught to write.*

*Johnny sailed from Liverpool on March 19 aboard
the S/S Atlantic, bound for New York, with 800 other
passengers. We understand they encountered a storm
on March 31, and the captain decided to head for
Halifax, since the ship was running low on coal. Then
at 2 a.m. on April 1, they hit an underwater reef. Over
five hundred people drowned, our Johnny among
them. It was the steamer's nineteenth voyage.*

*I'm sorry, this will come as a horrible shock to you
as it did to us, but I had to let you know.*

Your Da.

THE NEWS LEFT BELLA NUMB. She was stunned, racked with
guilt that she'd maintained no direct contact with Johnny
since leaving Galloway. What a pity, to have set out with
such lofty aspirations, and to die in a shipwreck so far from

home! Nobody could have asked for a better brother than he'd been to her when they were growing up together, and not once had she thought to tell him so. Why should it have happened to him, when the ship had already completed eighteen crossings without mishap?

Having lost wee Jimmy as a child, it was a cruel blow for her parents to lose their remaining son in his early thirties. It was good that they still had Thomasina and Mary Jane in the house, though Bella worried that her mother might seek solace in laudanum as she'd previously done.

Unlike her other letters from home, this was one that Bella had no desire to reread. She showed it to Will, then put it away with the others, hating the message it brought, yet unable to part with these last words she'd ever read concerning her older brother.

Coatbridge.
June 6, 1873

Dear Da,

We were very upset to read the terrible news about Johnny. I can't believe we'll never again be seeing him, and it must be even harder for both of you to accept. I wish I was able to come back to Gelston to be with you all, but it's an awful long way, and Aggie's too wee for the train journey. I'm sorry. You know I'm thinking about you.

Love, Bella.

She continued sewing while taking care of Aggie. But soon Bella was pregnant again, and another daughter arrived in the spring of 1874. Over Will's objections, she insisted on naming her Nicholas, after her mother.

'*Nicholas?* No, your mother's the only woman I ever met called that! The poor wee thing will have plenty hurdles to cross, without getting a laddie's name as well!'

But Bella was adamant. 'My Ma grew up with it, and some of our relatives. Nicholas is a common enough name for a girl in Galloway. The first bairn was named for *your mother*, this one gets named for *mine*.'

She was registered as Nicholas Turner, though from then onwards, the baby was known as Nichola.

> Coatbridge.
> October 10, 1874.

> Dear Ma,

> *I bought a bottle of the Atkinson's Infant Preserve for Nichola, as you recommended in your letter, and it seemed to help her. After Aggie, this baby presents a real challenge. She doesn't have much appetite, and isn't growing like her sister did at that stage. We worry.*

> *I hope you're all well. Give Thomasina and Mary Jane a kiss from me.*

> *Love, Bella.*

During the preceding two years, the Turners' flat had attained an unprecedented degree of comfort, with two upholstered armchairs, a rug by the fire, and thick curtains on the windows to keep out the draughts and the noise at night. The four of them slept in the kitchen, Nichola in the wooden drawer and Aggie in a hurly bed that was tidied away during the day. The bedroom continued to be used for sewing. Bella received a fixed sum per dress, and later the garments would be sold on for almost three times the cost of her labour. Having established a reputation in the town as an able seamstress, it appeared reasonable for her to ask for an increase in pay, but the appeal was met with derision.

'You must be joking, Mrs Turner! I couldn't spare you a penny extra,' said the dressmaker with a sardonic smile. 'I've got too many overheads. You'll earn more if you sew faster.'

'I can't do that, but a lot of customers request *me* for their orders. Doesn't that count for something? I'm experienced, and I've been on the same rate since I started,' Bella argued.

'Makes no difference, hen. I'll admit you're never slipshod, but if it wisnae you, I'd have some other lassie makin' the frocks. I'm sorry – that's business.'

* * * * *

By the evening, Bella's indignation still simmered.

'Would you believe, she laughed at me when I asked for a raise! Told me quality adds no value for her clients.'

'Och, forget it, you tried your best,' Will sympathised. 'We're doing all right as it is – money's not everything.'

'I'm not done yet,' she said, taking a notebook from the table drawer.

She placed an advertisement in the local paper offering reputable dressmaking services at competitive rates. Within three months, Bella was doing the same amount of sewing as before, and now she netted twice as much for her efforts. It was fine while it lasted.

With two youngsters, it would be difficult to visit her family in Gelston, but the birth of twins, Isabella and Mary, in 1875, rendered it virtually impossible even to leave the house. So many people in two rooms afforded neither the opportunity nor the energy for sewing. It was a strain even to get as far as the grocer's shop a few paces along the street. In addition to their four little daughters, Will and Bella welcomed a son, James, the following year, bringing their number to seven. The girls slept through in the bedroom. The new-born stayed with Will and Bella in the kitchen. No sooner was one meal finished than she had to think about the next. A mound of nappies constantly waited to be washed and dried, one or other of the kids would be crying out for attention, and Bella hardly knew which way to turn. Her neighbours observed her struggles – some with pitying glances, and others with glee.

Gossiping at the landing sink, Annie would sneer, 'Not so high and mighty since she's got trauchled wi' bairns, eh?' Her eyes glinted with malice at the signs of Bella's new pregnancy. 'Would you look at that, she's away wi' it again!'

'Aye, Lady Turner's getting her comeuppance,' Mrs Miller sagely observed.

With the birth of William, the Turners' second boy, in 1878, there were eight mouths to feed. The simple task of going to the Coatbridge Cooperative Society store on Baird Street for groceries had become a major operation. Like Mother Goose, Bella carried the baby with the five others trundling along in her wake. In bad weather, she would settle the four youngest down for their afternoon nap with a spoonful of Atkinson's Infant Preserve. The laudanum in the mixture sent them off to sleep, creating a breathing space when she could nip out to the shops with Aggie and Nichola.

As payday approached, money grew short and errands were fewer. Shifts of thirteen or fourteen hours at a stretch left Will dirty, weary and ravenously hungry, but supper often consisted of hot tea with bread and jam. Milk was brought daily to the tenement. A zinc canful was hung on each customer's door handle, a godsend to Bella and many other harassed mothers who were housebound. A butcher would deliver meat, but that was well beyond the means of the Turners.

Mornings began early, and by evening Bella felt she'd been through a mangle and hung up to dry. She envied Will as he took off for work, strutting out unencumbered, to talk to different people and view different scenery. For her, tomorrow promised only an avalanche of soiled nappies, smelly chamber pots to be emptied, crying babies to soothe, and sticky little fingers tugging at her skirts as she strove to feed and clothe them all on her husband's meagre wages. Once the children were asleep, socks had to be darned and garments made or mended before she tumbled, exhausted, into bed. The existence that was to be better than her mother's in reality was worse. She was more like a beast of burden than a human being.

Occasionally she yearned for the old days when she and Will were newly married. In retrospect it seemed a carefree era when he could buy gifts for her, when she earned extra cash from sewing, and they could do as they pleased. But that was ancient history, prior to their descent into this vortex of poverty. With each year they were sucked ever deeper into a terrifying tunnel of blackness, with no light at the end.

20
Upheaval

'It is a pity that doing one's best does not always answer.'
– Charlotte Brontë

BATHGATE, 1875

ISA SAT QUIETLY KNITTING by the fire one night, intermittently glancing up at the clock on the mantelpiece.

'I'm off for a wee walk with Billy,' her older daughter had announced as she left, but that was two hours ago.

She's late, Isa thought to herself, when suddenly the door was flung open, and Christina burst into the kitchen, her eyes dancing with excitement.

'D'you see the time? Where were you?'

The girl came to sit on a stool beside her mother's chair, unable to keep from smiling. 'Maw! You'll never guess what happened – I'm engaged!'

The clicking of Isa's needles stopped. She had anticipated something of the kind, but not quite yet. 'You're eighteen – too young to be as serious as this!'

'Too young? I'm nearly as old as you were when you married my Paw!'

'There are other fish in the sea, you know. You've not given yourself a chance to check what else is out there.'

'That's the point – from the very first, I knew Billy was the one for me! We're getting married next month, and we'll live with his folk until we get a place o' our own.'

'As quick as that? What's the rush? Enjoy this age you're at, while you've no responsibilities.'

'The best thing about this age *is* looking forward to getting married, Maw! You must have felt this way yourself, did you not?'

'Aye, I suppose I did, but things aren't necessarily what they're cracked up to be ... marriage is all very well till you get widowed wi' a squatter o' bairns round your feet, then woe betide you! You'll finish up on the scrapheap – like me.'

Wearily Isa picked up her knitting again, conscious of Christina's disappointment that she did not share her elation. She genuinely wished she could display greater enthusiasm, but at that moment she could have wept for her first-born, so full of youthful optimism, misguidedly viewing the future through rose-coloured spectacles. The novelty and anticipation of falling in love would fade.   Soon Christina would realise that the glamorous delusions of romance were a cruel trick of nature by which the yoke of childbearing was slipped round the necks of innocents.

* * * * *

With Christina's wedding, Isa aspired to becoming a grandmother. At forty, she assumed she had entered 'the change' others spoke of, so it came as something of a shock to discover she was pregnant in the spring of 1876. A daughter, Isabella, was born in September. Like two of her older siblings, young Isabella was registered as Inglis, but was known by the name of Barclay.

The arrival of her tenth baby was not Isa's only upset that year. Peter had an even bigger one in store.

'I'm moving somewhere else,' he announced out of the blue.

Isa's heart thumped faster. She must not appear clingy – he hated that in a woman.

'When did you decide this?' she asked, fighting to contain her emotions.

'No' that long since, but I've been fed up wi' my job so I went to Bo'ness. I'd heard there was work goin'. I spent the night ... had a good nose aboot.'

Trying to hide her alarm, Isa gathered up the dirty dinner plates. 'Bo'ness, on the Firth o' Forth? I've not been across there, but I bet ye it's nice, is it?'

'Nice? That's a matter o' opinion. Did you never study a map, Isa? There's more than one reason why they call it the Arsehole o' Scotland!' He grimaced. 'Anyway, Bo'ness didnae work oot, but they had jobs goin' beggin' at Broxburn. I'm startin' there on Monday.'

'This comin' Monday? I'm speechless, Peter! If you were plannin' to leave Bathgate, why did you not mention it to me?' she burst out, her control deserting her.

'It seemed pointless to talk about it till I had somethin' definite in mind.'

She was compelled to ask, 'When will I see you if you're in Broxburn?'

'On my day off. It would be an easy walk, it's no' that far.'

'Don't be so gallus! It must be six miles each way!' After some hesitation, she said, 'Or were you plannin' to take us with you?'

Her breath was fast and shallow, and she had turned pale at her own audacity.

He shrugged. 'Och, I dunno, I hadnae got as far as thinkin' aboot that. Of course I couldnae stop ye movin' there if you wanted to ... it's a free country.'

He leaned closer, to peer at her. 'Are ye aware your two front teeth are gettin' brown, Isa? Funny, I hadnae noticed that afore!'

She would not be sidetracked, not when her whole life was at stake. 'Well, there's nothin' particular to keep us here,' she continued in as level a voice as she could muster. 'I wouldnae be averse tae movin'. Were you goin' to rent somewhere in Broxburn?'

'Isa, Isa, Isa! *Come on*, that's not my style! Me? Sign a lease? Not on your nelly! I'm no' the type for such responsibility. No, I've got new lodgin's fixed up. If you fancy a move, maybe we could find somewhere for *you* to rent ... similar to our arrangement here.'

Relief surged through her at his use of 'we'. For an awful moment she had feared that this was the end of the line for them. Her fate lay in his hands.

'Is it no' kind o' silly for you to live in lodgings, if we all went to a new place? We could share the same roof, could we not?'

Inhaling deeply, he tilted his head back to stare up at the ceiling, his teeth clenched in exasperation as he snarled, 'Here we go again! You always steer things roond tae this – it's exactly why I've put off tellin' you! *You never give it a bloody break, do ye?*'

She hurried to appease him. 'No, no, Peter, I'm no' pushin' to get married. I know the score. Me and the weans, we'll still call ourselves Barclay. We could take a house in my name, with you as our lodger. That would be all right, would it not?'

He pulled a face. 'Aye, well, I suppose it might work, but then it might not. I'm makin' *no promises*!' he conceded somewhat grudgingly.

Hardly able to suppress her joy at escaping the damp, nasty little row home she'd hated for more than a decade, Isa said, 'Come on, we'll have another cup o' tea, and I'll see if there's a bit o' that cake left that's your favourite – give me a minute or two.'

It had been a strange night! Quite how it would be to live in Broxburn, she had no clue, but she would have Peter – and the prospect of living anywhere but Durhamtown was cause to celebrate.

* * * * *

On the road to his lodgings, with a few beers inside him, Peter had to congratulate himself on his resolution of the situation. Things had gone more smoothly than he'd hoped. He'd enjoyed watching Isa wriggle like a fish on a hook till he manoeuvred her into proposing their new arrangement. Now he'd have all the advantages of eating well and sharing her bed without ever being nagged about marriage or responsibility. If her brats got on his nerves, he'd go off on his own for a break, and she'd accept it, as always. It might be all right ... time would tell.

Isa's plan met with a mixed reaction. For her younger children, it was of no great import, but the others protested, led by James, whose resentment of Peter had festered for years.

'No, Maw, you can count me out. I'm not livin' in the same house as that wee bauchle,' he declared.

'That's enough o' you! How can you miscall Peter when he's provided for you since you were a wean? He's been like a father to you!' she exclaimed.

'*Paw* was my father. Peter Inglis may mean a lot to you, but he's nothin' to me.'

'Come on, son, don't be stupid. You'll get a position in Broxburn workin' at the oil-shale. They're desperate to hire, and the money's good.'

'No thanks! I'm coming up to eighteen, Maw, too old to be still livin' wi' my mother. I'll get lodgings here – you don't need to concern yourself about me!' James assured her.

And so early in 1877, Isa and her remaining brood of three Bartholomews and five Inglis tykes moved to Broxburn.

To their new neighbours, Peter Inglis was a quiet bachelor who lodged with the poor widow Barclay and her family.

* * * * *

Queen Victoria's daughter, Alice, had married Prince Louis of Hesse in 1862, and was made Grand Duchess when her husband succeeded his uncle as Grand Duke in 1877. Contracting diphtheria after nursing one of her seven children, she died on December 14, 1878, the seventeenth anniversary of her father's death. Alice was buried in Darmstadt, Germany. Struck by the coincidence of her husband and daughter's passing on the same date, the Queen wrote that she found it '*almost incredible and most mysterious*'.

Setting aside her grief, Victoria focused on matters of state. The Russo-Turkish war was raging in 1877–78, and she argued fiercely for British intervention. On five separate occasions she threatened to abdicate if Disraeli took no action but her threats were ignored. Already in 1878 Britain was involved in the Second Anglo-Afghan War and would become embroiled in the Anglo-Zulu War at the start of the following year. The Queen, nonetheless, justified her expansionist policies, writing:

> *If we are to maintain our position as a first-rate power, we must ... be prepared for attacks and wars, somewhere or other, CONTINUALLY.*

With John Brown's support, she was fearless. She could take on the world.

21
Feast and Famine

'Poverty is the worst form of violence.' – Mahatma Gandhi

O N THE ANNIVERSARY of Prince Albert's death in December, it was Queen Victoria's custom to visit his mausoleum at Frogmore, before boarding the train from Windsor to Portsmouth. A ship would be waiting to ferry her across the Solent to Osborne House on the Isle of Wight for Christmas, where she would remain until February. Her offspring regularly joined her, except for the Prince of Wales, who preferred to spend the festive season with his wife and family at Sandringham.

Great pains were taken with the decoration of Osborne for the Queen's arrival. Holly and ivy, yew and ferns draped chimney breasts, with poinsettias for added splashes of colour. Huge bouquets of flowers, bundles of cinnamon sticks and cloves perfumed the air, while garlands of brightly coloured glass beads glittered in the candlelight. Twelve Christmas trees in all were required, the largest of them placed at the foot of the grand staircase. All were hung with blown glass and tin ornaments, toffees, tinsel and bows but their candles would not be lit till Christmas Eve, when the Queen appeared at the staff party in the servants' hall.

Tables were laden with food and ale for the assembled company of the domestic staff, estate employees and their families. Each was given a Christmas gift – always of a practical nature – perhaps a bolt of cloth, a shoulder of lamb or a crock containing a plum pudding. Children received a toy, a book or an item of clothing, together with a gingerbread man. After the singing of carols and the national anthem, the Queen withdrew, to prepare for the next scheduled event.

The distribution of gifts to members of the royal household was a somewhat more lavish affair. The long tables in the Durbar room were piled high with expensive dressing gowns, gold cuff-links and watches for the men, and extravagant dresses, furs or jewellery for the ladies. Household luxuries – silver salvers and tea services, coffee pots, books, paintings and signed, framed photographs of the royals – were also presented. Similar tokens were exchanged between the Queen and her children. Later, they were set up for display, and Victoria inspected them while being wheeled up and down in a chair.

Christmas Day started with a church service, lunch at one and tea at five. At nine o'clock that evening a magnificent dinner would be served for which up to fifty turkeys, a 140lb baron of beef requiring ten hours to roast on a spit, hundreds of pounds of lamb, dozens of geese and cart loads of vegetables had been shipped from Windsor. Chefs created the Christmas mincemeat from eighty-two pounds of raisins, sixty pounds of lemon and orange peel, two pounds of cinnamon, over three hundred pounds of sugar, and two dozen bottles of brandy.

After the feast musicians and singers performed, until the Queen decided she was ready to retire for the night. Then the banquet was over.

* * * * *

COATBRIDGE, 1879–1880

Christmas in the Turner home came and went almost unobserved. December 25 was a normal working day, and the small bag of sweets each of the youngsters received was the sole hint of festivity. New Year was more widely celebrated in Scotland, but the dreary dawning of 1880 brought no party for Bella and Will. They were at their lowest ebb, barely managing to make ends meet, and expecting yet another birth in the spring.

The cash reserve in the envelope under the mattress had dwindled to the original two pounds, not to be touched except in the direst of circumstances. Once again Nichola was confined to bed, and the bairns coughed and sneezed their way through a bitterly cold January. When a weak sun filtered through the clouds, the weather improved and it seemed they were past the worst.

Inside her the foetus kicked constantly, reminding Bella of its presence. On February 13, 1880, Will had risen first as usual to light the fire. Bella poured glasses of milk for the children, cut up some bread and made a pot of tea. She scarcely acknowledged his farewell when he called, 'I'm away – it's the shale mine shuttle the day. See ye all at teatime!'

But these were his last words to them.

It was dark, ages after he should have arrived home from his shift, when there was a knock at the door. The blood drained from Bella's cheeks at the sight of two sombre-faced officials on the landing. Politely they asked if they could come in, refusing to divulge their agenda till she sat down. But already she knew, from the way one stood stroking his whiskers, unable to meet her eye, while the other hummed and hawed nervously and looked down at his clean nails.

It was their unpleasant task to bring terrible news, they said. Around two o'clock, as her husband's train was en route with a load of shale to the Pumpherston oil works, there was a crash. It happened at the East Calder viaduct in Linlithgowshire, and Will's death from a fractured skull had been instantaneous. Their meaningless mumblings of sympathy went unheard as Bella tried to reconcile her image of him as he left that morning with the ghastly pictures they painted of Will's mangled body, pinned by jagged, tangled steel, his dark head bleeding and broken.

Remorse hit her. She had not properly appreciated him, had always paid him less attention than he deserved. She'd even told him he was a galoot on occasion! That very day she'd been too busy feeding the family even to see him to the door – and now he was gone forever.

* * * * *

Life was cheap. In fledgling industries without enforced safety standards, gruesome accidents were frequent, and employees' rights few. In timely fashion, a railway executive arrived to conclude the settlement. Patiently he explained to Bella that workers' compensation was awarded on the basis of earnings, not on the number of dependents or length of service.

'So if you'll just sign here, I'll be off,' he said, eager to close the file.

Again she scanned the form, questioning how her husband – or anyone, come to that – could be valued at so little.

'Well, of course, it's not simply about the money, Mrs Turner. You'll be permitted to occupy this house for as long as you wish, provided that you *remain a widow* – and I must emphasise that condition. Your rent will be fixed at the current amount, which you have to agree is more than generous.'

Bella made no response. The gall of him, with his rosy jowls hanging over his starched white collar, assuming she would show humble gratitude rather than the bile of anger, misery and resentment that churned inside her!

Pointedly he took out his gold pocket watch, and still she did not move. He coughed and shifted uncomfortably in his seat, then pushed the document towards her. 'Please ... will you sign there, Mrs Turner?'

Finally she began to write.

He blotted the wet ink. Gathering his papers together, he said, 'And with your husband's funeral expenses all taken care of, that's one less concern for you. Such humanity is the hallmark of good management. We're fortunate.'

Fortunate indeed! She was not yet thirty four, her husband had been killed leaving six children fatherless, and she was due to give birth to a seventh in a matter of weeks, but she had nothing to worry about, the man said! Could this pompous jack-in-office understand how *lucky* she was feeling at that moment, accepting a pittance for the loss her husband, the father of all these little ones clustered round her, with hunger staring out of their eyes? The utter senselessness of their loss gnawed at her.

Without saying a word, she rose ahead of him, and held out his bowler hat as he departed. She might be poor and pregnant, but in her look he read no thanks for what she'd received, only withering contempt.

* * * * *

Gelston.
April 13, 1880.

Dear Bella,

   We were so glad to hear that wee John arrived safely, and I hope you're regaining your strength after all you've been through.

   Da and I want you to consider moving back down to Galloway. You can all squeeze in here till we find a bigger place because it's no use, being on your own in Coatbridge with so many bairns. I know you'll say you don't want to leave your home there, but maybe you should contemplate making a fresh start.

   Ma.

Moving south was not a viable proposition. Much as Bella loved and missed them, nothing would compel her to return to the stifling embrace of her family. She could imagine the gossips pointing out yon Isabella Pattie who married in a fine silk frock, then came crawling home nine years later with a string of brats and not a penny to her name. In Coatbridge she had a house, if she could pay her rent, and she would be reliant on no one but herself. The Turners *would* survive.

With a new baby it was impractical to think of offering dressmaking services. Only one alternative presented itself: she would take in a couple of lodgers. Another advertisement had to be written, not for the newspaper, but for the notice board at the train station. She could see no other solution. Unappealing though she found the idea of outsiders sharing her two-roomed flat, she had to earn or they would all starve.

So in May 1880 the Turners were joined by a pair of young railway guards from Ayrshire, both in their early twenties. Bob and Jamie were big lads with appetites to match. It took a lot of bread, soup and potatoes to fill them up, but their rent covered the household expenses, which was all Bella needed. She continued to sleep in the bed in the kitchen, with baby John and the twins beside her, while Aggie and Nichola shared the hurly bed. The bedroom became a male domain, with a double bed for the lodgers, and a single occupied by James and William.

When Bob and Jamie worked the night shift, some of the girls slept in their bed. Likewise the boarders could spread out, taking both the single and the double bed in the bedroom to catch up on their sleep during school hours – a Box and Cox arrangement. They were nice enough boys, but high-spirited and their presence crowded the flat. However much food they were served, they invariably looked for second helpings. Their loud voices and laughter echoed in the stairwell, bringing sharp comments from the neighbours. To control two obstreperous youths enjoying their first taste of freedom away from home seemed an impossible task. When they forgot to empty their chamber pot, they claimed not to object to the flies and the stench of urine that filled the room and came wafting through to the kitchen.

'*But I object*!' Bella screamed in frustration.

'You're lucky we don't leave chunks o' butter floating in it! Then you *would* have something to complain about, Missus!' they joked.

Obviously she should have been stricter from day one, but it was impossible to undo bad habits once they were established. She would learn from this experience. As it was, caring for her offspring and two lodgers used every ounce of strength she had. Her patience was sorely tried by the two overgrown schoolboys who had invaded her living space.

Sleep was her only respite. In her unconscious she travelled back to Galloway and Tam. It consoled her to remember how they used to laugh together, so young and light-hearted, her life of drudgery forgotten for an hour or two as she dreamed of what might have been.

Not a minute too soon for Bella, Bob and Jamie announced they were being moved elsewhere. Now, she calculated, they could live on the rent from one lodger if she also took in a bit of sewing to make up the difference. She'd keep her sons in the kitchen beside her. The single in the bedroom would be for a new boarder, while the four girls could sleep in the hurly bed and the double. With fewer children squirming and wriggling, scratching and giggling all night in the box bed, she might even wake up refreshed, with increased stamina.

It wasn't much, but it was the best she could look forward to.

* * * * *

In 1881 Queen Victoria appointed a resident medical attendant, named James Reid. It was the first time a monarch had a physician constantly on call. Wherever she travelled, he went along as part of the royal household.

Born in Ellon and educated at Aberdeen Grammar School, James Reid graduated from the University of Aberdeen as a Gold Medallist, the most distinguished scholar of his decade.

Having spent time learning German in Vienna, he was perfect for the position, since he could communicate with Victoria's visiting relatives in their native tongue. When Sir William Jenner was forced to retire through ill-health, James Reid succeeded him as Senior Physician-in-ordinary to the

Queen.   His accent, shrewdness and sense of humour all contributed to his appeal as doctor and confidant.   He dined regularly at the royal table in the company of Victoria and John Brown.

With two handsome Scots now in her immediate circle, the Queen was well pleased.

22
Collision Course

'There is a sort of jealousy which needs very little fire ...'
– George Eliot

BROXBURN, LINLITHGOWSHIRE, 1882

'COATBRIDGE IS MILES AWAY, SON! Why would they send you there?' Isa protested in dismay, when Charlie announced that he'd been given a job transfer.

'It's a promotion, Maw! I'll be a guard! You should be pleased, you'll have one less to cook for. I'll see you every second week. You're no' gettin' rid o' me *that* easy!'

He put his arm round his mother, desperate to soften the blow of his leaving. He wished he'd had the courage to go five years previously when they'd moved from Durhamtown, should have taken lodgings, as James had done, but he had lacked the guts. Now at last he would shake off the invisible net Maw cast over him.

The first thing he intended to do when he left home was to call himself Bartholomew again. He was sick to the teeth of the sham that they were all Barclays when in fact five of the family were Bartholomews and five of them were fathered by Peter Inglis. It was senseless! He'd no longer have to toe the line once he'd broken free of Maw's influence. He'd return to using his Paw's name, his *real* name, instead of maintaining Isa's pretence.

'I worry about you on these trains, Charlie. You read o' so many accidents in the paper,' Isa fretted as he wolfed down his sandwich.

'Would you rather I worked underground, like Paw did?'

'I wouldn't have let you get into that. It wisnae an option, not for *you*.' He was better than the rest. She hated to see him go, but there was nothing she could do to keep him close by. 'You said it's a widow woman you'll be lodging with?' she enquired for the umpteenth time.

'Aye, I told you earlier. There was an advertisement in the office. Her man was a railway guard – got killed in yon crash up at the East Calder viaduct not long ago. Mrs Turner's her name.' He stood up, his patience wearing thin.

'She's probably a poor old soul, glad o' the companionship. But if she disnae take good care of you, she'll have *me* to answer to!'

'Never fear, I can look after myself. Must get a move on – I'll tell you all about it when I see you in a fortnight. Cheerio, Maw!' he said jauntily, grabbing his bag.

Isa sighed. It wouldn't be the same without him. Alone in the kitchen, she wiped the table, then sat down by the fire and shed a few tears. She would miss Charlie's extraordinary warmth. He was considerate, regarded her as a real person, not merely part of the furnishings, there for his convenience – as it seemed everyone else did.

There was no rush to peel the potatoes. Peter would come stumbling back from the Green Tree Tavern on Main Street when he felt like it, and not before.

* * * * *

COATBRIDGE

The knock at Bella's door came at precisely the appointed hour. Her first impression was good of the lad who stood there, bag in one hand, his cap in the other.

'Is Mistress Turner at home?' Charlie said.

'That's me. You'll be Mr Bartholomew, is that right?'

'Just call me Charlie,' he replied with a grin, as Bella led the way into the kitchen.

'As you please,' she said, standing as tall as she could, braced to be firm. 'There's a few things I want to make clear from the beginning, Charlie,' she said. 'I've got seven children and many other families live in this building, so we must all make as little noise as we can on the stairs, especially at night. I don't object to you going to the pub, but I won't have you rolling in here drunk. A chamber pot will be provided for your own use, but I require you to empty it *yourself* each morning.'

As she spoke, she noticed a smile playing around his mouth. 'Have I said something to amuse you?' she demanded sternly. He needn't think he could get away with the same nonsense the other two did!

'Sorry, Mrs Turner, my mind wandered for a minute ... but I do understand it's a decent house you keep. I'll try not to cause you any trouble.' His brown eyes were wide with sincerity.

'In that case,' she said, showing him into the bedroom, 'I think we should get along fine. You'll be sleeping in the single, and your supper will be on the table in half an hour. I hope the bairns won't disturb you.'

Abruptly she turned and left the room. This time she would run a tight ship.

He set down his bag. That was him told! Charlie had been studying the amazingly pretty widow, had anticipated a wizened old crone, grey and work-worn, and instead he'd been lectured by an attractive redhead. No wonder he'd been tempted to smile, but Hell mend anybody who got on the wrong side of her! It would take a braver man than him.

* * * * *

A month later, Bella placed Charlie's dinner in front of him and snapped at one of the twins, 'Leave her alone, she got there first!'

'She did not, she shoved in! It's *my turn* to sit beside him. Isn't it, Charlie?' wee Isabella replied, smiling up adoringly at him while wedging her behind into a tiny space on the bench between her sister and the lodger.

Charlie moved along. 'Mary, you come and sit here, and then I'll have a bonnie lassie on either side o' me. How's that?'

At six years old, the twins vied shamelessly for his attention. It was as if he had always been part of the family. He read to the children, even went outdoors to kick a ball with the older ones in the street on mild evenings. Bella deliberately kept him at arm's length, but even she had to admit she enjoyed having him there.

Arriving back one afternoon as she was lugging a bucket of coal up the stairs, he said, 'Let me get that for you, Mrs Turner. You shouldn't have to carry such a weight!'

'I'm fine, I can manage. Thanks.'

She was damned if she'd become indebted to him – had to appear strong, otherwise he might think he could take advantage as the other two had done.

'Come on,' he insisted, taking the bucket from her. 'You don't keep a dog and bark yourself!'

From that day on, he made sure the coal bucket was full when he left for the station, and he filled it again after his shift, if necessary.

She couldn't help liking him.

His chivalry was noted by Mrs Miller and Annie McColl.

'I see things are perkin' up for Lady Turner,' Annie commented.

'Aye, she's got another man eatin' out o' her hand. Thinks she's the cat's whiskers, that one.'

* * * * *

BROXBURN

It was marvellous to have Charlie back in the house, even if only for a brief stop. Isa could scarcely wait to hear his news, and hung on his every word, probing ever deeper for information regarding Mrs Turner. Even the tiniest details were of interest. Must not seem *too* curious, though, she reminded herself, because then he might clam up and tell her nothing else.

'Is the flat clean?'

'Well, it gets messy when she's sewing, cloth and strands o' thread all over the place, but she can't help that. The worst thing was the atmosphere the first week – I didn't half get a frosty reception! I was convinced she didn't like me, but she actually managed to crack a smile one night, and you should've seen the difference, Maw!'

'Huh! She should count herself lucky you're there, and show some respect. But that's Glasgow keelies for you ...' sniffed Isa. 'And is she feedin' you well enough?'

'Aye, it's all right. A lot of soup and bread.'

Charlie wished the interrogation would stop and changed the subject.

On his next visit, the conversation again centred on Mrs Turner.

'And what kind o' age would you say she is, son?'

'She's a bit older than me, early thirties, maybe.'

Isa gave a start. '*Early thirties*? She'll be more than that, is she not, when she has seven bairns?'

'Well, she could be – I'm useless at judging folks' ages, and it doesn't matter anyway. She's slim, red hair, quite presentable. So there. Are you happy now?'

Isa's jealous curiosity knew no bounds. She knew Charlie was holding something back. 'An' I suppose she wears all the fancy outfits o' the day since she's a dressmaker! Gets herself done up to the nines, does she?'

Charlie sat unusually engrossed in the newspaper.

Still, she persevered. 'Aye, you're thinkin' *she's* not let herself go ... unlike your poor old Maw, eh?' she said half-jokingly, giving him a nudge, which he ignored. What could he say? He would not be drawn into the minefield of comparisons.

But Isa *was* only half joking. At forty six, having borne ten children, her looks were gone. Her stomach bulged and her breasts sagged. She was drab and heavy, with sallow skin and hair that was grey and lifeless. Her big brown eyes, once so bright, had grown dull and sad.

She heard the admiration with which Charlie spoke of his landlady in Coatbridge. Nonetheless, Isa would not rest till she'd wrung out every last detail because her interest in Mrs Turner was insatiable. It was like a scab she was compelled to pick at, fully aware that it would bleed afterwards, but the momentary satisfaction of uncovering what lay beneath made the sting worthwhile.

His knowledge of women was limited, but Charlie detected envy in his mother's voice. Wisely he resolved to hold his tongue about Mrs Turner in future.

In mathematical theory, parallel lines cannot intersect. Parallel lives, by contrast, can and do occasionally cross, as Isa and Bella were about to discover.

23
Romance

'Alcohol is the anaesthesia by which we endure the operation of life.' – George Bernard Shaw

COATBRIDGE

HE HAD THE SAME sense of humour and gentleness of manner. Physically he bore a resemblance to Tam, she decided, though perhaps his jaw was a tad too broad, his mouth too generous to call him handsome. Charlie was seldom at a loss for words. He was easy to be around, and the bairns loved his stories. With him there, the house was a happier place.

'I'm going down to the pub,' he said to Bella one evening after supper.

'Aye, on you go. I'll see you later,' she answered.

'They play some great tunes – folk say it's as fine a concert as you'd pay for at the music hall. Why not put on your hat and come for a wee while?'

'And have all the neighbours talking about me? I couldn't do that! Away and enjoy yourself, Charlie. I've plenty to get on with here.'

Within the hour he was back, with some beer.

'What's this?' Bella looked up from her sewing.

'I can't bring the tunes home to you, but we can at least take a wee drink together.'

She laughed. 'You're a bad influence on me, d'you know that?'

'No, I'm not. I just love to make you smile,' he replied.

Unbelievable as it seemed, she had to admit that this twenty-one year old somehow lightened her burden. More like a friend than a lodger, his happiness was infectious. Not since she became both mother and father to her brood had she felt so relaxed. Starved of adult company since Will's death, she finally had someone with whom she was free to be herself.

On Hogmanay, the last day of December, 1882, Charlie told the children a bedtime story then went out to the pub. Well after ten, he arrived home and set a pint of whisky on the table.

'I thought we might celebrate the New Year with a dram.'

'Oh, I don't think I should, Charlie. I haven't touched whisky since my wedding.'

'Wait a second!' he said, and shot out of the door again.

She wished she hadn't said anything. The girls were settled for the night through in the bedroom. Bella tiptoed to the box bed to check on the boys, who lay fast asleep, tugged the covers up to their little chins and drew the thick curtain that shielded them from view. Charlie returned in five minutes, with some bottles of ale.

'I'm sorry, I didn't realise you weren't a whisky drinker.'

'Oh, I can take it – it's just that I haven't tasted it in a decade!' she laughed.

'No problem, the whisky will keep,' he said.

She lifted her tumbler. 'Here's to you, Charlie. Thank you.'

'You've nothing to thank me for,' he replied. 'But there's one thing I have to ask: do I *have* to continue addressing you as "Mrs Turner"?'

'You could call me Bella, I suppose.'

'I'll drink to that. Happy Hogmanay, Bella!' he said as they clinked glasses and sat in convivial silence, both gazing at the flames of the fire.

Softly he said, 'You know, I never met anybody like you before.'

'That'll be right!'

'Really, I'm not kidding! There's something different about you,' he murmured, reaching across the table and taking both her hands in his, 'something *exotic*.'

Her eyes met his. She raised one brow and smiled. 'Me, exotic? That's a joke! Come on, let me go. I need to tidy up – must have everything straight by midnight for the New Year coming in, or we'll be at sixes and sevens for the twelve months after.' Reluctantly she pulled away and got to her feet.

Charlie stood up as well. 'I think about you all the time.'

'Stop it ... you must have loads o' girlfriends, a good-looking lad like you!' A blush came to her cheeks, the first in years.

In an instant he was by her side, and she was in his arms. 'Honest, I fell for you the moment I saw you, Bella.'

His lips were on hers, and they stood clinging to each other. Suddenly, neither the age difference nor the children fast asleep behind the curtain mattered, only the attraction that had been simmering between them for months. The clock ticked on, and there was no turning back. As 1883 began, their bodies were locked together, hot breaths mingling as they made love, right there on the rug in front of the hearth.

* * * * *

Their anxieties over the awkwardness of confronting one another at breakfast proved groundless. Next morning everything was absolutely normal. Charlie went to work, arriving home for supper with a bottle of raspberry cordial so that the bairns could drink a toast to the New Year while he and Bella took a nip of whisky. They were as one big happy family. He loved them and they loved him.

But Aggie immediately noted the change in Charlie's relationship with her mother. Unsure exactly what had occurred, she could sense a different closeness between them, as children do. For weeks she watched and listened, and irritation festered inside her.

When she could stand it no longer, she brought things to a head. Coming back with a loaf from the baker's, Aggie tossed the change on to the table, muttering, 'There's your bread, *Bella!*'

'What did you just say?'

'I said, there's your bread, *Bella*!' Louder and bolder this time.

'Don't be so cheeky, talking like that to your mother!' Bella's tone was sharp. 'You don't address me by my first name.'

'Well, it's very strange that suddenly Charlie does! You were always *Mrs Turner* till the New Year, when you got so pally with him!' Aggie squared up angrily, her face red. 'It wouldn't be "Bella this", and "Bella that" if my Daddy was still here!'

With that she ran out of the door and down the stairs, leaving her mother speechless. Aggie might have a point, but Will was long gone and Bella would not be ruled by a ten year old. She had rediscovered happiness, felt human, able to laugh, to get up with a lightness in her step, to relish the prospect of a new day. She'd had enough of ploughing through the blackness of depression and exhaustion. What harm was there in their encounters on the fireside rug, during these cold January nights? In having the comfort of his flesh against hers, the pulsing vibrancy of his embrace, and that tender bonding with another mortal that had seemed lost to her for eternity? It was perhaps a delusion, but to love and be desired let her feel whole, warm and alive again, if only temporarily.

* * * * *

It came without warning: she got sick at the taste of tea. When she told him quietly one evening in April that she was pregnant, he blanched.

'Are you sure?' he asked finally.

'Oh, I'm sure! With the number o' bairns I've had, I'm well acquainted with all the signs.'

'Well, don't vex yourself, we'll get married,' he said, putting his arm round her.

'Charlie, sit down. We have to think this through.'

'I won't run out on you. We'll do the right thing.'

'You wouldn't want a wife that's fifteen years older than yourself, would you? Folk would laugh at us wherever we went. They'd think I'm your mother!'

159

'Rubbish! You don't look your age, and why should I care what folk say? We'll do it for the baby's sake, if nothing else.'

She placed her hand on his shoulder. 'I appreciate that, Charlie. You're a good man. But we shouldn't make any rash decisions. Let's go on as we are for now.'

As spring turned to summer, they drifted on happily enough from day to day, and talk of the future was avoided.

Both were aware the crunch would come, but denial was easier than facing reality.

24
The Rent Collector

'Moral indignation is jealousy with a halo.' – H.G. Wells

ONE MORNING IN LATE SEPTEMBER, the rent collector was doing his usual weekly round at Sunnyside Road when he received a pleasant surprise. Mrs Miller invited him in for a cup of tea.

'This is very kind of you, Mistress,' he said, once they were both seated.

'Something to eat?' She held out a dish laden with thick slices of fruit cake.

'Don't mind if I do, thanks.'

'I hesitate to raise this topic with you, Mr Gordon, but I felt compelled to.'

'What does it concern?' he managed to say, his mouth full.

'Well, for want of a better name, I suppose you could call it blatant abuse of railway property. By that Mrs Turner up the stairs … the widow woman.'

'The one wi' the red hair? Lost her man three years ago, if I remember correctly.'

'Exactly, Mr Gordon,' Mrs Miller cut in. 'Tragic, really tragic, that crash. It happened not far fae Edinburgh.' She paused dramatically, then noticed her guest's plate was already empty. 'Will you have another piece?'

He couldn't believe his luck. It would be an hour or two till his break, when he'd be sinking his hungry rodent teeth into the greasy pie he bought at lunch time from a street vendor. He leaned forward greedily, ready to enjoy each bite. Might as well

161

savour it, he thought, because there would be a hefty price for being so royally entertained by a superintendent's wife.

'It's delicious, Mrs Miller, fair melts in the mouth! Home-made, I presume?'

'Oh, yes – what you buy isnae a patch on *my baking*, so Mr Miller tells me!' she simpered. 'But returning to our current difficulty ... the thing is, Mrs Turner's not quite the poor lost soul she may seem to be. She and her lodger, Mr Bartholomew, have been cohabiting as a married couple. As if that's not bad enough, she actually *gave birth to his baby a few days ago!*'

Mr Gordon sipped at his tea, and pensively picked a currant from the crevice between his front teeth. 'Had a bairn to her lodger, has she? Well, well now, imagine that! Is he an older man, this Mr Bartholomew?'

Drawing in a deep breath, Mrs Miller puffed up with indignation.

'Wouldn't be so bad if he was! In fact, it's shameful to behold, Mr Gordon. He's just a bit laddie, probably not much over twenty. Appeared nice, on the rare occasions I met him on the stairs. Then he fell into *her* clutches, and that was that, as God is my witness.'

She grimaced.

'Aye, it's very tricky, I have to say,' replied Mr Gordon guardedly, 'because of course, it takes two, if you see what I mean.' He paused, had to tread warily. 'Not that I'm necessarily defending the lady in question, you understand.'

Mrs Miller noisily clattered down her cup and saucer. 'I should certainly hope not, or you're not the man I took you for!' She bent forward menacingly, resting her forearms and bosom on the edge of the table. 'Listen to me: God-fearing people everywhere know that *it takes a bad woman to make a bad man*. There's no telling what depths she'll sink to next. If respectable folk turn a blind eye to that kind o' behaviour, where will it end?'

Without waiting for an answer, she continued, 'I'll tell ye where. We'll all be reduced to her level! I'm sorry, but she has to go before she starts bringing clients off the street up the stairs! We can't have her contaminating this building any longer. It says in Romans 6:23, "for the wages of sin is death".'

He knew Mrs Miller's type all too well, knew it was more than his job was worth to ignore a complaint from the wife of a railway superintendent. The venomous dumpling opposite him would have to be placated, which was unfortunate. Yet like any normal male he had a soft spot for Bella. Her door was one of the few he looked forward to knocking on during his round, because she was different from the others. There was something douce about her ... she stood out like a diamond among dross. Who could blame the lodger for succumbing to her charms? Lucky young devil!

'Aren't you being somewhat hard on her? She's not had an easy time of it,' he ventured, leaving no doubt where his sympathies lay.

His hostess sat glaring, her jowls hanging belligerently like those of a bulldog cornering a rabbit.

'I want her out. I mean it!' she growled, her aggravation mounting. 'We've been harbouring a *Mary Magdalene* in our midst, may the Lord forgive us! Something will have to be done about that baggage, and *you're* the man to do it.'

The rent collector was torn. The increasing pressure was fast eroding any lingering fancy he might still feel for Mrs Turner, but he said nothing.

'Let me pour you a wee drop more tea while we work out what action you're going to take.'

Theoretically the decision to investigate the allegation was his alone. Much as he resented her use of '*we*', he realised he had little choice in the matter. Bella Turner would have to be evicted. It was futile even to consider resisting Mrs Miller's demand.

He sighed and capitulated. 'I see your point, Mistress. Such conduct cannot be condoned on railway property. Rest assured appropriate measures will be set in motion.'

Having accomplished her goal, Mrs Miller blushed with pleasure. It had taken years, but she was getting the last laugh at

163

Lady Turner. They could do without her kind around there, and good riddance!

'Well, you wouldn't want to get folk into trouble, but you can't let your standards slip either,' she said, her voice dripping with poisonous piety.

Mr Gordon lifted up his cap from the floor. 'And never a truer word was spoken, if I may say so, Mistress! That was a lovely cup o' tea – thank you for your hospitality. I'd best be on my way since there's some unpleasant business to deal with.'

God forgive me for this, he muttered to himself, as Mrs Miller watched him climb the stairs, her eyes glistening with vindictive self-righteousness.

* * * * *

Bella could tell there was a problem when she opened the door at the rent collector's knock. Rather than his customary smile, Mr Gordon greeted her with a brusque 'Morning, Mrs Turner.'

'Good morning to you, Mr Gordon.' She had her money ready in her hand.

Normally he'd pocket the cash, and would fuss with his notebook, but instead he said loudly, 'I have to talk to you. Could I step inside for a minute?'

When he glanced over his shoulder and down to the landing where Mrs Miller occupied her position by the sink, Bella sensed what was afoot. She stood aside as he entered the kitchen where her new-born infant lay sleeping.

Once inside, he began sheepishly, 'I'm sorry about this, but a difficulty has arisen, Mrs Turner, an allegation that you and your lodger have been living under this roof as man and wife.'

'Mr Bartholomew resides here, as my lodger. He sleeps through in the bedroom – come later and speak to him yourself if you don't believe me.'

The rent collector grimaced. 'Aye, but you see, I'm in an awkward position ... it's been reported that you've a new bairn. Now, if it so happened that the kid isn't actually yours, let's say,

164

and you signed a statement that you're *just takin' care o' it* here, then there would be no issue, if you get my drift ...' He stared at her, his brows arching high in his forehead, willing her to catch his meaning.

But Bella had stopped listening. She could guess who was behind this! Blinded by rage at Mrs Miller's interference, the lifeline Mr Gordon tossed her way went unnoticed.

'I don't accept that my private circumstances are any of my neighbour's concern, or yours, provided I maintain a decent house, and pay my dues on time.'

She had a point, but if he showed too much sympathy for the tenants he dealt with, he'd be sacked. 'Yes ... but one individual in the block claims that you've flouted the rules – and it *was* a condition of remaining here after your husband's death that you lived *as a widow*. So your private circumstances, as you call them, really *are* of concern to the bosses. They keep tabs on what's going on in their properties.'

The baby started to cry. 'My status remains unchanged. I have not remarried,' she said, reaching across to the box bed. 'The birth of a child makes absolutely no difference to my tenancy.'

'That's not how it works, Mrs Turner. The regulations have to be observed. I don't want to do it, but I'm forced to register a complaint at the office.' Ashamed of the harshness of his message, he added apologetically, 'It's part o' my duties. You understand that, don't you?'

'Ah, yes, your duty ... throwing widows and innocents out on the street,' she shot back sarcastically, 'that's your duty. Tonight you can sleep with a clear conscience that you've done the right thing, eh? Well, there's what I owe you. I do *not* owe you, nor anybody else, explanations or apologies for my personal affairs. So go ahead, do what you must.' She opened the door.

'You'll be getting a letter. I'm sorry. Good day to you, Mrs Turner.'

Doing the right thing, both women had said. But who or what was *right*? Here was a responsible tenant. She was clean and paid her rent, so where was the harm in allowing her to stay on? Would it be so remiss to show some humanity? The birth of an illegitimate child seemed far less reprehensible than the bigotry spouted by the superintendent's wife, who used her modicum of power to trample on unfortunates. That she did so in the name of religion really stuck in his craw.

Having knocked on the remaining doors to complete his round, Mr Gordon exited the tenement to make his way along Sunnyside Road, slouched with self-loathing to have acted as such a heel. He had tried to help her. Such episodes made him hate his job, but his own survival hinged on adhering to company policy. There was no room for pity. In the face of adversity, Mrs Turner had demonstrated backbone and admirable restraint, which he had to admire.

She was a fighter, but this was one battle she could not win.

25
Jessie

'It is the property of fools to be always judging.'
– Thomas Fuller

BROXBURN, 1883

'WHAT ARE YOU LOOKIN' FOR?' Isa asked.

Charlie turned round briefly from the dresser, then continued to rummage in the drawer.

'Would my birth certificate be in here, do you think?'

'Your *birth certificate*? What d'you want with your birth certificate?'

He pretended not to hear, kept on rifling through the jumble of papers with his back to the room.

'Hey, I asked you a question! *Why* do you need your birth certificate?' demanded Isa.

'I'm going to register a bairn, that's why,' he answered mildly.

'You're *what?*' She caught hold of his sleeve.

'Let me go, Maw!' he said, trying to shake her off.

'I'll let you go, all right, but no' till you tell me what all this is about. Shut that drawer and sit down.'

Like a naughty six-year-old, Charlie obediently took a chair opposite his mother.

'So what exactly *has* been goin' on in Coatbridge?'

'There's nothing to tell, except Bella's had a wee girl.'

'Bella? Not your landlady, Mrs Turner?' Isa said, in astonishment.

'Aye. Fine you know who I mean. The baby's mine, so you're a granny again.'

'*No, son, no*! Tell me it isnae true! She's far too old for you! What were you thinkin'? If it was some young lassie your own age, I could sympathise, but an old woman wi' seven kids already? You must have been out o' your mind!' She paused to take a breath. 'I bet she got you drunk! That's how it happened, isn't it?'

'No, I *was not* drunk! And you needn't call her old – she's *a decade* younger than you.'

'Which makes her fifteen years older than you – she's still nearer my age than yours! Oh, my God! This is precisely what I was feared o'. She saw you comin' ... a soft mark, your first stint away from home ... she cast her bait, and bein' a chump, you swallowed it hook, line and sinker! She imagines she's found a meal ticket for herself and her squatter o' bairns, but she can think again!'

Red-faced, he rose from his seat. 'Stop it, Maw, just stop it right now! You don't know her, you're talking a load of rubbish. Are you going to tell me where to find my birth certificate or are you not?'

He stood up and moved towards the dresser once more, annoyed that she regarded Bella as a schemer, and him as a gullible fool.

'The kid maybe isnae even yours, did you consider that? You're young, you've no idea what tricks women can get up to! Nobody can tell how many other men the filthy bitch has been with!'

Charlie reared up in anger, raising his voice as never before when addressing his mother. 'Don't *ever* say such a thing about Bella! I'm warning you, Maw, I'll not have anybody miscall her!'

Isa shrugged, and watched him sullenly from the corner of her eye.

'You're a silly laddie, that's all I'm sayin'! And that's no' where your birth certificate is. I'll get it for you,' she grumbled, taking a box from the cupboard and unlocking it with a little key she kept in her pocket. Leafing through various documents, she ultimately held out what he wanted.

'You should let her go herself to the registrar. She'll have been often enough already.'

He took the piece of paper, and lifted his cap. 'How can you say that? *You of all folk?*'

Then he made for the door, paying no attention to her cries as he strode down the street towards the station. He'd had as much as he could take for one day.

She'd simply spoken the truth, Isa fumed as she poured herself a cup of tea. This baby was the landlady's headache, not Charlie's.

* * * * *

COATBRIDGE

Having seen the five older children off to school, they went together to register their daughter. Like a married couple, Charlie and Bella walked down the street, with the baby in her mother's arms while William and John each took Charlie's hand. For ages they'd debated what to call the new arrival, till Bella remembered admiring the infant Jessie Maxwell of Munshes in her perambulator, all those years ago in Galloway. Perhaps having a Maxwell name would give this one a good start in life.

Both parents' names were entered on the birth certificate. When he unnecessarily blurted out that he was her lodger, Charlie received a sharp nudge from Bella, but the fact was duly recorded. His agitation became visible when the word 'illegitimate' was added. He squared up to protest, and Bella gently pressed her foot on the toe of his shoe, to avoid further embarrassment.

Rain fell as they traipsed miserably along Sunnyside Road.

'I wish we'd got married before Jessie was born … it would have saved that pompous ass from branding her illegitimate!' Charlie fretted, the minute they stepped into the flat.

'It's neither here nor there,' Bella replied airily. 'No point in getting married until we've really thought it through.'

169

'Aye, so you say, but I've told you about my Maw, and how she struggled to bring up our family herself on a pittance from Peter Inglis. The last thing I want to do is bring more kids into this world to live as we had to. Any offspring o' mine will have better than that.'

'Come on, Charlie, you take things too much to heart. Jessie's going to be fine.'

'Not as fine as she'd be if we were married. Maybe we should tie the knot, and be done with it,' he said, yet his voice lacked conviction.

'And is that what *you* honestly want?'

'Well ... I suppose I really wish I could turn the clock back,' he said wistfully.

'There's no point in wishing for what you can't have.'

Bella's patience was exhausted. He needed to snap out of this mood he was in! She had no desire to marry anyone, certainly not someone who had barely reached manhood. At such moments, he was nothing more than a big bairn, and she had enough of them to cope with as it was.

* * * * *

An official letter arrived, and she put the envelope on the table beside Charlie's plate that night when he sat down for supper.

'See what came today? I'm to be evicted. They say you and I are living here in a common-law marriage, and Jessie's birth proves it.'

'They couldn't actually throw you out on the street because you've had a bairn, could they? *Surely* they wouldn't do that!'

'They *are* throwing me out on the street, there's no *would* about it! It was understood that I was a charity case, after Will died. They're happy to get rid of us, so they can increase the rent on the house.'

'We'll fight it!' said Charlie. 'They're not getting off with this.'

'There's not a thing we can do.' She threw up her hands. 'They own the place, they can choose who occupies it. No use in

170

antagonising them – they'll sack you! Let's cut our losses and move on ... I've been thinking it over since the morning. I'd fancy Glasgow, perhaps Bridgeton. It won't be long till Aggie finishes school and there's jobs galore there. The city would be cheerier than this hellhole, anyway!'

'Where does that leave us?' asked Charlie.

'Us? We can carry on as we are, only we'll live in Glasgow.' Bella raised her chin. 'It'll do us all good to get a change, away from this dump. That letter's not the end, it might be the start of something better. It'll all work itself out.' With more confidence than she felt, she smiled at him and the seven tykes gathered around the table.

Charlie ate his meal in silence, unsure what to say or do next.

In the box bed, Jessie's eyelids were white and heavy with sleep, and her mouth formed a small, perfect circle as she yawned, unaware of the turmoil her presence had caused.

26
Mammy's Boy

'All that I am or ever hope to be, I owe to my angel Mother.'
– Abraham Lincoln

BROXBURN, 1883

'Y E'RE GOIN' SOMEWHERE ELSE? I knew you would come to your senses eventually! Thank God, you've seen the light,' said Isa. 'Did you find new digs in Coatbridge?'

'No, that's not what I meant,' said Charlie. 'Bella has to move, so we're going to look for a place in Glasgow. We might get married.'

His mother cried out in disbelief. '*No!* You have to be kiddin'!' Her eyes grew wide and welled up with tears.

'I'm serious! I've told her I'll marry her if that's what she wants.'

'*Over my dead body!* You're not going to throw yourself away on the likes of her.'

'Why are you so down on her? I'll get married for Jessie's sake, if nothing else.'

Charlie waited for a response but none came.

Isa had bowed her head, fingers covering her brow. Her shoulders shook and she began to sob.

'Och, no, Maw, don't cry! I didn't want to distress you!'

He became ashen. He hated to see anyone in tears, his mother most of all.

'It's all my fault,' she moaned. 'If I'd done a half-decent job o' bringin' you up, you wouldnae have been so soft, getting trapped the minute you left home. But I did the best I could, son – I wanted you to get on in the world. Never did I expect you to fall into the clutches o' the first bad woman that lured you into her bed!'

'Now just a second! You're shocked, but I'll not have you calling Bella *a bad woman*! For your information, if anybody's to blame, it's me. I was the one that did the running. I initiated the whole thing,' he protested.

Isa continued to weep. 'Oh, Charlie, this is so typical of you. You'll defend her, you always were loyal. But marry her? I can't stand aside and watch that happen. Get away fae her for a spell. You're not thinkin' straight.'

'I want to play fair with her and Jessie. She's already losing her flat over this business, and it'll be months until she can get working again, with a new baby to care for. How will they survive, Maw? You can't ask me to watch while they get put out on the street! I couldn't live with myself if they land in the poorhouse because of me.'

His mother choked back a sob. 'You know I wouldn't wish the poorhouse on anybody, son, but it makes me ill to even *think* o' you gettin' railroaded by that woman.'

'Nobody's railroading me. You've been in the same position yourself – Bella's done no different from what you did! I'm fond o' her, and I'll give her a ring if she wants it. It wouldn't be perfect, but it's more than Peter ever did for you. Even after having five weans to him, he wouldn't marry you!'

Isa was wounded. 'At least I was no cradle-snatcher! Peter and me, we're roughly the same age. Let me ask you *two things* before you rush into something you'll regret.'

He raised his arms, palms outwards. 'Enough! You can talk till you're blue in the face,' he said brusquely, 'but I'm leaving it up to Bella to decide.'

Stretching determinedly across the table, Isa took hold of his wrist. '*Indeed you are not!* Listen to me. Out there,' she said, pointing at the window, 'at this very moment, you could have your pick o' plenty fresh young lassies hopin' for the right man to come along. And in Coatbridge, there's a widow that's been through the mill, fifteen years older than you wi' eight bairns clingin' to her skirts. Now, who would you rather have as your wife? Eh?'

Charlie avoided her eyes, and said, 'That's not a fair question.'

'Oh? Well, here's somethin' else for you to think about ... can Mrs Turner really care much for you if she'd contemplate saddlin' you – *an innocent young laddie of twenty-two* – with the seven she's had to somebody else, not to mention that she'll be old and grey when you're thirty?' There was a wildness in Isa's expression as she bent towards him. 'Don't let her make a fool o' you. Her youth's spent, but yours is in front o' you! It breaks my heart to imagine you sacrificin' yourself!' Her voice rising in hysteria, she slumped forwards to give a loud sob, and hot tears trickled down her cheeks. 'Please, I'm beggin' you, don't do this. It would kill me!'

Her distress brought Charlie dangerously close to crying himself. Holding one of her hands in both of his, he pressed it to his cheek.

'Och, Maw, don't say that! I hate to make you weep. I'm sorry.' He bit his lip to control the quivering. 'But ... say Bella and I didn't get married ... how could I leave Jessie? I have to stay for her sake. It's one almighty mess, isn't it?'

He was seeing her point of view, and Isa's spirits soared, though it was too early to stop blubbering quite yet. She burrowed into her apron pocket and produced a grubby pink hankie.

'Will you let history repeat itself by movin' wi' her and her weans to Glasgow? You make on you don't want to go down the same road as Peter and me, but that's exactly what you'd be doin'! In no time she'll be up the stick again, and you'll never shake her off. You've as good as said you don't really want to marry her, so why prolong the agony?'

They stared at each other in silence, and Isa could tell that she had finally struck a chord. He was the first to glance away, blinking so hard that his mother saw she had him. Victory was hers! Poor, gentle Charlie, he might have fathered a child, appeared to be a grown man, but he would *always* be her wee boy. She could still reach his inner being.

'I don't know what to do. I don't know anything any more!'

He put his head in his hands.

Isa dabbed her eyes and sniffled into her hankie, then rose up and filled the kettle.

'I'll get us a cup o' tea and a biscuit. Don't get yourself worked up, we'll sort somethin' out. There's an answer, if you search hard enough for it.'

'What would I do without you, Maw?'

She went to stand behind him, and triumph lurked beneath her smile as she patted Charlie on the shoulder. There was nothing like crying together to cement the bond between a mother and her son.

No one knew that better than Isa.

27
Breaking Up

'Like some wines, our love could neither mature nor travel.'
– Graham Greene

COATBRIDGE, 1883

SOMETHING WAS BITING HIM. He'd been abnormally quiet since he returned from Broxburn, but Bella would not ask why. It would come pouring out sooner or later in any case – it generally did with Charlie. With the other bairns tucked in for the night, she sat by the fire nursing Jessie, the last feed of the day, while Charlie seemed engrossed in the Glasgow Herald.

Tiredness washed over her in huge black waves, and she got up from her chair, mumbling, 'I'll have to go to bed.'

He lowered the newspaper. 'No, hang on! We need to talk this through, get something worked out.'

Tenderly she laid the infant down to sleep, and began to undress.

Charlie scowled, and extinguished the flickering gas light before retiring to his single bed through in the other room.

* * * * *

He lingered at the breakfast table next morning.

'Look at the time – you'd best hurry up,' remarked Bella.

'No bother, I switched shifts. There's something I have to say to you.'

'Well, let's hear it, then.'

'I'm going into new digs in Coatbridge instead of moving to Glasgow.'

'Oh? Why the change of heart, all of a sudden?'

As if she had to ask! It never failed after he'd been to Broxburn. He came back different, remote almost; for Isa to alter Charlie's mindset was as easy as shaking up the crystals in a kaleidoscope.

'I'm sorry,' he said, 'I hate to blow hot and cold, but the thing is, I don't think it's such a clever idea for us to get married. In fact, I think it would be best if we had a ... had a *break* from each other.'

He gulped at his own daring, to have uttered the words he'd silently rehearsed over and over.

Bella's pulse was racing.

'A break, did you say? Well ... we could, if that's what you want, or we could give ourselves a bit more time. Just days ago you were agitating to get married!'

Calm. Keep calm, she told herself, as panic stirred inside her.

'Och, Charlie, come on! Won't you help me to find another flat? If you're with me it'll be easier. Once Jessie's weaned, I'll get sewing again. Just stay as a lodger till I get back on my feet, that's all I'm asking, then you'll be a free agent.'

But as she spoke, he sat as if frozen, afraid to speak in case he lost his resolve. God knows, it had been difficult enough to break the news, let alone try to justify his decision!

Seldom had he appeared so young and vulnerable.

'So this is what was bothering you, eh? I could feel there was a storm brewing. I should have seen this coming, when you'd been to Broxburn!'

'I'm sorry, I didn't want it to end this way ...'

It was going from bad to worse!

'So you're dumping me, are you?'

'You don't need to put it like that, Bella. We were good together, you and me, but it wasn't really going to work out, was it? Not in the long term.'

'Nobody was talking long term, Charlie. A few months is all I'm asking for, not a lifetime commitment. A few months, I promise. No more.'

The spectre of the poorhouse loomed closer with each minute that passed. Blood pounded in her ears and her heart beat faster and faster. How could she have got herself into this situation again? When she fell pregnant with Thomasina fifteen years ago, she'd been young and inexperienced. On this occasion there was no excuse. She loathed herself, loathed the despicable self-indulgence that had led her to jeopardise her family's wellbeing. And for what? Some cheap thrills? That was all it amounted to.

He refused to look directly at her, and she knew it was finished.

But she would not beg. Never would she be reduced to that.

'No wonder you hid behind the paper last night! You had your fun, land me out on the street thanks to your bairn. Now you haven't the guts to face me, since you've been *got at* by your mother! She *had* to put her oar in.'

'Leave my Maw out of it. This is between you and me, Bella, nobody else.'

She gave a dry, humourless chuckle. 'Oh? We were getting on fine until yesterday, and now you're ready to take flight. All it took was an hour or two on your own with your Maw, and immediately we're history. She's put a wedge between us, because she can't bear to lose you!'

'Stop it, you're exaggerating! You wouldn't speak that way if you knew her. She's a good woman – nobody could ask for a better mother. She devoted her whole life to rearin' the ten of us. Her weans mean everything to her.'

'Aye, and to hell with the rest of us, eh? Forget Jessie and me. She says jump and you ask how high – that's how it goes.'

'I'll have no more of this! If I stay with you, I'll be as bad as Peter Inglis, that's what it comes down to.'

178

'And if you leave, it'll destroy me and my eight bairns, one of them yours. Isn't that worse? You *know* I'll never get a lease on a flat by myself: not with no income, let alone a new baby and no man by my side! We'll be beggars, dependent on the parish.'

Taking a deep breath, he got to his feet and clenched his jaw. 'What if I was to take Jessie?' He stood gripping the chair so tightly that his knuckles shone white.

With a contemptuous flash of her blue-green eyes, she shot back, 'How can *you* take Jessie?'

'There's a place for her at Broxburn,' he stammered. 'Maw says she'll take care of her. Then you'd be able to sew again and lease a flat on the strength of your own income.' He paused. 'What do you think?'

The truth had revealed itself. They were all pawns in Isa's game. *She* was calling the shots, and would nab Jessie under the guise of helping solve the problem. Bella could accept her terms, or condemn her whole family, including the infant, to destitution.

It all seemed surreal. In a daze Bella looked round the home she and Will had struggled so hard to cobble together. To some it might seem shabby, but it was her whole world. If she once lost what little she had, it would be impossible to start afresh. Sink as low as the poorhouse, and the bailiffs confiscated everything. The Turners would be reduced to nothing, with no hope of climbing up out of the gutter. The odds were weighted against her. She blinked, as though emerging from a deep sleep, and glared at Charlie, ruing the day she'd encountered this stripling who chewed her up and spat her out.

Emboldened now that he'd laid his cards on the table, he demanded yet again, 'What do you think of Jessie living at Broxburn?'

Frustration welled up inside her. 'I'll tell you what I think, Charlie. I think your Maw's won, that's what. She finally poisoned you against me! There she is, pushing fifty, no use to anybody any more because all she's ever done is breed. But now she's got you where she wants you. You'll be kept on the end o' a

179

string till the bairn grows up. She'll just need to raise a finger, and you'll come running!'

'Hold your tongue! You don't know what you're talking about!' he said, his temper rising. 'My mother's got no axe to grind – it's what's best for all of us, especially Jessie. There's no sacrifice Maw wouldn't make for her own flesh and blood, and she asks nothing in return.'

'You can't see through her, can you? She's *Saint Isa* as far as you're concerned. Well, she's welcome to you. You don't have the guts of a louse! You'll be no use to any other woman as long as she's on this earth – you'll forever be a *Mammy's Boy*!'

'Shut your mouth, for goodness' sake! How can you say such things about somebody you've not even cast eyes on? You're distraught, or you wouldn't speak like this!'

Further inflamed by his words, she became aware of a hairpin that had worked free. Angrily she shook loose her red mane.

'*Don't you dare tell me to shut my mouth in my own house!*' she snarled. 'You think I'm distraught? Well, you're not wrong ... I'm so distraught, actually, that I can't stand the sight of you!' Seizing on one of his shirts that was hanging to dry in front of the fire, she balled it up and threw it at him. 'You'd best gather your stuff and get out this minute!'

His face took on a greenish tinge. Unnerved by such a display of temper, he went to the bedroom and sat with his head between his knees for a few seconds, afraid he was going to be sick. By the time he emerged carrying his bag, Bella had wrapped up the baby in a tartan plaid.

'Here you are. You want a clean break, so you can take your brat with you today,' she cried, thrusting the child at him. 'I won't have you or your kind round here any more!'

Silently Charlie clasped the little red-haired bundle to his chest with one hand, lifted his bag with the other and left. He'd got what he asked for, he supposed, as he shakily negotiated the stairs.

The door slammed behind him.

Silence and emptiness filled the kitchen.

And immediately Bella began to regret the things she'd said. She'd been wrong to miscall his mother, but fury had distorted her reasoning. With greater diplomacy, she might have finessed a different outcome. Despair and guilt alternated with a towering rage at her own impotence.

Much as she wanted to keep Jessie, it was impractical. She had an image of herself and her seven children on one end of a seesaw, with Charlie and Isa seated opposite, and the baby precariously perched somewhere near the middle. If Jessie slid to the Turner side, Bella and the brood of eight were sent careering downwards into destitution. Putting the infant with the Bartholomews made the beam teeter slightly, but eventually it steadied to restore balance in both families. It was the only sensible solution.

The poorhouse was no place for a newborn, she told herself repeatedly. Letting Jessie go to Isa had to be the proper course of action. The Bartholomews would be happy, the Turners saved from total ruin. Yet she would eternally be haunted by the memory of Charlie's departure with Jessie wrapped in the red tartan plaid.

Logic prevailed. Hurt would inevitably follow.

* * * * *

BROXBURN

Isa was sweeping the kitchen floor when the door opened, and in walked Charlie.

'What are you doin' back here?' she said, in amazement. 'In the name o' God, is that the wean ye've brought wi' ye? Give her here, till I take a peek at her!' She set down her broom and held out her arms. 'Oh, but she's beautiful!'

Charlie presented her with the bundle and stood awkwardly holding his cap. 'Bella threw us out. I hope you were serious when you said you would look after Jessie,' he mumbled.

'Of course I was serious, there's always room for another here, son.'

Isa continued to study the baby's features. 'The red hair certainly didnae come fae you, but she's like our side, too, wouldn't you say?'

Shuffling his feet uncomfortably, Charlie cut in, 'I suppose so ... Maw, I'm sorry, I have to run. Are ye sure it's all right to leave her here?'

'Aye, off you go! Don't worry about Jessie and me. We're goin' to get on just great, aren't we, darlin'?' cooed Isa, smiling at the infant, and lifting her tiny fingers to kiss them. Few things matched cradling a new bairn, even one that came from Bella Turner – and that would soon be forgotten.

Charlie was on his train to Coatbridge before Isa discovered a document carefully tucked in between the folds of the plaid. She shook her head as she read the baby's birth certificate.

'Your Daddy's a silly big laddie, isn't he? But never mind. We'll put this away in my secret box,' she whispered, 'because you'll not need it for years and years, darlin'. You're *Jessie Barclay* now, aren't you? Yes you are, my wee sweetheart, and I'm *your Maw*!'

Jessie Barclay gave a contented gurgle in reply as she gazed round her new home.

* * * * *

That same year, disaster struck Queen Victoria with the sudden death of John Brown at Windsor Castle. She was inconsolable. Her loyal servant had fallen prey to a chill which proved his undoing, and the loss affected her deeply. In the grounds of Osborne House, a granite seat was erected in his honour, with the inscription:

> *A TRUER, NOBLER, TRUSTIER HEART,*
> *MORE LOVING AND MORE LOYAL,*
> *NEVER BEAT WITHIN A HUMAN BREAST*

She wrote to Viscount Cranbrook that for the second time in her life she had been deprived of what she needed most. The passing of Prince Albert had been almost more than she could bear: but the loss of her highland gillie, to whom her attachment was equally strong, left her devastated.

'Mrs Brown' was once more a widow.

28
Reaction

'When you get into a tight place and everything goes against you, till it seems as though you could not hold on a minute longer, never give up then, for that is just the place and time that the tide will turn.' – Harriet Beecher Stowe

COATBRIDGE, 1883

A STRANGE LISTLESSNESS overcame her. Following Charlie's departure with Jessie, Bella had been in shock. Barely paying attention to William and John, she brooded silently, wondering where was the caution, the good sense that age was supposed to bring? How could she, at thirty-six, have got herself into this predicament? Did she really fall for a young boy fifteen years her junior? What kind of madness made her risk losing what little she had, for a few stolen moments of pleasure by the fireside while her children slept? The foolish delusion that her youth could be rediscovered had cost her dear. She'd lost her home and her baby too.

The letter from the railway company stated the date on which her lease would be terminated. Twelve days was all she had, to vacate her flat. In the event she, her family or any of their belongings still remained there, bailiffs would forcibly clear the premises. How stupid to sit wasting valuable hours, punishing herself for mistakes that could not be undone! Reflection was a luxury she could ill afford – repentance would have to wait. The clock was ticking.

William and John were busy playing together at the table with a basin of water, some cups and spoons – a foolproof way of keeping them amused – and Bella sat busily unpicking a dress when the girls returned from school that afternoon.

'Where's Jessie? Is she through in the room sleeping?' asked Aggie.

'No, she wasn't well, so Charlie took her away to the doctor at Broxburn.' The lie came out so smoothly, Bella surprised herself.

'Broxburn? Why would he take her there?'

'Because that's where the Bartholomews live. Jessie's better to be with them during our move.'

Aggie glared dubiously at her mother. 'How could she be better with folk she doesn't know?'

Bella did not reply, and Aggie could tell something didn't ring quite true.

Nichola fingered the brown silk. 'What's this, Mammy?'

'It was my wedding dress. I wore it to get married to your Daddy twelve years ago, and it's lain in a box ever since. That's why you haven't seen it before.'

Aggie folded her arms and narrowed her eyes. 'Don't say you're getting married to *Charlie*, are you? Is that what all this is about?'

'Don't be silly, of course not. I'm making myself a new frock, that's all. I paid too much for this material to wear it only once. It's time I got more use of it.'

'Phew! We can be grateful for small mercies, then!'

Bella pressed her lips together at Aggie's insolence, but continued undoing a seam. She had more pressing problems to consider, would not be drawn into a confrontation.

Aggie was kept off school to care for the two youngest boys while the brown silk was remodelled into a fashionable, straight dress. Gone were the flounces and full skirt that had been so stylish in 1871. Some matching trim on Bella's good hat was all it took to complete the ensemble. If there had been a few shillings to spare, she might have invested in a new shawl, but such extravagance was out of the question. What she had would have to do.

She rose at the crack of dawn next day to catch the first train into Glasgow.

'When will you be back?' Aggie demanded.

'At supper time. See that this lot behave themselves,' she said, pointing at the younger children, 'and be careful of the fire!'

Bella went hurrying down the stairs, nodding curtly as she passed Mrs Miller and Annie McColl by the landing sink.

'Lady Turner's quite a toff the day, isn't she?' Mrs Miller remarked. 'Did ye notice the fancy outfit? You'd think gettin' herself all dolled up would be the last thing on her mind!'

'Aye, but when the bailiffs come to throw her out, they'll put an end to her airs and graces,' Annie scoffed.

* * * * *

In her wooden third-class seat, Bella rested her eyelids as the guard's whistle blew and the locomotive slowly puffed its way out of Coatbridge station. How different this was from that other journey, when she'd travelled in this same brown silk! Excited and apprehensive, she had sat with Will by her side as they rattled towards Coatbridge, her hopes high for a future with unlimited possibilities. They had it all, she had believed, with the grand new life that awaited them. No one could have foreseen quite where that journey would lead. The anticipation had been more pleasant than the reality that followed.

Now there was no Will, no income, no roof and seven children to provide for. She was hurtling into the void, totally alone. Somehow by the close of business, she had to find a job and a place to live. Perhaps it was lunacy to spend money taking a train into Glasgow, a harebrained scheme to set off alone to Bridgeton where she knew nobody! But she had to try, had to prove to herself that she could start over and put things straight again, regardless of her misdeeds. The Turners _would_ survive. Rarely had security seemed so precious or elusive.

Jessie came into her thoughts. She'd be all right with Charlie's mother, wouldn't she? Or would she be cruelly treated?

Bella's muscles tightened to imagine the horrors that might befall her baby. She pinched the back of her left hand. The sharp jabbing of the nails of her third finger and thumb hurt, leaving a raised ridge, a reminder that she had to be calm and focus on what was attainable, not on what lay beyond her control.

Stepping off the train at Bridgeton Cross, she inhaled the malty steam of breweries that mixed with acrid smoke from steel works, sewing machine plants and textile producers. Brick factories, tall chimney stacks and high tenements stretched as far as the eye could see, leavened solely by the huge expanse of open land they called Glasgow Green, along one side of London Road. Somewhere among all this, there absolutely had to be a house and a job for her!

She envied the self-assurance of those who went so purposefully about their pursuits. Like sleek, well-fed cats they would go padding back to soft cushions in front of blazing fires, while she was a stray on the prowl for any meagre scrap of food or refuge she could find. On and on she trudged, her spirits beginning to sink. She spied a 'House to Let' sign in an upper flat window, and entered the hallway. Upstairs, she knocked on one of the landing doors and it opened just a crack.

'Whit d'ye want?' a woman enquired, peering out at Bella.

'Is this the house that's for rent?'

'No it is not! The notice is nothin' to do wi' me. You'll have to go and talk to old McGee, at the paper shop. He owns the buildin'.' The door was quickly slammed shut.

At the newsagent's, Bella's query was met with a violent bout of coughing. Then the bent old hag by the counter shrieked, 'Wullie! Ye'd better come through. I've a wummin here wantin' tae speak tae ye aboot a hoose!'

Wullie duly appeared, a gruff little man with a mass of frizzy white hair. 'Yes? What can I do for you?' Before Bella could speak, he said, 'I gather this is aboot the flat in London Road?'

'Yes, could I see it? My name's Mrs Turner.'

'And I'm Mr McGee,' he stated, brusque and unsmiling. 'It's two rooms, shared sink. Coalhoose, privy and dryin' green are ootside. No animals allowed. Rent due *in advance* every Friday.'

'That might suit me fine,' Bella smiled, undaunted by his abrupt manner.

'Hang on. I'll get the keys,' he muttered, shuffling through to the back shop.

Mr McGee led the way, hobbling up the street. The flat was big and airy, nicer than she was used to. Both the kitchen and the bedroom were square rooms, their windows yielding decent light, the entry and staircase tidy and well kept.

'Has it been vacant for long?'

'A week. A couple had it till the wife died. The man's moved in with his daughter. Where d'ye live at the moment?'

'Coatbridge.'

His questions were fired at her like bullets.

'So what brings you and your family here? I take it you *have* a family?'

'Yes, indeed, I've got seven children.' Almost inaudibly, she added, 'And I'm a widow.'

He gasped. 'Oh! I'm sorry for your situation, Mrs Turner. That's a shame, but I've heard enough.' Moving towards the door, he said over his shoulder, 'No offence – it's nothing personal, ye understand, but I'm no' a gambler, and you're a bad risk. I'm interested in tenants that can pay their dues, or there's no deal.'

She forced a laugh. 'And with good reason, I'm sure, Mr McGee! You have to be on your guard. I would feel the same if I was in your shoes.'

'Is that so? And what security could you offer me, if you've no husband?'

'I'm a dressmaker. I've already got a position lined up in Bridgeton,' she lied, giving her most charming smile. 'I'll be happy to lay down a deposit, provided we can agree on the price.'

From an envelope in her dress pocket, she produced her two pound notes.

Mr McGee glanced down at the cash, then at Bella, and laughed out loud. 'Are ye jokin'? That won't take ye very far in Glasgow! This is one o' my best houses, it's no' goin' cheap.'

Her heart sank when he mentioned what the rent would be. She looked around the room, disappointed. 'Is this the *only* place you've got available?'

The landlord weighed her up doubtfully, trying to gauge her degree of desperation.

'There's a couple o' wee rooms in Bernard Street. I'll let you see them, but they're no' up to much.'

The second flat was at the very top of a crumbling tenement. As they climbed three flights of stairs, Bella shuddered at the stained treads that creaked with each step they took, at the stains on the walls, and the stale air that reeked of cooking, beer and garbage.

He opened the door to reveal the gloomiest, filthiest dwelling she could imagine. Low ceilings sloped sharply along one side of both rooms, being directly under the roof. Instead of proper windows there were two skylights. Adjacent to one of these was a mildewed bulge in the plaster, where water had seeped through. The hearth was caked with burned-on food and strewn with rubbish. Eyeing the thick film of grease and mouse droppings that covered the floor, Bella could scarcely hide her dismay.

'See? I knew ye wouldnae like it! Can't blame ye, I wouldnae fancy livin' here myself,' he said. 'Somethin' else will turn up.'

It sounded so simple! Something else *would* turn up, but maybe not before the bailiffs were rapping at her door, geared up to seize all her earthly goods and kick her out on the street.

Mr McGee held the door open, ready to leave, but she continued to stand surveying the dismal kitchen.

'Wait! What kind of rent are you asking?'

He shrugged. 'Whit are ye offerin'?'

'I'll give you a third of what you wanted for London Road.'

'*A third*, did you say? Och, come on now, Mrs Turner, I'm not made o' money!' he retorted uncompromisingly. 'I don't think so.' For all that she was smart and well-spoken, sentiment and business were not to be mixed.

Bella wanted to tell him to keep the pigsty that was unfit for human habitation, but it would beat going home empty-handed. She stood her ground.

'D'you think I came up the Clyde on a bike? You're lucky to get any offer at all, the state this is in!'

He stood scratching his chest for a minute and gazed about him. It would be a pity to have the flat on his books for another six months, bringing no income. This woman would spruce the place up; he could tell from her looks. For once, he'd met his match. She had spunk, he had to grant her that.

'Fair enough, we have a deal. I need to get back to the shop. Come on, we'll hae a cup o' tea wi' Lizzie, and get things organised. But nobody else in the buildin' gets tae hear aboot the bargain you got fae me, right?'

They'd have somewhere to stay, unappealing though it was. With the most important item on her agenda settled, next she'd to find a job. Her reputation as a seamstress in Coatbridge counted for nothing in this new town. She would be starting from scratch again, with no credentials, but Bridgeton offered long-term advantages. Jam tomorrow, forget the misery of today. Having trailed through a maze of streets for what seemed an eternity, Bella found what she was searching for and entered a shop doorway.

'Yes? How can I help you?' a shrill voice cried out from behind a screen.

'I saw the notice in your window,' Bella called.

A scrawny old crone appeared. 'You're a dressmaker?'

'I am ... with eleven years' experience.'

She approached to stare more closely at Bella, then touched the sleeve of her dress. 'Hmm, not bad. Nice material. Made it yourself, did you?'

'Yes.'

'I assume you've a machine of your own?'

'I have a Singer.'

'Aye, but where do you live?' she demanded. 'It's no use unless you're nearby.'

'Bernard Street,' replied Bella, without batting an eyelid.

'Oh, really?' Her mouth drooped in distaste: not much could be expected of anyone from *there*. 'Well, we'll give you a try,' she said with a sniff. 'You can begin on the first of the month.'

When her train pulled into Coatbridge station that night, Bella knew her strange elation would not last. It had not been a pleasant or an easy excursion, but she'd achieved her goal. The removal of the Turners' possessions to Bridgeton would be organised as soon as possible, for a new chapter of their lives to be written.

* * * * *

Everything and everyone had been safely loaded. The driver flicked the reins for the horse to move, when suddenly Bella let out a cry.

'Stop a minute! I forgot to empty the coal bunker!'

'Naw, haud on, Missus, that wisnae in the deal,' he stated flatly. 'I could shift your fuel for you, if you had it bagged up. I don't shovel coal, and we're short o' time as it is!' Staring sullenly ahead with his clay pipe at the side of his mouth, the carter hoped she would abandon this idea.

But already she had jumped down to the ground, when another thought occurred to her. Sacks! She had none, but her coal was too valuable to leave.

'You'll have to wait till I rake up something to put it in,' she said.

He searched under the box seat. 'I have potato bags, but it'll cost ye.'

'That's fine. Nichola, watch our stuff!' Bella ordered. 'And the rest o' you, sit where you are! Come on, Aggie!'

Tsking his annoyance, he grumbled, 'How long is this goin' to take? I don't have all day, you know! I want to be back here fae Bridgeton afore it's dark.'

'We'll be as fast as we can!' Bella called.

She and Aggie went marching into the close and out to the bunker. 'Hold the bag open and I'll shovel,' she commanded.

'Och, Mammy, our clothes will get filthy, and everybody's going to see us!'

Ignoring her daughter's protests, Bella kept on shovelling. 'Open the sack wider, for any sake! I'd rather get dirty than not have heat when we get to Bernard Street.'

'I'd rather stay put and forget about Bridgeton altogether.'

'Aye, well, that's not on the cards, and you'd better accept it.' Noticing the girl's trembling lip, Bella softened her tone. 'Come on, we're nearly done!'

Aggie muttered to herself under her breath.

The bags were filled with coal, but still the firewood remained. 'Run and tell the driver to come and pick these up, and ask if he has another sack. If not, bring the old sheet that's on the Singer!'

With obvious resentment the carrier loaded the coal. The curved box of Bella's prized sewing machine lay open to the winds, while the sticks were securely tied up inside its cover. Mrs Miller and Annie McColl had plenty to gawp at as she and Aggie climbed up to sit on the wagon, their faces and clothes streaked with coal dust. But the Turners got themselves and their possessions out of there, and nothing else mattered.

Dirty or not, she had a house and a job to go to, and Bella held her chin high as she and her family rode out of Coatbridge under the leaden skies of a December morning.

29
Bridgeton

'We are all in the gutter, but some of us are looking at the stars.' – Oscar Wilde

BRIDGETON, GLASGOW, 1883

AGGIE INSPECTED THE FLAT, and said in horror, 'Is *this* it? What a dump!'

'It'll be all right once it's been scrubbed out … a bit o' elbow grease can do wonders!' Bella sounded more confident than she felt.

'How could you bring us to a stinking hole like this? I *hate* Bridgeton already.'

'That's enough of you, stop whining. Go away down for a pail of coal so I can light the fire and make some tea.'

'This is all your fault.'

'What did you say?' Bella peered in disbelief at her daughter.

'You heard me,' replied Aggie. 'I said it's *all your fault*, what's happened to us.'

'I don't know what you're on about!'

'Well, you must be the only one, because all the neighbours in Coatbridge knew why we got kicked out of our house!'

Bella's chest tightened. 'Go and get the coal this minute,' was all she managed to say as she roughly steered the girl towards the landing door.

Through her hunger and exhaustion, she somehow created order among the chaos for her seven children to sit and eat at the table. A pot of hot tea with bread and cheese – that was supper.

The cost of the move, plus the extortionate sixpence she was charged for a few dirty sacks, had used up her last coins. Her purse was empty. Bella pondered where their next meal would come from, but consciously set that worry aside for later. She could do nothing till she got some sleep.

* * * * *

'I have to go out for a wee while. Keep the bairns in their beds, and don't open the door to anybody,' she whispered to Aggie early the following morning. 'I've lit the fire, and I'll bring something for the breakfast.'

Pawn shops were ten a penny in Bridgeton. The money she got for her engagement ring didn't seem much, but sufficient unto the day, she told herself. When the aroma of freshly-baked bread came drifting out of a bakery, her mouth watered to imagine biting into a warm, slightly salty Glasgow roll with its thin, crisp outer shell that gave way to an incredibly soft, chewy dough inside. She would get a bagful for the kids, she decided, and butter too, as a special treat.

But first she would call by Mr McGee's shop.

When he noticed her at the end of the queue of customers waiting to be served, he braced himself for a barrage of complaints about her flat: that was usually why a tenant appeared so soon after moving in. Well, if that was her game, she'd get short shrift. There had been no trickery, he'd tell her! Prior to viewing, he'd warned her it wasn't up to much ... nobody compelled her to sign the lease.

As Bella arrived at the counter, he said brusquely, 'Well, Mrs Turner, you got settled in, did you?'

She smiled wanly. 'We did, thanks, Mr McGee. It's all fine, but I ... I just wanted to say,' she stammered, 'if you had any odd jobs needing done, anything at all, my oldest girl could help you at opening time, or when she gets out of school at four o'clock.'

He studied her, no longer business-like in brown silk and perky hat, ready to negotiate the cheapest deal on a rental agreement. Now she stood shivering with a flimsy old shawl clutched round her thin shoulders. Her eyes sought his beseechingly, pleading for any scrap of human kindness he could muster. Her hair was roughly drawn back, her cheeks sunken and skin so translucent that he wondered when she'd last eaten a square meal. Perhaps she was ill? The ice in his heart melted a little; she was the embodiment of desperation, this woman so ravaged by grinding poverty that renting his hovel in Bernard Street was her sole option. Ashamed, he stood drumming his fingers and eventually he bent towards her, to speak in a voice so low that only she could hear.

'I could maybe use another pair of hands to sweep up, or sort the papers and help wi' the delivery round – but she'd have to be here at six sharp, every mornin'! You can send her along to see me.'

'Thank you, Mr McGee. Thank you very much,' she said, and hurried off.

If he even paid Aggie tuppence a day, it would help buy some bread.

* * * * *

'Why me? *Girls* don't do paper rounds. Folk are going to laugh at me!'

'Nobody will laugh because nobody knows you!' Bella replied. 'Or do you want to go to bed hungry every night?'

Aggie glowered, but knew she was beaten. 'It's just not fair!'

Between six and eight, she was a general dogsbody at Mr McGee's shop. When she left for breakfast, he thrust a newspaper at her, always with the message, 'This is for your mother.' He hoped no one overheard. He wouldn't have folk thinking he was an easy touch.

Bella's repeated scrubbings had failed to eliminate the damp smell that persisted in the flat but they learned to tolerate it, and gradually the place felt more like home. The children attended school, which established a sense of order. Bella got busy sewing, though Jessie was often on her mind. The baby would be cutting her first tooth. Frequently she re-enacted that last scene with

Charlie, aware that remorse would make her weep and grieve as though the child had died. How *could* she have dumped Jessie on him and sent them both packing? Had she been possessed, to behave so abominably on that awful day? Yet what else was she to do? There had been no alternative.

She regarded her unhappiness as a punishment for her actions; guilt made her welcome the countless chores that had to be done. The antidote to her misery was to toil from dawn till dusk, almost to the point of collapse. The faithful old Singer hummed for hours on end, bundles of fabric were ferried up to her flat and churned out as tailored dresses. Together with Aggie's earnings, Bella's income put food on the table and covered the rent. When she had saved enough, she reclaimed her ring from the pawnshop. She could not pretend to be happy, but a semblance of normality was restored.

* * * * *

Her immediate neighbours in Bernard Street were Maggie Reilly and her husband Danny, a tyrant with a weakness for drink. Maggie and Danny existed not in a partnership, but in a constant battle for supremacy. Each Friday, with many other wives, Maggie made her way to the factory gates at finishing time. When her husband emerged clutching his pay packet, she demanded cash on the spot, and headed straight for the cooperative store, where she converted the money into tokens that would help feed and clothe their eight young children. Anything Danny had managed to retain would be spent on liquor. Come Saturday evening, he'd be itching to get back to the pub.

'Gie's back some o' the coins I gave you, Maggie!'

'I'm skint. All I have is up in the tin.' His wife's reply seldom varied.

Stretching up to the top shelf to discover nothing but tokens there, Danny's rage would explode. 'Many a man wid knock you intae the middle o' next week for this, Missus!'

'Oh, wid they? But *you're* no' many a man.'

However much he shouted or shook his fist in frustration, still Maggie would taunt him, 'Ye're a big man, but a wee shirt fits ye!'

'Come on, gie's a bloody sixpence, will you no'? I work hard, I deserve to get oot tae the pub for an hour at the weekend!' he wheedled, fully aware that it was a pointless charade since there was no money to be had.

'Ye've had yer chips. You're gettin' out to *no* pub the night!'

Danny stood shadow-boxing in front of her, his clenched fists coming within an inch of her face. 'One o' these days, you'll go too far, wummin!'

'Lay a finger on me, and you'll no' dare sleep again. No' when there's a poker lyin' in the hearth,' his wife would smirk.

'I'll *swing* for you, yet, ya old bitch!' Danny bawled as he slammed the door and went stomping down the stairs to hang about at the street corner.

There he and others as disgruntled as himself would while away the time with idle talk that fuelled their resentment of the petticoat government their wives tried to impose. It was all wrong, women should be kept in their place: they were just good for one thing, right? Aye, very true, they all agreed.

Climbing the dark stair, Danny was ready to show who was *really* the boss in his house. Maggie was lucky he wasn't like his cronies, who battered their spouses for the least offence. She thought she wore the trousers, but he disabused her of that notion between the sheets. Her impudent mouth was silenced when he took his pleasure as often and as roughly as he chose. He was aware of the first stirrings of anticipation as he reached the landing. Before daylight, she'd be beggin' him for mercy!

* * * * *

Her sewing machine chuntered on from morning until late into the evening, but it was impossible for Bella not to overhear the constant bickering through the thin walls that separated her from the Reillys. It would not always be thus, she told herself. The more she sewed, the faster they'd be out of there. Her fate would not be decided by a cretin like Danny, and for that she was grateful.

Her relentless struggle to climb out of the slum she clearly despised did nothing to endear Bella to the gossips in the hall. Their chatter came to an abrupt halt at her approach. It irritated them that she remained unaffected by their scathing glances. As she went back and fore, ferrying another batch of newly stitched garments or a bolt of material for the next assignment, they watched with a mixture of contempt and curiosity. Envious of her looks, her style and her talent, they treated her as an outcast. Only a brazen hussy would dare to make her own way in the world.

Maggie and others like her were to be pitied, Bella told herself. Let them talk if that made them happy. The raw squalor of Bernard Street was perhaps all they'd known, and ever *would* know. She fed on their hostility. It increased her self-discipline, and strengthened her resolve to rise above it.

No matter how much she'd to sew or how great its toll, she'd get herself and her family out of there – or die in the attempt.

30
Charlie and Ellen

'Freedom is the right to tell people what they do not want to hear.' – George Orwell

IN HIS BOOK *QUEEN VICTORIA*, Lytton Strachey describes the monarch's relationship with John Brown.

... Far from making a secret of her affectionate friendship, (Victoria) took care to publish it to the world. By her orders, two gold medals were struck in his honour; on his death, in 1883, a long and eulogistic obituary notice of him appeared in the Court Circular; and a Brown memorial brooch – of gold, with the late gillie's head on one side and the royal monogram on the other – was designed by Her Majesty for presentation to her Highland servants and cottagers, to be worn by them on the anniversary of his death, with a mourning scarf and pins. In the second series of extracts from the Queen's Highland Journal, published in 1884, her 'devoted personal attendant and faithful friend' appears on almost every page, and is in effect the hero of the book.

* * * * *

BROXBURN, 1886

Charlie had popped in to visit his mother and little daughter. More than two years had passed since he had taken the baby to Broxburn, and she was thriving.

'Charlie's here, Jessie! Come and show him your new teeth, hen,' called Isa.

The girl came running through from the bedroom, and obligingly opened her mouth for Charlie to see. She was a beautiful child, with big brown eyes and golden curls that tumbled on to her narrow shoulders.

'Getting big, aren't you, eh?' he said fondly, giving her a bag of sweets.

Leaning across the table towards Isa, he confided, 'I've got something to tell you, Maw. I'm getting married.'

'Tae that lassie fae Hamilton? You just met her!'

'Aye, but ... well ... things moved faster than we expected.'

'So it seems.' Isa set down her teacup thoughtfully. 'Don't tell me ... you've not done it again, have ye?'

'We were going to get married in any case! Even before this happened we'd discussed it, so we'll bring the wedding forward a bit.' Charlie raised his eyebrows defiantly. 'It comes to the same thing.'

Isa shook her head in disbelief. Would he never learn? Yet *another* older woman had got her claws into him, but at least Ellen Russell was only three years his senior. It was bound to come, and *anyone* was preferable to Bella Turner!

'And where will the two of you live, may I ask?'

'Bathgate. I've found us a room in Marjoribanks Street.'

Isa sat back and folded her arms. 'I suppose you've got a date fixed too, have you?'

'End of this month. On the twenty-ninth, in Hamilton.'

'Very good!' she bristled.

He'd suspected it would annoy Maw, to be cut out of the arrangements. But this was how Ellen wanted things done, and he couldn't please everyone. As he left, he heaved a sigh of relief that the session was over with.

They were wed under the name of Bartholomew, the surname he'd enjoyed using during his spell in Coatbridge. But when Charlie and his bride settled down to married life in Bathgate, they became Charlie and Ellen Barclay. It was not feasible to do otherwise. With the births of Peter Inglis's children, Isa had thrown the Barclay name like a blanket over all her offspring to unite them as one family. Convenience had blinded her to future problems. Awkward queries would arise if Charlie suddenly used the Bartholomew name near where he'd grown up, and he'd die first, rather than disgrace his mother.

Charlie and Ellen welcomed a son, Charles, that July.

Isa was tickled pink to have her favourite living within a few miles once more, because she'd been apprehensive when Charlie mentioned dating a Hamilton lassie. At least he'd got himself out of Coatbridge … the further away he stayed from Bella Turner the better!

Now if she could persuade the three of them to move to Broxburn, her happiness would be complete.

31
Life and Death

'Human life is everywhere a state in which much is to be endured, and little to be enjoyed.' – Samuel Johnson

BRIDGETON, 1886–1887

AGGIE WAS AT WORK in a carpet mill, where she was a weaver's apprentice, and Bella's other children were all in school except for John. From an early age, he had caught every infection that was going, and was unable to shake off that hacking cough of his, causing his mother increasing anxiety about his health.

A letter from home had compounded her vexation.

> *Gelston.*
> *January 5, 1886*

Dear Bella,

> *I'm sorry for what I have to write and tell you. Your Da's ill. A while back, he told me he'd felt funny all over, weak and trembling, but it seemed to pass. Then three weeks ago, he had a terrible turn – collapsed on the kitchen floor, and you've no idea what a struggle it was to get him up into his chair. He hasn't been well since, and he can't move his right arm or leg. His face went stiff down one side, and he can hardly speak. He finally agreed to let the doctor come in to see him, but the news wasn't good. We're told things probably won't improve.*

Thomasina's well established in her position in Yorkshire, and she writes regularly – unlike Mary Jane who's in service somewhere up north, but hasn't even sent us her new address yet.

I pray you and the bairns are fine.

Ma.

Her poor, dear father! Bella wished it was feasible for her to get on a train for Galloway there and then. How could she have let fourteen years go by without visiting her family? She might never see Da again, let alone hear him speak. She thought of her mother, having to soldier on alone, and wanted to make the journey, but she could not contemplate travelling. Apart from anything else, the return train fare was beyond her means.

125 Bernard Street,
Glasgow.
January 26, 1886

Dear Da,

I was sorry to receive Ma's letter saying you were ill. It must be frustrating not to be able to do what you once could, but I hope things will improve and that you're not in pain. I've been thinking about you a lot.

I would come down, but I just can't leave the bairns. Aggie's working full-time, and John's off sick. He's scarcely managed to go to school at all for the last two months, his chest is so bad. I trust I'll be able to come south before long. Take care of yourselves.

Love,

Bella.

* * * * *

It was the Golden Age of the circus in Britain, and even Queen Victoria was a fan. She enjoyed the spectacle in privacy and comfort during special command performances that took place at both Sandringham and Balmoral Castle.

When the circus came to Glasgow, the Turners sat on coarse wood benches in a stuffy tent, surrounded by several hundred other spectators. They found the clowns on stilts funnier than anything they'd seen in their lives. Tightrope walkers had them sitting on the edge of their seats, and they gasped in amazement when the lion tamer placed his head inside the great beast's mouth.

Practically on Bella's doorstep, the Green hosted the Glasgow Fair, which was the highlight of the summer. Coloured bunting fluttered in the wind, strains of music floated from the marquee, and the aromas of fried food, sweets and toffee apples mingled with the smell of freshly mown grass and horse dung. Barkers called from the side shows, vying for customers to demonstrate their prowess at Wild West shooting, to try the coconut shy or come and view the ugliest bearded lady on earth. Glasgow's toughest youths stood eager to compete for worthless prizes by surviving one minute in a boxing ring with an aging, half-blind, punch-drunk Irishman fired up with cheap whisky. Allegedly he was a world champion, and the crowds lapped it up, roaring their approval when one of their own was still standing at the end of the round, albeit with a bleeding nose.

But most thrilling for Bella's youngest son, John, were the carousels, powered by the massive, gaudy steam engines that would haul this wonderland of delights on to another venue. Afterwards he spoke dreamily of the brightly painted prancing horses, their nostrils flared and teeth bared as they waltzed round and round to the music of the steam organ.

The image of these horses sustained him when he got ill again. With the arrival of winter, their garret was colder and damper than ever, and the boy grew visibly weaker, coughed harder and spat up blood. On his worst days, Bella would remind him of the Fair: speaking of the sounds, the colours and the horses helped cheer him up. Four months later, when he had shrunk to a transparent shell of his former self, seven-year-old John quietly slipped away. His parting words were about those horses.

Even before the end, Bella and her other children had grieved. But however well prepared they imagined they were, John's passing was a shock. His relief from suffering was their consolation.

The situation was equally dire in Gelston. For months James Pattie had hung on, paralysed on his right side, while his wife struggled hard to cope with nursing him on her own. Four weeks after losing John, Bella received news of her father's death.

She took it hard. Gone was the one man she had always relied upon to take her side when she needed him. Yet for so long, she'd been far off, unable to spend even a few hours with him. Her entire family was trapped in a maze of tragedy from which there was no escape. Would her mother be next? She'd written complaining of chest pains and breathlessness; perhaps she, too, was ill. Instead of becoming wiser with age, Bella's confusion increased, as she asked herself what meaning this existence of perpetual strife and torment could possibly hold.

* * * * *

One night, she sat with Aggie and Nichola by the last embers of the fire when a knock came at the door. There on the shadowy landing stood a young woman, soaking wet, her dishevelled hair straggling around her shoulders. Clutched close to her chest was a tiny baby, snuggled inside a shawl. A cloth bundle lay at her feet.

'I'm looking for Bella Turner,' said the stranger, peering through the darkness. 'Is this the right house?'

'I'm Mrs Turner,' Bella replied, warily. 'What can I do for you?'

'You don't recognise me, do you? It's me, Auntie Bella, your sister's lassie. I'm *Mary Jane*! Oh, let me in, for any sakes, or

I'll faint after all these stairs!' she said, gripping the doorpost with her free hand.

'Mary Jane Pattie? Well, come on in and get warmed up. Sit yourself down there,' Bella said, leading her across to a chair by the hearth.

The young woman trembled as Aggie shovelled more coal on the fire and Nichola put the kettle on to heat. *Was* this the daughter of her sister, Agnes? Bella eyed the newcomer suspiciously. When she and Will had married in December 1871, the girl was a mere toddler ... and yet, it was conceivable. She bore a definite resemblance to Agnes.

Mary Jane sipped at a cup of hot tea while Bella held the baby and feared the worst.

'I have to say, this is unexpected. Ma said you'd gone into service, but she hadn't heard from you.'

'Aye, I was in a big mansion out in Bearsden, very posh,' Mary Jane responded with a shrug.

'I hadn't even realised you were anywhere near Glasgow. Are you still living there?' Bella inquired hopefully.

She snorted. 'Fat chance! With *that*?' She pointed at the infant.

Bella frowned. 'Are you feeling well enough? You're most terrible pale!'

'I'll be fine, I'm just tired. I've walked and walked for hours – I remembered you were in Bridgeton, nothing else. God knows how many doors I've knocked on, but I had to find you! I've nobody else to turn to.'

'And the bairn ... when was it born?'

'Ten days ago.'

'And does it have a name yet?'

'Jane Hamilton, but I call her Jeanie. She got her father's name, but that's all she'll get from him.'

'And is he in Bearsden?'

Mary Jane attempted to smile. 'Oh, aye! He's the son at the residence where I worked – used to creep up to my room at night, said he loved me, and promised we would run away together. I was stupid enough to believe him. I thought he meant it, Auntie Bella! When I told him a bairn was coming, he said not to worry. He'd take care o' me, but it was to be *our secret*.' She began to cry. 'Then his father found out, and stormed up to my room, roaring and shouting that I was a disgrace to the household. He wouldn't listen when I tried to explain I was carrying *his grandchild*, and it was his laddie's fault as much as mine. He laughed at me, said I was finished, and I was never to darken their door again or he'd get the police. He sent for his carriage and before I knew it, I was hustled down the stairs and off to Camlachie Street! The same thing happened with the last maid – so the driver said.'

'And have you seen the father since the birth?'

Mary Jane gave a sob. 'Aye, when he came by to say he'd register Jeanie – as if he was doing me a favour – but he'll be cut off without a penny if he has any further contact with me. So that's it – I've no money, and nowhere else to go.'

Aggie and Nichola sat wide-eyed, saying not a word. Bella looked aghast.

'You have to help me, I've got nobody else!' Mary Jane pleaded.

'I don't know what to say. Of course I'll help. You can stay for a wee while, but it couldn't be a permanent thing, you have to understand that. My flat's already bulging at the seams. The three of us sleep here in the box bed and the hurly, and my four other kids are through in the bedroom.'

'Just a breathing space, Auntie Bella, that's all I need. Any tiny corner you can spare would be fine, till I get my strength back.'

32
Trauma

'I must lose myself in action lest I wither in despair.'
– Alfred, Lord Tennyson

S HE HAD SEEMED REASONABLY PLEASANT on that first evening, but Mary Jane's gratitude quickly turned into disgruntlement. It was clear she had inherited her mother's peevishness. She might be irritating but she was family, and had to be made welcome. The 'wee while', however, turned out to mean an indefinite period. Three months later, nine people, including Jeanie, remained in Bella's two cramped attic rooms in Bernard Street.

In the mornings, Mary Jane watched the twins, now aged eleven, leave for Mr McGee's, as Aggie and Nichola had done.

'This is ridiculous! You two shouldn't have to be working before school starts. Go on, tell your Mammy that!' she whispered maliciously, till one day Bella overheard.

'Tell their Mammy what?'

'That it's a shame, making them get up so early to go out and slave at old McGee's, for all they get paid! They're only bairns!'

'I'm afraid that's how it is in this house. Once you're old enough, you have to earn what you can. And I'll thank you to show more respect for Mr McGee – he's been a good friend to us. There's nothing for nothing in this life!' Bella replied coldly. Mary Jane could take that however she liked. 'I'm away down to the shop with these two dresses. Tidy up the table and wash the dishes, would you?'

When she returned with an armful of fabric for her next orders, Bella found her niece sprawled in front of the fire reading the newspaper. The baby lay screaming, red-faced and angry.

'Are you still sitting there?'

Mary Jane glared round insolently. 'What does it look like? I'm tired. You'd be tired too, if you'd to sleep on two chairs shoved together!'

The girl's voice grated on her, but Bella would not lose her temper. 'I'm sorry, but it's the best I can offer you. Maybe if you did more when you're awake, you'd sleep at night. I keep telling you, it's bad for you to sit about so much.'

'Aye, you're a real expert at solving everybody else's problems!'

Wordlessly Bella laid down the bale of cloth, picked up the baby, and the crying stopped. 'Here, take her for a wee minute till I go and get some water.'

One of these days she would let her niece hear a few home truths, she thought as she bathed Jeanie and changed her nappy.

But Mary Jane was powerless to control her depression: she hated her life and the helpless little mite she had produced. For long periods, she stared with dead eyes at nothing. When she did speak it was to criticise or complain, exactly as Agnes, her mother, had done years earlier.

'You're not making soup *again,* are you?' she grumbled, when she saw a pile of chopped vegetables ready for the stock pot. 'I'm sick o' soup!'

Daily Bella reminded herself that Mary Jane was young – seventeen – and she was a blood relative. Her temper rising, she said, 'What would you suggest, then? Or were *you* going to do the cooking for a while?'

'I'm fed up eating the same thing – fed up with everything in fact! There's no peace with that brat. Each time I see her, there's something else to be done!'

'Sshhh, I know. That's how it is when they're so wee, but you'll get through this. We all feel that way at first.'

'I'll never be free! I wish I could go out, get a bit o' excitement!'

209

Bella put a hand on her niece's shoulder.

'That's enough o' you. You need a wee break, that's all. Here, take your shawl – off you go out for a breath of air. Check out the shop windows in the town, eh? That'll cheer you up. I'll watch Jeanie.'

No further encouragement was required. In a jiffy, Mary Jane was off, leaving Bella alone by the fire, cradling the infant in her arms. To feel that tiny body nestled against hers brought an unaccustomed feeling of peace and contentment.

She could almost imagine she was holding Jessie again.

* * * * *

Mary Jane took to going out regularly on her own. Whether or not her mood improved was difficult to say, but Bella found a guilty pleasure in being rid of her. One afternoon, the girl came running up the stairs, burst into the house and slammed the door shut.

'*How you can stand this*?' she screeched.

Calmly Bella looked up from her sewing, pins gripped between her teeth. 'Stand what?'

'Living in this hovel! There's rats in the lobby again – they're all over the building, everywhere!' There was an edge of hysteria in her voice. When Bella showed no reaction, the girl continued, 'How can you ignore such things? Do you *hear me*, Auntie Bella?'

'I hear you, but I save my energy for what counts. If the rats don't get inside my flat, I don't get alarmed. I have other priorities.'

Mary Jane's expression was one of incredulity.

'Does it not get on your nerves, this room where you can't even see out of the window? What could be more dreich than these skylights? And it drives me nuts when it rains, the noise of the water *drip, drip, dripping* from the ceiling into the pail!'

Bella sighed. 'It's not all bad – the light's good for sewing.' she said. 'I'm trying to complete this sleeve and get on to the other one before the bairns come home from school.'

'Sewing and making money – that's all you think of!'

Mary Jane sat down. Only the rhythmic click of the sewing machine disturbed the quiet of the room.

'Didn't you ever think it would be easier just to end it all?'

Startled, Bella replied, 'End it all? *No I did not*, what a thing to ask!'

'With what you've been through, don't you wonder why you bother to carry on?'

'How could I, when I'm all the kids have? I brought them into this world. I have to provide for them – it's my job as a mother.'

'I'm not like you. I feel I've got nothing to offer Jeanie – she'd be better off without me. I'm not cut out to have a kid,' Mary Jane whimpered.

'Come on, Jeanie's a part of you, she needs you.'

A fine one *she* was to speak, having thrust Jessie into Charlie's arms and ordered him to go on that awful day. Bella's own hypocrisy shocked her. But there was one important difference: Jessie was part of *him* too, though it didn't necessarily justify her action.

'It's all right for you, Auntie Bella, you find ways of coping with things, but I don't think I can take much more.' Mary Jane snatched up her hat and shawl. 'I have to get out of here, I feel stifled under this roof.'

'*Now* where do you think you're away to? Your tea's nearly ready. Come back here!'

Bella reached out and caught hold of her, but Mary Jane broke loose to go running out of the door and down the stairs.

By late that evening, she had not returned. The family had eaten supper, and the twins and the two boys went through to bed. Jeanie had her last bottle and was bedded, but still Mary Jane failed to materialise.

'Should we go out and search for her?' asked Aggie.

'But where we would start? She's been gone for hours, she could be miles from here.'

211

There was no telling what Mary Jane might have got up to, given her state when she left. Would she have made for Bearsden, to pay an impromptu call on Jeanie's father? Bella doubted that; she'd get no cuttings there. With no money, it was even less likely that the girl would try to make for Gelston.

A tiny paragraph subsequently appeared at the foot of a page in the Glasgow Herald, so insignificant it could have been easily missed. The police had discovered the body of a young, unidentified female floating in the Clyde. From the description of the victim and her clothing, Bella knew in her heart it was her sister's daughter. It would have served no purpose to voice her suspicions. They'd all had their fill of death and sadness for one year. If it was Mary Jane, she decided, it was best to let her rest in peace.

* * * * *

On the west side of Glasgow, the Victoria Park was opened, complete with its boating pond in the shape of a crown, in honour of the Queen's Golden Jubilee. Contributions were sought towards a personal Jubilee offering, and a leaflet sent out on general distribution, which read:

> The women and girls of the United Kingdom, of all ages, ranks, classes, beliefs, and opinions, are asked to join in one common offering to their Queen, in token of loyalty, affection, and reverence, towards the only female sovereign in history who, for fifty years, has borne the toils and troubles of public life, known the sorrows that fall to all women, and as wife, mother, widow and ruler held up a bright and spotless example to her own and all other nations. Contributions to range from one penny to one pound. The nature of the offering will be decided by the Queen herself, and the names of all contributors will be presented to Her Majesty.

The money raised reached £75,000. Most of it was spent on a replica of Baron Marochetti's Glasgow statue of Prince Albert, to be erected in Windsor Great Park, opposite the statue of Queen Victoria. What was left went on founding an institution to educate and maintain nurses who would care for the 'sick poor' in their own homes.

For the royals, the Jubilee celebrations were spread over two days. June 20, 1887 began quietly with an outdoor breakfast beside the resting place of Prince Albert at Windsor. Queen Victoria then caught the train to London, where a banquet was held in Buckingham Palace, with fifty foreign kings and princes included on the guest list. The assembled company sat down to a splendid family dinner at a horseshoe-shaped table, while the gold plate glittered in the light of hundreds of candles. After the meal, the company retired to the Ballroom where a band played.

Next morning the Queen travelled in an open landau to Westminster Abbey, escorted by Indian cavalry. Mark Twain wrote that the procession through London '*stretched to the limit of sight in both directions.*' Refusing to wear a crown for the occasion, Victoria insisted instead on a bonnet with her long black dress. She was cheered by huge crowds when she appeared on the balcony at Buckingham Palace. For a different audience in the evening, however, she was decked out in a splendid gown embroidered with silver roses, thistles and shamrocks. After a feast attended by diplomats and Indian princes, she was wheeled outside to sit and watch the fireworks in the garden.

Later, the Queen wrote:

> *I am anxious to express to my people my warm thanks for the kind, and more than kind, reception I met with on going to and returning from Westminster Abbey with all my children and grandchildren.*
>
> *The enthusiastic reception I met with ... has touched me most deeply, and has shown that the labours and*

anxieties of fifty long years – twenty two years of which I spent in unclouded happiness, shared with and cheered by my beloved husband, while an equal number were full of sorrows and trial borne without his sheltering arm and wise help – have been appreciated by my people. This feeling and the sense of duty towards my dear country and subjects, who are so inseparably bound up with my life, will encourage me in my task, often a very difficult and arduous one, during the remainder of my life.

The wonderful order preserved on this occasion, and the good behaviour of the enormous multitudes assembled, merits my highest admiration. That God may protect and abundantly bless my country is my fervent prayer.

As the Jubilee events wound up, two new servants from India joined the Queen's household. They had travelled from Agra to Windsor Castle, and first served the royal breakfast on June 23, 1887 at Frogmore House. Victoria wrote admiringly of the one who had particularly caught her eye: Mohammed Abdul Karim was tall and handsome, the son of a doctor. By the end of that week, she was so delighted with the two Indians that she had them wait regularly at her table. Karim introduced her to curry, which was so much to her liking that a portion of the kitchen was given over for the preparation of Indian dishes.

Already proficient in several languages, the Queen developed a passion for Urdu and Hindustani. She routinely met with the twenty-four-year old Karim for language lessons and at his request, in August 1888 Victoria promoted him to the position of 'Munshi' or 'teacher'. He was placed in charge of the other Indian servants, and had responsibility for their accounts. In her writings, the Queen expressed a tremendous fondness for him, and was voluble in her praise.

Not everyone in her circle shared her approval, least of all her offspring. His swift rise to prominence brought the Munshi great rewards, giving rise to jealousy and friction amongst Victoria's staff, who tried to discredit him. But the Queen would hear nothing against him. She wrote letters to him daily in his language, sometimes ending with a flurry of kisses. He accompanied her on all her travels, and occupied the room that had formerly been John Brown's at Balmoral Castle.

In Karim she had found another rare exotic pet: one who looked, talked, dressed and behaved unlike anyone else at court, whose sole allegiance was to her, and who afforded her a glimpse into an alien universe beyond her own. Now she could not – or would not – live without her faithful Muslim servant by her side.

* * * * *

1888. Such an auspicious-sounding number might bring better luck, or so Bella hoped. Something good had to come, to help shake off the pall that had been hanging over the Turners. Since Nichola had begun work as a hemming machinist, the family exchanged their squalid garret in Bernard Street for a flat in Preston Street. Though still only two rooms, it was airy and bright, with high ceilings and large windows.

With just Jeanie as her daytime companion in the house, Bella was able to devote many hours to sewing, allowing herself a break once each month to ride the horse tram to Kelvingrove Park with Aggie and Nichola. They would have a walk, before treating themselves to afternoon tea with freshly-baked scones in a restaurant. But in March of 1889 Nichola was not up to the usual jaunt.

'You two go yourselves. I'm not feeling great. I'd rather stay here at the fire,' she said listlessly.

Bella wanted to believe it was a common cold, but a stab of fear shot through her when the girl's cough lingered for eight weeks. Something was amiss, and she suspected consumption

215

was tightening its grip on another of her children. By April, Nichola was no longer fit for work. She coughed throughout that spring and summer, becoming too frail even to leave the flat; if she went downstairs, she had to be carried back up again. She passed most of her waking hours by the window, watching what happened below in the street. Snippets of news from the others were the highlight of her evenings.

Aggie arrived home later than normal one night, to announce triumphantly, 'I've been round at Templeton's in William Street, Nichola! I'm starting a new job with them next Monday.'

'I thought the new factory wasn't ready yet?'

'It's not. I'll be out in the old sheds for a wee while, but it'll be great – they're to have the most modern equipment, *and* I'm getting more money!'

'Maybe they'll take me on too, when I'm fit.'

'I bet you they will, after you're over this.'

With her siblings, Aggie maintained the pretence that Nichola's condition would improve, despite knowing otherwise.

Unlike any other mill in Glasgow, the new Templeton's was to be erected in grand style, to avoid offending the eyes of the wealthy residents in nearby Monteith Row. Production of Axminster carpet would take place behind the walls of an elegant construction featuring arched windows, modelled on the Doge's Palace in Venice. It would be an instant local landmark, designed to elevate the tone of the city's industrial architecture.

Joining well over a hundred machinists from the east end, Aggie began at Templeton's. But scarcely had she taken up her new position when tragedy struck. For all its style, Templeton's unfinished Italianate façade was unable to withstand the gale force winds that descended on the city on November 1, 1889. A wall collapsed on top of the old weaving sheds, burying fifty girls beneath the rubble. Rescuers struggled in the dark to uncover the victims, many badly injured and twenty-nine female employees who had been killed outright.

Aggie sustained an injury to her leg which was trivial in comparison with the fates of numerous co-workers, but left her with a permanent limp. The accident at Templeton's transformed her from a bright, bouncy young woman into a timorous, withdrawn creature, reluctant to leave the safety of the house, let alone go near William Street. Irritable and jumpy, she could not tolerate any sudden loud noise. The crash of thunder made her physically ill. For as long as she lived she would remember the growling rumble that grew to a deafening roar, heralding death and destruction. By night, awful images haunted her dreams, and she would wake up screaming.

Months passed till she was willing to venture out on her own.

'There was a card in the window of Kelly's Bakery. They were advertising for a counter assistant,' she remarked out of the blue one evening.

'Oh?' said Bella, offhandedly, hiding her relief that Aggie's confidence was returning. 'Would you be interested?'

'I'll have to be, I've got the job.'

But as Aggie healed after her narrow escape, Nichola went into decline. Too weak to leave her bed, she grew visibly paler and thinner, simply faded away until her suffering reached its conclusion, and she was at peace. One more Turner child had succumbed to the dreaded disease.

Not for the first time, Bella queried whether there really was a God. Why would Nichola have been taken, when she *wanted* to live? She might not have been strong, but she was affectionate, hardworking and intelligent, unlike Mary Jane who cared about nobody but herself, and chose to throw her life away. There was no justice!

Subsisting in such close proximity to each other, packed together like sardines in a can, it seemed that Bella and her family faced equal exposure to the root cause of consumption. Had poor nourishment left John and Nichola susceptible to the malady? The slightest hint of a cough filled her with a fear she could barely conceal.

Often she woke up in a cold sweat, imagining infection was attacking another of her brood. She would rise and feel her way from bed to bed in the dark to check on them, filled with gratitude to hear their quiet breathing.

It was one of her few comforts.

33
Reconnecting

*'The bitterest tears shed over graves are for words left unsaid
and deeds left undone.' – Harriet Beecher Stowe*

WHILE BELLA MOURNED the loss of her two children, Queen Victoria revelled in the companionship of Mohammed Abdul Karim. Though less than half her age, the Munshi had the Queen's full trust, and their relationship constantly scaled new heights. He and his family were showered with honours and material wealth which included lands in India.

On formal occasions, when a servant would normally have sat with others of his station, Victoria insisted that the Munshi remain close by her, among the gentry. An incident at Balmoral in September of 1889 sent shock waves through the entire household when Victoria and Karim spent a night alone together in a remote cottage at Glas-allt Shiel, by Loch Muick, on the royal estate. This same cottage had been the scene of many assignations with John Brown, and she had sworn never again to sleep there after his death.

That year brought an unfortunate accusation of theft against Karim's brother-in-law, Hourmet Ali, who tried to sell a brooch belonging to the Queen to a Windsor jeweller. The episode was quickly smoothed over by the Munshi's explanation to Victoria that 'finders keepers' was an Indian custom, leaving no charge to be answered.

When an inflamed boil appeared on the Munshi's neck, the royal physician, Sir James Reid, was instructed to attend to him. Having performed an operation to drain the boil, Reid noted that the Queen was extremely attentive, visiting Karim twice each day for language lessons and generally fussing over him.

In her bedroom, Victoria now displayed portraits of Prince Albert, John Brown and Karim. Her dedication gave rise to grave concern among her courtiers and family, but with a man by her side, she could weather any storm.

* * * * *

Bella, meanwhile, toiled feverishly, not permitting herself, nor any of her offspring, to sit moping. At her insistence, everyone kept busy, and slowly a new normality was established.

Aggie settled into her job at Kelly's Bakery, and was paid the handsome sum of nine shillings per week. The twins, Mary and Isabella, aged fourteen, walked together each morning to the mill where Mary was a curtain folder, and Isabella was a power loom weaver. Thirteen-year-old James worked as a clipper boy. His younger brother, William, was still in school, but was determined to find employment at the earliest opportunity. He envied his siblings' earning capacity, and had set his heart on one of the metal bicycles that had recently come into fashion.

Jeanie was indulged in ways the Turner bairns rarely were. Where they had worn ugly hand-me-downs, the toddler had the prettiest of dresses. In the afternoons, Bella took her for a stroll that invariably led to Mr McGee's shop for sweets.

One day, the newsagent whispered across the counter. 'Just a quick word, Mrs Turner. I've got a flat comin' up on London Road. You might like it – gas mantles, *plus* a coal bunker and a sink in the kitchen. No more trailin' outside for your coal, or down to the landin' for your water ... think aboot it.'

It seemed fortune had begun to smile on the Turners. With the move to London Road, Bella's aspirations for a dwelling with every modern convenience at her fingertips were realised. Were hope and prayer the same thing? Perhaps there was a God after all, she would think, as she stood at her kitchen window to view Glasgow Green and a few hills on the horizon.

Filled with an extraordinary feeling of contentment, she knew she had finally come home.

* * * * *

Despite her repeated attempts to rein in her children's spending, Queen Victoria commissioned a cottage to be built specially for the Munshi at Balmoral, and named it 'Karim Cottage'. No expense was spared in its construction, nor in the redecoration of Frogmore Cottage at Windsor, and Arthur Cottage at Osborne, both of which also became his.

He wrote of his particular fondness for Balmoral Castle in summer, where the surrounding hills were covered in purple and white heather, and the crystal-clear waters of the Dee flowed close by. The scenery reminded him of the highlands of India. Glasgow inspired less enthusiasm, however, and he described it as a very dirty industrial city, situated on a river so polluted that no fish could survive in its filthy waters.

* * * * *

1890

It weighed heavily on Bella's conscience that she'd allowed so much time to pass without visiting her mother, but at last she was in a position to make the trip south. Leaving her offspring to fend for themselves for a week, she set off with Jeanie. In her excitement, she felt almost young again.

Jeanie's initial consternation at the fearsome huffing and puffing of the steam locomotive quickly gave way to delight as they rattled through the countryside. When the girl fell asleep, Bella savoured the prospect of her first trip to her childhood home in two decades. It was oddly appropriate that Ma had arranged to meet her on the station platform at Castle Douglas, the same spot from which Bella had left for Coatbridge as a bride.

Such green all over! How could she have forgotten the joy of fields, trees and rolling hills, with not a tenement or industrial

221

chimney in sight, and the smell of clean, fresh air? She recalled leaving with Will, agonising that it would all have changed when she returned. Now she saw she'd been wrong. People come and go, but Galloway's unique character would survive.

She climbed down from the train. Looking expectantly along the platform, she caught sight of an elderly couple sitting on a bench. As she and Jeanie walked towards them, the old woman got up, her arms outstretched.

'You came, Bella!' she cried. 'I was scared you would never manage back! Here's your uncle Thomas – he's driving us to Gelston.' As the elderly man got stiffly to his feet, Bella was caught in the embrace of the stooped, white-haired stranger that Mrs Pattie had become in the nineteen years since they'd seen one another.

Uncle Thomas deposited them at the cottage door and took his leave. With trepidation Bella entered the house: smelled the burning peat as she crossed the threshold, heard the clack of her heels on the flagstone floor, saw the bed hidden by the same curtain that had always hung there. She noticed the familiar shabby furniture, but could not bear the sight of her father's empty chair.

'I can't get over your hair, Bella! I'm amazed you're not grey by now.'

'We've all aged, Ma, just in different ways.'

Virtually nothing had changed. The room was duller and a bit the worse for wear – like Mrs Pattie and Bella herself.

'Aye, but I note you still dress at the height of fashion!'

Where once her mother's comment might have been taken as a rebuke for her stylishness, Bella heard it as a feeble bid to banish the oppressive silence. How peculiar that the conversation would be dominated by inconsequentialities! Bella lowered her eyes – only then noticing Ma's feet, which were shod in the same old button boots from a quarter century earlier – and gave a sad smile. In this house, the bare necessities sufficed.

Mrs Pattie's fatigue began to show early that night, and she retired to the box bed. As Bella lay with Jeanie at her side in the darkness of the other room, she struggled to get her thoughts straight, to reconcile reality with fantasy. Da had lived to be an old man, and now was gone. Ma was Jeanie's great-grandmother, now a frail, shrunken old woman, instead of the robust, middle-aged mother of her imagination. But Bella would eternally visualise her parents as they had been when she left on the train to start married life with Will. The image of them waving from the platform had crystallised in her memory, and was one she would always carry with her.

By day, she and Jeanie retraced her childhood steps. Bella was painfully aware that her own children had no concept of simple country pleasures like wandering through the woods, or of dewdrops strung like glistening diamonds on a spider's web. Never would they know the shrill alarm of a blackbird's warning cries to its mate when a hawk silently hovered overhead. All *they* had experienced was the noisy congestion of Coatbridge and Glasgow. It was impossible to share Galloway with them.

There were some people in the village she recognised from a bygone era, but few spoke until she did. Bella had become an outsider, the chasm between her and old acquaintances too wide to be bridged. At home, she spent hours at the fireside with Ma, who talked relentlessly of the past. The same stories were rehashed and layers of time were slowly peeled away, as was the veneer each had acquired in the intervening years until their former selves gradually emerged.

Bella was inexplicably moved upon reading a pile of letters her mother had received from Thomasina – pages written by her firstborn, whom she'd so carelessly relinquished. But how much worse was it, she wondered, to have cast off a *second* child? Thomasina was loved as well as anyone could be, of that she had confidence. What might Jessie have endured, thrown on the mercy of Charlie's mother, the woman who twisted her family round her little finger, yet was revered as a saint? Isa's cunning was boundless. She had circled dark and soundless above them, talked Charlie out of staying for even a brief period and swooped down to sink her talons into her prey. Because of that woman, Bella had been forced into the cruellest choice she'd ever had to make ...

Mrs Pattie stretched out to touch her daughter's knee. 'Are you all right? Tell me what was going through your head there.'

Jolted back to the present, Bella's response was automatic. 'I'm fine! Sorry, Ma ... it was nothing,'

'Oh, aye? It didn't seem like nothing to me!'

'I'm tired, that's all,' Bella lied.

'Come on, out with it! You don't keep secrets from your own mother, do you?' She might have grown old and frail; nonetheless her tone and her stare demanded an answer, as they had in the past.

For a moment Bella wavered, was close to being a silly young lassie again, felt almost as she did when Ma wrung out a confession of her misdeeds with Will. But in this instance, she would not obey. She would not be badgered or bullied into a confession she'd regret.

She was in control. Ma's power was gone. The episode with Charlie and the birth of Jessie had not been – nor would be – mentioned in Galloway. Her worlds would not collide.

'Did you ever hear what came of Agnes?' she asked brusquely.

'No. There was not a word from her after she'd gone. It's as if she died. Indifference is such a brutal thing.' Mrs Pattie expression glazed over as she looked into the fire. 'I've fretted that she'd had an accident, but I think she just had no further use for us. It sounds as if Mary Jane turned out the same way, eh?'

Ma knew only that Mary Jane had disappeared, leaving her child behind, and Bella's discomfort grew. That name awakened unpleasant memories of Bernard Street, and she shuddered.

All she said was, 'Don't be too hard on her, Ma. I hope she's happy, wherever she is – and she gave us Jeanie. I'm grateful for that.'

Jeanie, whose arrival had been a miracle, the most precious gift of all. She was Bella's second chance, an opportunity to shower affection on the unwanted child of another and atone for her guilt over Jessie.

* * * * *

They agreed it had been a lovely visit. Bella felt she and her mother deserved that week together, had to reconnect before it was too late, but the past was wearing. What mattered was the present and the future.

At the suggestion she go back with them to Glasgow, Mrs Pattie smiled wanly.

'I would love to meet my grandchildren, but the journey's too much at my age. I've spent all my days here, and this is where I'll see them out.'

Bella had no good reply. 'Well, let me know if you change your mind, won't you?' As she and Jeanie left on the cart, they waved until the old woman standing at the cottage door faded from view.

Two years on, in March of 1892, Mrs Pattie passed away, bringing another chapter to an end for Bella when she embarked on her first and last solo trip south for the funeral. Then she travelled home to Bridgeton for good.

* * * * *

Glasgow hosted a spectacle different from anything previously witnessed there when the East End Exhibition Buildings in Dennistoun were converted into a 7,000-seat amphitheatre to accommodate Buffalo Bill's Wild West show. 'The Drama of Civilisation' featured Miss Annie Oakley, a herd of buffalo, real live cowboys and American Indians who engaged in amazing feats of shooting prowess and horsemanship.

The cast's fondness for Scottish beer and whisky caused a temporary rise in the number of arrests for public drunkenness on Glasgow's streets, but Buffalo Bill's true legacy was the single-handed creation of new heroes for countless children on both sides of the Atlantic. Unwittingly he had laid the foundation for the Hollywood movie industry that would be born a mere twenty years later.

34
Assertiveness

'The robbed that smiles, steals something from the thief.'
– William Shakespeare

BROXBURN, 1892

AT NINE, JESSIE WAS the apple of Isa's eye. With only four people in the house now, Isa revelled in the time she could lavish on the child. It brought such joy, to teach her all that she'd have taught her own family, had circumstances permitted. What seemed disastrous, when the news first broke of the girl's birth, had turned into a godsend.

As she helped Isa fold some laundry fresh from the washing line one afternoon, Jessie casually asked, 'What's a bastard, Maw?'

Isa gave a start. There was no telling what the bairn would come out with next! 'Where did you hear that bad word?'

Jessie blinked. 'Somebody at the school told me I was a bastard, said my name's not really Barclay, it's Bartholomew. Is that true?'

'They don't know what they're talkin' about, hen. Our name was Bartholomew, but ...' Isa paused, and worked at smoothing a sheet. 'But it's so long and awkward to write, we decided it would be easier to use Barclay instead. A lot of folk called Bartholomew do that.'

Jessie appeared satisfied, and Isa heaved a sigh of relief.

* * * * *

To combat any feeling of homesickness, Queen Victoria granted Mohammed Abdul Karim generous leave, when he could return to India. After six months abroad in 1892, he was permitted to bring his wife and mother-in-law back to Britain with him. The Queen wrote of them:

> *The two Indian ladies ... who are, I believe, the first Mohammedan purdah ladies who ever came over ... keep their custom of complete seclusion and of being entirely covered when they go out, except for the holes for their eyes.*

The Muslim women travelled extensively as part of the royal household, and always sat together in a curtained train compartment. Since each royal estate had a cottage reserved for the exclusive use of Karim and his family, the Queen could visit them regularly. Often she popped in for tea, with such female guests as the Empress of Russia and the Princess of Wales in tow, to meet the Munshi's relatives.

* * * * *

Wee Jessie Barclay up a tree,
B! – A! – S! – T! – A! – R! – D!

The class bully began reiterating the ugly taunt in the school playground. A gang of others joined in, even some Jessie had counted as friends, their chant growing ever louder. They made her cry, then left her alone; they'd had their fun for that day.

When she could stand it no more, the girl felt compelled to raise the question with Isa yet again. 'Why do they say I'm a *bastard*, Maw? What do they mean?'

'The wee devils!' Isa muttered to herself, and took a deep breath. 'Well, I've told you I'm your Maw, right?'

'Right,' Jessie said apprehensively.

'I'm your Maw but I'm not the one that gave birth to you. That person, she was *a bad woman*. She had you to a man she wisnae married to, and she gave you away. That's why they use that dirty, horrible word, darlin'! Pay no attention to them, you couldnae help where you came from. You were brought to me, you're just like *my own bairn*, and forever will be. That's what counts, isn't it?' Isa reassured her, hoping the discussion would end there.

Jessie sat anxiously chewing at her lower lip. Was it that creature's unmarried state, or being rejected that made her a bastard? That wasn't clear. She caught the condemnation in Isa's tone when she spoke of the character who had given her life, yet what exactly did it imply when Maw said she was a *bad woman*? There was so much she wanted to ask, but the topic was a delicate one.

Jessie could not bring herself to grace the bad woman with the title of 'mother', but in a final, desperate bid for understanding, she continued, 'So what happened to my ... to the one that had me? Did you ever ...?'

Abruptly Isa cut in, 'Och, I think she died, hen. That's enough, you're far too young to concern yourself wi' such things!' She got up from her chair to glance out of the window. 'It's brightened up, the rain's off. You should go out and play. Go on, and I'll shout on you when your tea's ready.'

The girl's mind was in turmoil. She would have done *anything* rather than go out to play at that moment, would have gone through to the bedroom to curl up in a ball on top of the bed – or even better, *under* the bed, away in a safe, dark hidey-hole where she could be alone, out of sight, where no one would see her confusion, or laugh and tease her. She wished she'd asked about her father, and about her birthplace, though obviously Isa would have preferred the issue not to have arisen at all. Still, she *had* to find why they kept calling her a bastard, and ultimately she did ... kind of.

Swamped by a strange flood of memories and emotions, it occurred to her that she'd always felt slightly different from the others, alone on the wrong side of an invisible fence. At home, Maw was her anchor, both mother and father to her. But with the others she regarded as her family, Jessie sensed a disconnect.

Isa's offspring had left her in no doubt that she was an *outlin*, a parasite clinging to its host, tolerated but not fully accepted. The lodger, Peter Inglis, paid no more notice to Jessie than he did to the rest of the family. He sometimes showed up at mealtimes, otherwise his waking hours were evenly divided between his work and the Green Tree Tavern. So was she a Bartholomew, a Barclay, or what? From what she had recently learned, it was hard to tell. Perhaps she was really nobody. Nothing. Worthless.

The taunts in the playground were not baseless. There was a reason she'd been branded a bastard and it cut her to the quick that everyone else knew it before she did. How she envied her classmates, all seamlessly linked to Mammies and Daddies, brothers, sisters, grandparents, cousins, aunts and uncles while she herself had been deemed unacceptable, rejected by the one who bore her, who was a bad woman and now was dead. From emptiness and self-loathing, tears of frustration pricked the back of her eyes, the tears of a child carrying a burden of shame not rightly hers.

Isa went to the door and held it open. 'I thought you were goin' out to play?'

Obediently lifting her skipping rope Jessie went outdoors into the sunlight, treading around the puddles that lay on the road. From the far side of the street somebody yelled out, 'Jessie! Are ye comin' for a game o' tig?'

But all Jessie could hear were raucous voices that roared *'bastard'* and reverberated through her brain, repeating Maw's words.

She was *a bad woman,* the one who gave birth to her.

Jessie began to skip. Disappointment and rage rose and fell inside her with each leap as she whispered rhythmically to herself.

She gave / you away / I think / she died.

Jump … jump … up and down!

Bitterness swirled inside her as she tried to imagine the feckless being who had borne her and thrown her out like a piece of garbage. Why wasn't she normal, born to someone who loved her, instead of a bad woman who didn't want her?

She gave / you away / I think / she died.

Jump ... jump ... up and down!

Isa said she was pretty, she was smart at her lessons, yet she had not been worth keeping. A bastard was good only for tormenting, for cruel jeers and patronising looks. That was her lot.

She gave / you away / I think / she died.

Jump ... jump ... up and down!

The dry rope whipped faster and harder on the pavement as she skipped, her anger mounting at the *bad woman* who gave her away. She missed a step, and the next thing she knew her foot had become tangled and she tripped. She reached out to save herself as she tumbled, then hit the ground and lay motionless for a few seconds, conscious of the sharp, stinging gravel that had lodged itself in the heel of her hand. As she picked herself up to wipe the blood from her grazed knees, Isa came hurrying out towards her.

'What happened, hen?'

'Nothing, Maw,' she lied, 'I'm fine.'

No sooner had Jessie spoken than her stomach heaved, and the swirl of emotions inside her rose up into her gorge. She bent over to retch, and a torrent of vomit spewed forth: a stinking, acrid stew of pain and fury. In disgust at the mess splattered on the road, she scrambled to her feet. Wiping her mouth on her pinafore, she disregarded Isa's outstretched arms, and walked shakily towards the house. She had to get over this on her own. She would learn to be tough, to hold everyone at a distance, even Maw. She would steel herself against the corrosive insults that wormed their way inside her. No longer would the class bully or anyone else be afforded the satisfaction of seeing her cry.

She could not alter the truth of being born a bastard, but she could hide the anguish she felt inside, even if that concealment brought its own pain. Better to hurt herself than permit others to do so.

Vulnerability invites attack. Self-control would be Jessie's shield.

* * * * *

A few miles distant, in Bathgate, Charlie and Ellen had experienced their share of joys and sorrows since their wedding six years previously. From their first encounter, Ellen believed Charlie to be good husband material, mistaking his unwavering consideration for his mother as respect for women in general. Surely it took a kind man to tolerate Isa's interference! Too late, she saw that he invariably chose the path of least resistance.

Ellen had borne four sons and one daughter. Two of the boys had died in infancy. Charlie, however, assigned as much of his leisure time to Isa as to his wife and three little children. When playing second fiddle to his Maw really began to rankle, Ellen decided that they had to get away – as far off as possible. Like an irritating mosquito, Isa buzzed constantly in the background, draining him of energy he might otherwise devote to others.

As they lay snuggled up in bed one night, Ellen murmured, 'Do you love me?'

Charlie grunted. 'Don't be so daft, you know how I feel. There's nothing I wouldn't do for you!' Declarations of love made him squirm. He shuddered to think what might follow, when Ellen was in this kind of mood.

She smiled to herself in the darkness. 'Well, here's something you can do for me: get yourself a job in the Glasgow area.'

Charlie was silent for a moment. 'Are you not happy *here*?'

'Now *you're* being daft! Of course I'm happy, but I miss my Mam, and she's getting old. If we were in Glasgow, I could visit her more, and you'd *still* be able to drop by your Maw's every week. Go on, the change would do us good! See if you could get a transfer, will you not, eh?'

Charlie lay quiet. Ellen had a point. Apart from the temporary upheaval of a move, it would make no difference to his daily routines. It might even be easier with just one woman

232

to please. Trapped between his wife and his mother, each one demanding his attention, he often feared he'd be ripped apart.

To Isa's chagrin, the family relocated to Glasgow. Largely out of her sphere of influence, Ellen and Charlie enjoyed greater freedom than before, becoming known as Bartholomew. It was at their new home in Salamanca Street, in the Camlachie area of Glasgow, that another daughter was born in December of 1894.

As a peace offering for having abandoned his Maw, Charlie suggested calling the baby Isabella Graham Bartholomew, and Ellen readily agreed. It seemed a small penalty for breaking her mother-in-law's stranglehold over them.

* * * * *

Although thirty years had passed since the death of his father, the attitude of Queen Victoria towards the Prince of Wales showed no sign of mellowing. Lytton Strachey writes in his book, 'Queen Victoria':

> *The Prince of Wales, in particular, stood in tremendous awe of his mother. She had steadily refused to allow him the slightest participation in the business of government; and he had occupied himself in other ways. Nor could it be denied that he enjoyed himself – out of her sight; but, in that redoubtable presence, his abounding manhood suffered a miserable eclipse. Once, at Osborne, when, owing to no fault of his, he was too late for a dinner party, he was observed standing behind a pillar and wiping the sweat from his forehead, trying to nerve himself to go up to the Queen. When at last he did so, she gave him a stiff nod, whereupon he vanished immediately behind another pillar, and remained there until the party broke up. At the time of this incident the Prince of Wales was over fifty years of age.*

35
Mirage

'Mostly it is loss which teaches us the worth of things.'
– Arthur Schopenhauer

BRIDGETON, 1895–1898

S ATURDAY WAS A REGULAR working day for thousands of men, but the town was always crowded since food for the whole weekend had to be laid in. The law in Scotland dictated that every business establishment should stay shuttered on Sundays.

On one particularly chilly April morning, Bella and Jeanie threaded their way homewards along the busy sidewalk, laden with heavy bags of shopping. A family was crossing the cobbles towards them, and Bella watched as they dodged between the horse-drawn carriages and carts on the road. The woman carried a young baby wrapped in a plaid, and the man held the hand of a young boy. After them trailed an older son and a daughter with a woollen tammy pulled down over her ears. Something about the father caused Bella to look twice at him, and her heart missed a beat to realise it was none other than Charlie, apparently with his wife and children. In the nearly twelve years since she'd seen him he had gained weight, even seemed taller than she remembered.

She kept her eye on them as they mounted the kerb and went walking away from her. On the spur of the moment, she caught Jeanie's arm. 'You go on with this stuff, I'm goin' back to get sugar at Lipton's. I'll not be long.'

Bella about-turned to track Charlie, watching the top of his dark head in the crush till they entered a shop. She followed, to stand outside on the pavement, as if engrossed in the window display. Why on earth was she doing this? Insane, she thought fleetingly, she must be going insane! But there she remained, her pulse racing, possessed by a madness that kept her rooted to the spot.

She peered at them through the dirty, streaked little panes, desperately seeking out the face of the daughter. Could that possibly be Jessie? In her innermost soul, she wanted it to be her lost child, *prayed* that it would be her, inside the store. Foolish euphoria bubbled up inside her, to think that they might be so close. Jessie would be twelve by now. But wasn't that girl too young? Her last shred of optimism vanished when the older boy playfully snatched off his sister's tammy, exposing her dark pigtails: dark hair like Charlie's. Bella sighed and her shoulders sagged with disappointment, but she lingered on, mesmerized. It was ridiculous to be lurking there, spying, yet it was as if she was in a trance, devoid of free will.

Charlie reached inside his pocket. He glanced up, and their eyes met. The woman was talking earnestly at him, her back to the window, but he continued to stare past his wife towards Bella. He appeared to nod and cast a nearly imperceptible smile in her direction, before he paid the storekeeper.

Bella stood frozen, unsure if he'd even noticed, let alone recognised her. He'd seemed lost in contemplation. She *wanted* to believe he'd knowingly nodded and smiled at her, but more probably he was responding to his wife. She would never know. Suddenly the girl began tugging on her tammy and the whole family moved towards the door. The shop bell jangled and the spell was broken. When they emerged on to the street, Bella had already seized her bags and wheeled round to take off towards London Road.

Could Charlie be living near Bridgeton, almost on her doorstep? On subsequent Saturday shopping expeditions she half hoped to run into him again. Sometimes she wondered if she was delusional, if it could really have been him that she'd spotted, or if her imagination had run away with her. No, she knew full well it *was* Charlie Bartholomew she'd seen in Bridgeton. Perhaps the child over whom she'd tortured herself for years, was there too ... yet it was unlikely that his wife would be raising his bastard daughter, when his mother was willing and able to take that responsibility.

Bella harboured no illusions that an attempt to make contact would be welcomed, but if she could be certain that Jessie had not been mistreated, could once have seen her or heard her voice, she would have given all she possessed. Any red-haired young girl she passed who might be around Jessie's age was carefully scrutinised: it became her obsession.

* * * * *

In March of 1897, the members the Queen's household decided they could no longer tolerate Karim's continuing presence. As they prepared for the annual visit to Cimiez on the French Riviera, they took the unaccustomed step of banding together to insist that the Munshi should, on that occasion, be excluded from the royal party. Their decision was conveyed to the Queen via one of her maids of honour, Harriet Phipps. If their demand was not met, she announced, the entire staff would resign in protest.

In a blind rage at such insubordination, Queen Victoria immediately swept everything from her desk on to the floor, accusing her courtiers of jealousy and racial prejudice. The trip went ahead as planned, but the bad feeling persisted.

In April, the Queen's Private Secretary and Keeper of the Privy Purse, Sir Henry Ponsonby described the Munshi as '*a thoroughly stupid and uneducated man, and his one idea in life seems to be to do nothing and to eat as much as he can.*'

* * * * *

Seeing Jeanie off to bed one evening, Bella bent down to say, 'Night, night, *Jeanie Jingo.*'

The little girl chuckled. She always liked the funny name game.

236

'Night, night, Mammy. If I'm to be Jeanie Jingo, well you can be ... umm ... you can be ... *Bella Bartholomew!*'

'Oh! Where did you pick up that one?' Bella asked in astonishment.

'At the school. There was a lassie called Bartholomew.'

'Is that right? And what's her first name?'

'Janet. But everybody called her *Wheezy,* because she couldn't run without her chest whistling!' Jeanie said, bursting into a fit of the giggles.

'Hmm ... and where does she live?' Bella inhaled, almost afraid of what was coming next.

'Mammy, I said there *used to be* somebody called that! She was in my class for a wee while, then she got moved up and I don't see her now,' said Jeanie with a yawn, losing interest since the amusing bed-time ritual had taken a serious turn.

It was a false lead sent to tantalise. Yet again Bella's hopes were dashed.

* * * * *

Queen Victoria's relationship with her family and household reached a crisis in June of that year. Not content with allowing the Munshi unrestricted access to all her correspondence, Victoria regularly consulted him on the problems in India between Hindus and Muslims. Her pro-Muslim missives to the Viceroy of India were not well received. In addition, there was concern that the presence of a Muslim at the heart of the British court might pose a threat to the stability of the monarchy and the Empire.

An undercover investigation of Karim's background was instigated by the Viceroy, who sent an envoy to Agra. It was discovered that the Munshi had embellished his history, claiming to be the son of an Indian army surgeon, when actually his father was an apothecary at the local prison. Karim himself had once been employed there as a clerk.

Sir James Reid, the Queen's outspoken Scottish physician, did not mince his words when confronting Karim with the evidence. He expressed the opinion of the whole royal household when he told the Munshi that he was presumptuous and arrogant, an impostor from a low class who could never be a gentleman.

Queen Victoria was outraged.

As revenge for discrediting her favourite, she announced to her courtiers her intent to bestow a knighthood on him. Already Karim had been promoted over those whose families had served the royals for generations, but this was the final straw. On all sides, she was confronted with hostile resistance. Threatened with the mass resignation of her household, she countered that she would abdicate on the eve of her Diamond Jubilee if her wish was not granted. But with the support of the Prince of Wales, Sir James Reid called her bluff. Any further effort by her to honour the Munshi with a knighthood, he said, would result in drastic action.

He would be forced to declare her insane.

The Queen had to accept defeat with a good grace.

Now crippled with arthritis and more frail than before, Victoria passed the first day of her Diamond Jubilee celebrations with her family at Windsor. Next morning she sent a telegraph message throughout the Empire, which read:

From my heart I thank my beloved people, may God bless them.

Then to loud cheers from crowds lining the six-mile route of the procession, she was driven in an open state landau to St. Paul's Cathedral, where an open-air service was held in her honour.

A longer message to the nation said:

In weal and woe I have ever had the true sympathy of all my people, which has been warmly reciprocated by myself. It has given me unbounded pleasure to see so many of my subjects from all parts of the world assembled here, and to find them joining in the acclamations of loyal devotion to myself, and I wish to thank them from the depth of my grateful heart.

* * * * *

When Bella encountered a client who had moved from Broxburn, she found the temptation too strong to resist, and inquired, 'Did you have any neighbours called Bartholomew?'

'Oh, aye, Linlithgowshire is full of Bartholomews!'

'There was a wee girl I knew from there, she'd be about fourteen now. Red hair, she had, and she was brought up by her granny. She was called *Jessie Bartholomew*,' Bella said, shy at uttering that name aloud.

The woman pondered for a moment, her head to one side.

'I can't say that rings a bell, no. I'm sorry,' she said, and paused. 'There were a few folk o' that name, but there wisnae a Jessie Bartholomew in Broxburn. Not that I remember, and I was there for ten years.'

'Oh ... well ... I must be mistaken. It doesn't matter.'

Bella tried to hide her dismay. There was a greater chance of finding a pot of gold at the end of a rainbow than of hearing news of Jessie.

36
East, West

'Travel is fatal to prejudice, bigotry and narrow-mindedness.'
– Mark Twain

CAMLACHIE, GLASGOW, 1899

THE EARLY YEARS IN GLASGOW were exciting. Ellen and Charlie showed their children the People's Palace and the Winter Gardens that had opened in Glasgow Green in 1898. For a penny each, they experienced their first run on an electric trolley. Horse-drawn trams would soon be a thing of the past in this city that embraced all things modern.

Happy as they were in their new surroundings, Ellen's ambition to ease her mother-in-law's grip over them was only partially realised. All it took was a cup of tea with his Maw, together with some gentle probing, for Charlie to pour out everything that was in his thoughts when he visited Broxburn. Not content with ferreting out miniscule details of her son's marriage, Isa fearlessly volunteered her opinions.

Janet's asthma was a case in point. The girl's chest ailment had developed after their move to Glasgow. Though the air quality in Linlithgowshire had rarely been the best, it was like nectar from the gods in comparison with the city smog.

'Don't say I didn't try to warn you, son,' Isa said when Janet's breathing was again the topic of discussion. 'I could have told you that air's unhealthy. It's bad for folks' chests *and* their bones. That's why Glasgow bairns all have bowly legs! I've read the fog's so bad, they hardly get a blink of sun, and that's why they get rickets.'

She folded her arms self-righteously. It was a sin that her grandchild's wellbeing had to suffer just because Charlie wanted to please that wife of his. Maybe now she could make him see sense.

At that minute, Jessie breezed into the kitchen.

'Hello, Charlie! How're you getting on this week?'

'Not bad. Yourself? Where are you away to in such a rush?'

'I'm great, going off to work. I'll have to hurry up or I'll get the sack, I'm late! Say hello to Ellen for me. Cheerio, Maw!'

Isa nodded proudly in the direction of the door as it closed behind Jessie.

'She's turned out to be a fine lassie, that! I sometimes ask myself what I'd have done without her. She's a quiet one … doesn't let on what she's thinkin'. Other lassies o' that age, they blether a lot o' rubbish, but no' her – very down-to-earth, seems quite happy wi' her housekeeper's job. She's shapin' up to be a rare wee cook, in fact!'

Rummaging among a pile of newspapers beside the hearth, Isa selected one and delightedly thrust it in front of Charlie.

'Here's what I was talkin' about. The article on rickets was in the paper recently. Did you no' see it?'

'Give it a rest, Maw! Not every bairn in Glasgow has rickets, you're exaggerating!'

He wanted to protest that there were plenty of tall, robust youngsters in the city, but their life of privilege meant they seldom saw the inside of factories, nor did they constantly breathe the pollution that hung like a sooty veil over Camlachie and Bridgeton. It annoyed him that Isa prattled on with such conviction when she'd not actually been in Glasgow. She'd barely left the confines of Linlithgowshire, but kindness kept him from pointing that out. He wished he hadn't brought up the issue of Janet's lungs.

'All I'm sayin' is that the quicker you get your wife and family out o' there, the better,' said Isa. 'You'll learn from your mistakes. *East, west, home's best.*'

'Aye, that's true. I'll get on my road, Maw,' said Charlie, resolving to persuade Ellen that they should go east again. There was sense in what his mother said. It had been a stupid idea to relocate to Glasgow.

* * * * *

He got back to Camlachie that night in a good enough humour, but with less to say than usual. In bed, he tossed and turned.

'You might as well tell me what's going round in your head, otherwise neither o' us will get to sleep, with your stramashing,' his wife complained.

Charlie clutched the sheet tighter round his chin. This was no hour to open up the kind of discussion they needed to have, but Ellen persisted.

'Come on, was it something your Maw said today?'

'Och, nothing we haven't heard before. The same old guff, how she hardly gets to see us, and what a rotten place this is to be bringing up our weans in. I shouldn't have mentioned Janet's asthma, it gave her an inroad again. *East west, home's best*, she says, and we should have stayed where we were. Perhaps she's right.'

It was terrible to be torn, Charlie was thinking. If he agreed with Isa on the poor quality of the Glasgow air, he was betraying Ellen, who had been the driving force behind their move. They each had a point, that was the trouble. It seemed he just opened his big mouth, and one or the other of them took offence.

For thirteen years, Ellen had fought Isa's efforts to undermine them, but the liberty she craved remained elusive. Charlie was so pliable, that a few minutes alone with his Maw could change his opinion on virtually anything. It was almost comical, the way he fell for her trite phrases! *Never* had she voiced a single original idea, Ellen wanted to yell, but it would be counter-productive; there was nothing to be gained from criticism. Instead she would redouble her initiatives to keep her

242

mother-in-law at bay, to prevent her tentacles reaching any further into their marriage.

Ellen had one weapon in her arsenal that his Maw could not use. She cuddled into Charlie, who lay despondently facing the wall. As they snuggled like two spoons, Ellen's arm stretched over to fondle and stroke him, and she whispered soothingly, 'Come here, you! I'm worried about Janet and all, you know.'

When he turned towards her, she continued, '*Of course* you have to tell your Maw what news there is of the weans. She wouldn't be a normal mother if she didn't put in her tuppence-worth! She means well, but we have to decide things for ourselves. We'll find a solution.'

Charlie began to relax and dropped off to sleep, while Ellen spent what was left of the night figuring out how to outwit Isa in her latest bid for control.

* * * * *

BROXBURN, 1899

'*Portobello*, did ye say? Why would you go there?' Isa cried, her eyes wide with disbelief.

Charlie was sitting at the kitchen table, and had braced himself for this moment. He knew his mother would disapprove, but as Ellen said, the sea air would help Janet's chest.

'Come on, Maw, it's not the end of the earth, and we're getting a flat with four rooms!'

Isa frowned her disapproval of this new scheme, all signed and sealed before she heard a word of it. Four rooms in Portobello, if you please! That had unquestionably been Ellen's doing. Charlie wasn't one for that kind of showiness. 'And just what are you goin' to do with such a huge place? You'll be payin' through the nose for space you don't need.'

Ignoring her sour tone, Charlie continued, 'No, we were amazed, the rent's scarcely any higher than we're paying in

Camlachie. With wee Charlie's pay coming in as well, we'll easy manage.'

'Well, you've *no' half* been busy since I last saw you, to have got all this fixed up! There was I, fair hopin' that you'd be coming back where you belong.' Isa paused to dab at a tear. 'But you've got your own life to live, and I *would not* try to hinder you ... except you'll be *right at the far side* of Edinburgh from here. It's a terrible distance away.'

'It'll be handier for me to pop in and see you, Maw. And with all that space, you might even come to us for a wee holiday, eh? You'd love the beach!' he said without thinking. When the image of his wife came into his mind, he felt like kicking himself. Chump that he was, would he never learn? Ellen would have his guts for garters if Maw took him up on his offer!

'Me, travel the country? That'll be the day!' replied Isa, to her son's relief. 'I'm gettin' to be an old woman, comin' up to sixty-four, Charlie! I'll no' be here for much longer, maybe.' She sniffed petulantly.

Gratefully Charlie put his arm round her shoulders. 'You're a spring chicken. That's enough of that kind of talk!'

It was true, she was showing her years, and he wouldn't always have her. On the journey to Glasgow, he determined to visit her more often after they'd moved. Ellen would air her displeasure, but it would be preferable to her wrath if Isa ever darkened their door in Portobello.

He sighed; his existence was one continuous balancing act.

* * * * *

Peter Inglis was employed as a retort man at the oil works in Broxburn, a dangerous, dirty job that earned sufficient for a reasonable living, an occasional pound to lay aside and as much beer as he cared to drink at the Green Tree Tavern. Isa was thrilled that they could afford nicer home furnishings, and her adult children were apparently happy that their Maw enjoyed such unprecedented security in her old age. Equally evident was their resentment of Jessie. It galled them to remember their childhood deprivations in Durhamtown, while this cuckoo in the nest wanted for nothing – or so it seemed.

Charlie could not deny the girl's undoubted resemblance to Bella, her mother, which increased as she matured. Jessie frequently was conscious of his searching looks, but unlike those of his siblings, Charlie's bore her no ill-will.

Prior to his wedding, he had divulged the circumstances of Jessie's birth to Ellen, when he'd felt obliged to speak frankly about his illegitimate child. Then the matter was laid to rest. Charlie found it easier to bury the past.

Isa's youngest son, Hugh, had enlisted in the Royal Scots Dragoon Guards, and a treasured gilt-framed photograph of him in uniform graced the kitchen mantelpiece. (Treasured not simply because Hugh had ventured to the distant shores of southern Africa, but the formal portrait was the first ever taken of any of Isa's offspring.) A photograph was an expensive luxury. In her eyes, it was proof that Hugh had moved up in the world, and its presence enhanced the status of the whole family. It tickled her to see her baby boy, now a handsome soldier, standing there proudly in his kilt.

Unpatriotic though it sounded, she would have preferred that Hugh stay in Scotland, instead of fighting in the Boer War. But he hadn't listened to her, said he wanted some excitement before putting down roots.

With advancing years, it was a mother's due to have her children close by, she wanted to say. Without them, she would have nothing.

* * * * *

As if they were a means of holding on to the past forever, Queen Victoria took great pleasure in her vast collection of material possessions. Lytton Strachey writes:

She gave orders that nothing should be thrown away –
and nothing was. There, in drawer after drawer, in
wardrobe after wardrobe, reposed the dresses of
seventy years. But not only the dresses – the furs and
the mantles and subsidiary frills and the muffs and the
parasols and the bonnets – all were ranged in
chronological order, dated and complete. A great
cupboard was devoted to the dolls; in the china room at
Windsor a special table held the mugs of her childhood,
and her children's mugs as well. Mementoes of the past
surrounded her in serried accumulations. In every
room the tables were powdered thick with the
photographs of relatives; their portraits, revealing
them at all ages, covered the walls; their figures, in solid
marble, rose up from pedestals, or gleamed from
brackets in the form of gold and silver statuettes. The
dead, in every shape – in miniatures, in porcelain, in
enormous life-size oil-paintings – were perpetually
about her. John Brown stood upon her writing-table in
solid gold. Her favourite horses and dogs, endowed
with a new durability, crowded round her footsteps.
Sharp, in silver gilt, dominated the dinner table; Boy
and Boz lay together among unfading flowers, in
bronze. And it was not enough that each particle of the
past should be given the stability of metal or of marble:
the whole collection, in its arrangement, no less than its
entity, should be immutably fixed. There might be
additions, but there might never be alterations. No
chintz might change, no carpet, no curtain, be replaced
by another; or, if long use at last made it necessary, the
stuffs and the patterns must be so identically
reproduced that the keenest eye might not detect the
difference. No new picture could be hung upon the
walls at Windsor, for those already there had been put
in their places by Albert, whose decisions were eternal.

Victoria's imperiousness did not wane with age. Many anecdotes are told of her insistence on punctuality and protocol. At mealtimes, no one could continue eating after the Queen laid down her fork and knife. Likewise, the regime for after-dinner conversation in the drawing room had to be observed. Lytton Strachey again:

> The Queen, at the fitting moment, moved towards her guests; one after the other they were led up to her; and, while dialogue followed dialogue in constraint and embarrassment, the rest of the assembly stood still, without a word. Only in one particular was the severity of the etiquette allowed to lapse. Throughout the greater part of the reign the rule that ministers must stand during their audiences with the Queen had been absolute. When Lord Derby, the Prime Minister, had an audience of Her Majesty after a serious illness, he mentioned it afterwards, as a proof of the royal favour, that the Queen had remarked "How sorry she was she could not ask him to be seated." Subsequently, Disraeli, after an attack of gout and in a moment of extreme expansion on the part of Victoria, had been offered a chair; but he had thought it wise humbly to decline the privilege. In her later years, however, the Queen invariably asked Mr Gladstone and Lord Salisbury to sit down.

37
Ups and Downs

'The past, the present and the future are really one: they are today.' – Harriet Beecher Stowe

FOR MONTHS QUEEN VICTORIA'S health had shown signs of deterioration. Easily tired and occasionally confused, she took a turn for the worse on January 17, 1901. Her physician, Sir James Reid, wrote in his notes that she clearly had suffered one of several small strokes. After a brief rally on January 19, she lost consciousness and her children were summoned. At 6.30pm on January 22, 1901, Queen Victoria died at Osborne House on the Isle of Wight. Present at her bedside were her son Bertie, who would become King Edward VII and her eldest grandson, Kaiser Wilhelm II of Germany. At her death, the Queen had thirty-seven living great-grandchildren.

James Reid's diaries reveal surprising details of his doctor/patient relationship with Victoria. Despite attending to her for twenty years, the first time he actually saw her in bed was during her final short illness. Draughts or potions he personally had prepared for her at all hours of the night had always been administered by her maids. Following her demise he performed a physical examination of the Queen, to discover that she had a ventral hernia and prolapsed uterus.

The instructions for her burial reflected her excessive fondness for John Brown. Alongside her in the coffin were to be laid not only Prince Albert's dressing gown and a plaster cast of his hand, but also a lock of her Scottish gillie's hair, his photograph, some letters he had sent her, and a gold ring of his mother's.

The new king, Edward VII, subsequently set about removing or destroying all of his mother's tributes to John Brown. Likewise the King demanded the return of all photographs and letters from Victoria to the Munshi, and had them burned. Mohammed Abdul Karim had the satisfaction of being the last to view the Queen in her casket, and he was granted permission to be in her funeral procession. Immediately afterwards, however, he and his relatives were summarily dismissed from court and sent back to India.

With the passing of the monarch, the Boer War in its closing stages, and smallpox breaking out once more, the organisers of the International Exhibition were justifiably concerned. There was a risk that their upcoming celebration of recent achievements in art, science and industry might be greeted with less public enthusiasm than they had anticipated. Given the tremendous degree of planning and expense invested, however, it was decided that the show should carry on as scheduled, and it was hosted by Glasgow in May of 1901.

Conventions were held to coincide with the milestone occasion, and the railway companies offered special excursion fares from England. From all over Britain and beyond, a total of almost twelve million people flocked to Glasgow. Rarely had the city known such a prolonged period of good weather, nor such crowds. Regardless of the horrors they expected, visitors from south of the border were impressed by the city's friendly sophistication, its underground train network, and its new electric trolley buses. Kate Cranston's Tea Garden was a favourite tourist venue.

The architect James Millar designed elaborate buildings that covered one hundred acres of Kelvingrove Park and its surroundings. People could view a model farm with a functioning dairy and windmill, and ornate pavilions showcased the cultures of many corners of the earth from as far afield as Japan, Persia, Russia and Africa. Everything new under the sun was on display, such marvels of modernity as electric light bulbs, the telephone, and a model of the newest steamship. Elevator rides were available for twopence, and the latest motor cars were demonstrated and tested.

One of the most popular attractions of 'the Groveries', as the exhibition was locally named, was the Canadian water chute, which cost sixpence a turn, and ended with a chilly plunge into the River Kelvin. There were athletic contests, football matches and a gymkhana. A track was built exclusively for bike races. Amusements included a rifle range, a switchback railway at threepence a ride, and two gondolas from Venice that sailed on the River Kelvin. Glaswegians affectionately nicknamed the gondoliers 'Signor Hokey' and 'Signor Pokey'. Marching bands played daily. The Grand Concert Hall, with seating for three thousand, hosted performances by orchestras from all over the globe. Kelvingrove Park was *the place* to be seen: it had a museum, art galleries, a sports stadium complete with grandstands, and the famous Industrial Hall whose 'Statue of Light' appeared to float above its golden dome. Even The New York Times reported that Glasgow's International Exhibition was truly unique, and for six months the city proudly held the world in its hands.

* * * * *

Queen Victoria's resident physician continued in the same capacity for King Edward VII, but the duties of Sir James Reid also involved other challenges. In 1904, blackmail threats arrived at the palace from one Alexander Profeit, factor at Balmoral, claiming possession of notes written to him by Victoria, about John Brown. The good doctor was deputised to resolve the dilemma and after a six-month negotiation, he met with Alexander Profeit's son, George. A tin box filled with the Queen's letters was presented. Reid read them, noting in his diary that many of them were *'most compromising'* before delivering them to the King. What was paid for the letters, or what eventually happened to them is not known. Queen

Victoria's voluminous correspondence was thereafter examined and sensitive areas expunged by her descendants. Princess Beatrice devoted the next thirty years to the mammoth task of editing her mother's diaries.

Succeeding monarchs would be more circumspect when committing pen to paper.

* * * * *

As Glasgow's popularity grew, the Turner household rapidly shrank. The twins each became engaged: Isabella's marriage to Wullie Gillan at the end of 1901 was quickly followed by Mary's to Andrew Jamieson. James and William, both stone polishers, branched out on their own, leaving Aggie and Jeanie at home with Bella. Aggie still served at the counter in a bakery, while Jeanie was employed in a confectionery warehouse.

Age began to take its toll on Bella. She was hard of hearing, and her eyesight deteriorated so badly in the early 1900's that sewing was impossible. Like Queen Victoria, she had developed cataracts, and blindness left her feeling redundant. Where once she'd peered through a smeared shop window to spy on Charlie and his family, now she constantly peered through a similar haze, straining desperately to make sense of her own life.

Her hours alone dragged. Her thoughts frequently drifted back to her childhood in Galloway, and to her time with Tam prior to Will's arrival on the scene. Then came Thomasina, who had only really seemed hers in the moments after the birth, till Mrs Pattie assumed ownership of her. As if it were yesterday, Bella could remember leaving for Coatbridge, and she smiled to think of the fun she and Will shared together, before poverty sucked all the joy from their existence. How weird, that circumstances had driven her to surrender both her first child and her last to others! Thomasina and Jessie were bookends to her middle seven.

She reproached herself: when her sight was good, she should have made an effort to track Jessie down. She could have taken a day ticket to Broxburn, just to see where she had been reared, to breathe the same air she had breathed. Yet it would have been pointless. Even if they met, no words could heal the wounds she'd inflicted on the child she gave away.

Eternal regret was her penance.

* * * * *

A new group called the Suffragettes was waging an aggressive campaign for women to be given the vote. There were news reports of scandalous protests where acid was poured into mailboxes, fires were set at Leuchars Railway Station and Ayr Racecourse, windows were smashed and portraits of the king were slashed. Not content with chaining themselves to railings, the Suffragettes heckled at public meetings then spat and kicked, shouted and slapped at the police who arrested them. Never had females been guilty of such mob behaviour.

Standards among in the male population were also slipping. In April of 1909, there was a Scottish football cup final match at Hampden Park between Glasgow's two rival teams, Rangers and Celtic. The game resulted in an unprecedented riot, where grown men battled one another and caused destruction to property.

The country had changed and Bella no longer felt part of it, nor wanted to be.

38
Sorrow

'Almost all our desires, when examined, contain something too shameful to reveal.' – Victor Hugo

BROXBURN, 1911–1912

D AVIE PRESENTED JESSIE with a gold engagement ring set with five tiny stones – three rubies and two diamonds. But their plans for an autumn marriage were put indefinitely on hold when illness struck both Peter and Isa. Like a dutiful daughter, Jessie resigned from her housekeeper's position to work at home as cook, cleaner and nurse.

'What about us?' asked Davie. 'Peter and Isa might go on for years yet.'

'I've told you, I can't leave them as they are. He can hardly take two paces without having to sit down to catch his breath, and Maw looks worse each day.'

Davie gave an easy-going shrug. The reply was as expected, and Jessie was worth waiting for.

In December 1911, Peter Inglis had a massive heart attack. The chore of going to the registrar fell to one of his sons, who signed as a witness on the death certificate. As his name he entered '*Peter Barclay*'. In the box specifying his relationship to the deceased he wrote '*a neighbour*'.

These months were the worst Charlie had experienced. Against his better judgment he'd been persuaded by Isa to move back to Broxburn.

'Portobello's too far off. I'd be far happier if you were here, son,' she had said. 'Get yourself a safe wee job, save us all constantly worryin'. It's terrible, you read o' a train crash nearly every week in the paper. How will Ellen and the weans manage if anythin' happens to you?'

He shouldn't have listened to her! He'd give anything to be in Portobello again, instead of just a street away from his Maw. Her deterioration so horrified him that on occasion he'd even thrown up after visiting Church Street. This slow torture couldn't be how a man was meant to remember his mother! When he decided he couldn't take it any longer, his calls grew less frequent.

It was lucky they had Jessie there, he reflected ... but women were more used to coping with illness. Her resilience certainly hadn't come from him. She was strong, somehow remained indifferent to it all. The girl was a survivor.

At the close of January 1912, Ellen turned up at the house with a bag from the baker's. 'How is she?'

'Not great,' whispered Jessie softly. 'She's terrible weak, can hardly even get out of bed. The doctor should be here shortly.'

'Has she been able to keep anything down this morning?'

Before a reply came, there was a scuffling noise, and Isa's ghastly figure appeared, her hair stringy and dishevelled. With a mouth too big for her face, and cheekbones that nearly protruded through her pallid flesh, she stood framed in the doorway to the bedroom. Her scrawny arms stuck out at either side of her grotesquely swollen stomach, like a scarecrow's.

'I thought I heard voices,' she murmured, beginning to trundle unsteadily into the kitchen.

Jessie rushed to steady her.

'Well, hello there! I brought you a fresh-baked scone, to try and tempt you to eat something,' said Ellen brightly.

Isa took a seat and smiled wanly, her cracked lips sticking to dry, discoloured teeth.

'Have a wee sip of water, Maw,' said Jessie, offering her a glass.

'Thanks, hen.'

Having taken one mouthful, Isa turned to Ellen. 'How's Charlie?'

'Fine. He's at his work, but he'll maybe manage round later.'

'Aye, maybe. Ye could hope.'

Ellen glanced sharply at Isa. Was she being sarcastic? It didn't matter a tuppenny damn anyhow!

'It's good that you're up and about.' She stood up and gingerly patted her mother-in-law's shoulder. 'You're less pale today. I'll away, then, if the pair o' ye are all right ... have to get the dinner on. Cheerio!'

With that she made her escape. As she hurried home, Ellen smiled to herself.

Isa might have succeeded in getting Charlie and his family close by her in Broxburn, but her struggle had been in vain. Her number was nearly up. The doctor had said as much.

Charlie would forget the nightmares that had haunted him since his Maw had been stricken, and they would be free of the chains that had bound them so tightly. Bartholomew, Barclay or whatever – they'd adopt any name they liked!

Isa's reign was nearing its end, and Ellen was nothing less than jubilant.

* * * * *

Peter Inglis' passing had both eased and added to Jessie's burden. Devotion was a double-edged sword.

Apart from her, only the doctor was permitted to view Isa's ailing body, and rarely had the girl undergone such a harrowing time. The interminable sessions alone with Maw, when it grew increasingly tricky to maintain the delusion that she would soon turn the corner and regain her good health, left Jessie exhausted.

Half-hearted offers of help from her offspring were firmly rejected by Isa. 'No, I lick my wounds in private. It's enough that you pop in to see me. Jessie and I get on fine, don't we, hen? She's a great wee nurse – she feeds me, bathes me and keeps me company.'

The fleeting appearance of any visitor was the highlight of many tedious hours, before the two of them once more were left alone in the house. What guests had said and how they said it – even the clothes and shoes they wore – provided fodder for conversation. Such minutiae filled the void. When all else failed, Jessie would lift down the photograph of Hugh from the mantelpiece for Isa to study it yet again. Together they admired the noble figure who posed proudly in uniform. Poor Hugh's enthusiasm for adventure had been quickly dampened by the horrors he endured in Africa. He was killed in a pointless war that claimed twice as many lives from disease as on the battlefield. Isa wept to think he was gone, and squeezed her eyes shut to block out the pain of it all.

At the mention of her relationship with Davie, Jessie winced, because inevitably Isa would rail about the selfishness of men.

'Don't forget what I've always told you – they're interested in just one thing. Keep your hand on your ha'penny till you have a weddin' ring, or he'll treat you like dirt.'

'*Maw*! Come on, I'm twenty-eight, I can take care o' myself!' Jessie protested.

'It doesn't matter what age you are. Believe me, I know. Men are all the same.'

Having had her say, Isa mercifully would doze off, and Jessie's cheeks burned at such intimate talk.

* * * * *

'Bring me a pen, a sheet o' paper and an envelope, would you, hen?' Isa said, a nerve at one side of her mouth twitching in agitation.

'Are you going to write a letter, Maw?' inquired Jessie cautiously. Such an event was a rarity.

'You could say that, I suppose,' replied Isa with a nod.

Silently mouthing the words to herself as she composed a few lines in her unaccustomed hand, she finished writing. She folded the paper and placed it in the envelope.

'Put a dab o' red sealin' wax on this for me,' she said, holding out the letter to Jessie. 'You're to open it after I'm away.'

'Don't ... you're going to recover. Look at you today, you're stronger than I've seen you for a while!'

But Isa slumped back in her chair, exhausted. She pointed to the locked box in which she kept her personal papers and mumbled, 'I need to put this in there.'

Jessie saw her safely into bed, and she sank into a deep sleep, content to have accomplished that final task.

The doctor's house calls increased in frequency, and when the patient's pain grew unbearable, a morphine mixture sent her drifting into lengthy periods of unconsciousness.

Stress began taking its toll on Jessie, until she found relief by taking an aspirin powder, which helped dull her agony as she cried herself to sleep in bed at night. Patented by the Bayer Company in 1900, the popularity of aspirin had grown and it was widely regarded as a cure for almost every malady.

When Isa seemed relatively lucid, Jessie grabbed the opportunity to say, 'There's a question I have to ask you, Maw.'

'What is it, hen?'

'You said I was given *to you* when I was an infant. But why here, why to you?'

For years she had wanted to ask these things, but her courage had always failed her. It was bad enough to be a bastard without dwelling on it. Yet with Isa so sick, this might be her last chance.

'It's all water under the bridge, hen. Don't start rakin' up the past.'

'Oh, I wish you would tell me! Please, Maw,' pleaded Jessie, placing her fingers on Isa's wrist and squeezing gently, as if that would help refresh her memory. 'You said my mother was a *bad woman*, but I must have had a father as well. D'you have any information about him?'

'You were brought to me by Charlie, darlin'. Get him to tell you how it happened ...' Isa breathed, halting in mid-sentence. Her eyelids closed and she nodded off.

She became unable to leave her bed, the same one in which Peter Inglis had died eleven weeks earlier. From the brown, foul-smelling urine in the bedpan, Jessie instinctively knew that Maw had reached the terminal stage of her illness. The doctor did his best to ease the patient's misery, till eventually Isa sank into a peaceful sleep from which she would not wake. Jessie sat by her bedside, watching and waiting, while other members of the family dropped by periodically to join in the vigil.

As the end drew near, Isa's rasping, frenzied gasps echoed in the darkened room as she strove to fight her way out of death's grip. For thirty six hours that seemed like an eternity, she fought valiantly, then the battle was over.

Isa drew her last breath in February of 1912.

39
Revelations

'It is better to be hated for what you are than to be loved for something you are not.' – André Gide

THE WHOLE FAMILY reacted calmly to Isa's passing since each of them had mourned during her horrendous suffering. There was palpable relief that it was over and they could resume their normal lives.

Charlie was ready to assume control of the proceedings.

'I'll go down to the registrar's, but I need Maw's birth and marriage certificates out of the box. Where's the key?'

'Maw used to keep it in her pocket ... I don't know what happened to it after she took to her bed,' responded Jessie.

Ellen rummaged in the bedroom, averting her eyes from the corpse laid out on the bed, and Charlie rifled through the pockets of Isa's clothes till finally the key turned up in a ruby glass jug on the window sill. The place could do with a thorough gutting, Charlie thought. It stank of illness. After the funeral they'd attend to that, once they'd divided up the house contents.

First they'd to get to the registrar's before the office closed for the day.

* * * * *

Jessie watched them go, relieved to have an hour on her own. Exhausted, she sat at the table with a cup of tea, and idly began emptying Isa's box, curious about what had merited such purposeful concealment for so many years. On top, there still lay the envelope that was to be opened following Maw's demise. Jessie set it to one side: she'd wait for Charlie. She focused her attention on a stack of birth certificates, eager yet afraid to discover her own one. At the very bottom, under many other yellowed documents, she found what she wanted.

The evidence she sought was here, right under her nose, all this time! Her birth certificate had lain undisturbed for twenty-eight years. Jessie gasped and her hand shook as she read and reread it. *Charlie* was her father! Feeling as though a stone had hit her between the eyes, she let the paper drop on to the table. But again she returned to the names of her biological parents, and ran her finger over the lines that bore their actual signatures: *Isabella Turner, maiden surname Pattie,* and *Charles Bartholomew.* Why hadn't she realised it before? Her naiveté must have provided endless amusement for the family! Were Charlie's offspring, her half-brothers and sisters, also in on the secret? Barclays, Bartholomews or whatever they were – at that moment she hated them all.

The nameless, faceless couple who gave her life had previously seemed unreal. Now in front of her, in black and white, were the marks of those living, breathing, humans who had created her and gone together to register her birth in Coatbridge. Doubts lingered in her mind. *Could she* have been born there, in a place she'd barely heard of, or was it all a mistake? Never had any link with Coatbridge been mentioned.

She tried to picture the one who had carried her for nine months, whom she quite possibly resembled – or maybe not – the same person who hadn't wanted her, who had blithely cast her out, thrown her away. And what of the man Jessie had considered a sort of older brother, who had always been kind, but gave no inkling of their relationship? With a little effort, Charlie could have made a world of difference to her self-confidence. Knowledge would have been ammunition against the taunts she endured at school. Instead Maw told her she'd been created by '*a bad woman*' and some nameless man. That was why she was called a bastard.

What kind of people were they, those Barclays, whose conspiracy of silence let her believe she was a foundling? She'd felt like a stray kitten picked up off the street, while *they* knew full well that she was one of their own!

Conscious that Charlie could arrive at any second, Jessie hurried through the other items in the box, fumbling with every scrap of paper because the more she read, the more she *had to* read. She scanned the certificates documenting Isa's marriage to Charles Bartholomew, and the five children they had together. What caused her heart to race faster were the papers naming Peter Inglis as the father of several of Maw's offspring. To think the Barclay name had been pure invention! For four decades, Isa had lived a lie. There was no denying her breathtaking hypocrisy. The evidence was right there on the table. Maw, who condemned Bella Turner as '*a bad woman*', had herself borne five illegitimate children after being widowed, yet how smoothly, how cunningly she had spun her web of deceit!

Jessie felt sick. At the sound of footsteps by the front door, she bundled the pile of papers back into the box.

'Are you all right?' Charlie asked as he entered the kitchen. 'Why are you looking at me like that?'

She made no reply.

'For a minute there I thought you'd seen a ghost!' he ventured.

'The ghost o' my father, perhaps.'

He shivered.

'Were you ever goin' to tell me how I landed here? Or did you hope I wouldn't ask?'

'Och, Jessie, it was when you were an infant, and Maw must have explained ... I brought you to Broxburn, because I'd nowhere else to take you.'

His mouth had gone dry. If Ellen had come with him, Jessie would have been less ready to attack him. He wanted to head for the door, but there was no escaping the awful moment of truth.

'*Why* didn't you let on that you were my father? Wasn't I entitled to know where I came from?' Her voice was controlled, but inwardly she shook with anger.

Desperately he tried to avoid her gaze.

'It was best not spoken about. You had a family here, and Maw gave you a decent upbringing, didn't she? There was nothing wrong with that ... it was the best solution to a tough situation.' He stood with his arms folded defensively in front of him.

'You've no clue how important this is to me, have you? My history's a sham. I've been conned by everybody I trusted. You got them all to play dumb, since you *weren't man enough* to tell me about your caper with the landlady!'

'Come on, hen, it's been a terrible day for all of us. With what you've come through, it's no wonder you're overwrought. There was no intent to deceive you.'

He moved to put a hand on her shoulder but she shook him off in exasperation.

'No deceit, but no honesty either!'

'Don't, Jessie. You shouldn't say such things. You'll just regret it. You're not alone, there's a lot o' folk in your position. Some folk even claim the Queen's illegitimate!'

'Aye, but I'll bet she wasn't told her mother was *a bad woman!* For years, I imagined I'd been born to a *prostitute* and one of her clients.'

'*No! That's a lie!* Maw called her a bad woman, not me!'

'And Maw was a fine one to speak, wasn't she? I was an idiot to think *I* was the only bastard around here!'

Beneath the shadow of his dark stubble, a green-tinged pallor spread across Charlie's face. He wished he'd gone straight home and turned to leave, but Jessie sprang up and blocked his way.

'No you don't! You're going nowhere till we get it all out in the open, once and for all! I'll not let you make a fool of me again!'

He willed her to stop, wanted to be anywhere at that moment rather than be involved in this confrontation and stretched out a hand, hoping to placate her. 'Nobody wanted to make a fool of you. You have to believe me.'

'*Believe you*?' she retorted, shrinking away from him. 'That's a good one! Why don't you tell me about *Bella Turner*?'

He flinched at the mention of that name. 'There's nothing to tell ... I was a young laddie on my first job in a strange place, living in digs. Bella was a widow, a bonnie woman, with red hair like yours in fact.' He fell silent, embarrassed.

'And ...?' Jessie paused for him to continue.

'And nothing. That's it.'

'Surely there's more than that! Did you think of marrying her?'

'Och, Jessie, I had a fling with her nearly thirty years ago, that's all. She was lonely and so was I. She was older than me, already had seven weans, so how could I be expected to marry her? I brought you to Maw, because Bella couldn't keep you.'

'Did she not want me?'

'That didn't come into it. Whether she wanted to or not, she *couldn't* keep you ... you have to understand that. The best solution was to bring you to Broxburn, that's all I can say.'

He shuddered to remember that last morning in Sunnyside Road.

'Granted, I wasn't much o' a father to you, but I saw that you were cared for, had a roof above your head and food in your belly. If that wasn't enough, I'm sorry, but I did what I could.'

Jessie paused. 'So what came of her? Maw said that she had died ... or was that another fib?'

'I wish I could tell you, but I can't. She might still be in Coatbridge for all I know.' He sighed. 'Nobody meant things to happen as they did. I sowed some wild oats, that was all.'

She stared at him. 'I see,' she said frostily, and tossed Isa's envelope across the table in his direction. 'You should open this. Maw wrote it a few weeks back, wanted it kept till she was away.'

Cautiously Charlie picked up the letter, as if afraid it would bite him. A bemused expression spread over his face as he read its contents and then laid it down.

'If you had any doubts about bein' one o' us, this should change your mind,' he said. Without a word, he put on his cap and walked out, slamming the door behind him.

Isa's instructions, written just prior to her lapse into unconsciousness, left Jessie stunned. Late into the night she lingered in the kitchen, oblivious to the chill that descended once the fire went out, staring round the room without seeing. She felt swathed in a cool blanket of tranquillity. Seldom in her memory had the house been so empty. In this kitchen she had often experienced loneliness, as a solitary being among a noisy crowd who claimed a genuine connection to the place. Yet now there *was* no other living soul, and the chair she sat in, the bed she slept in – indeed all Isa possessed – was hers. For the first time, she knew the feeling of truly *belonging*.

In the aftermath of that day's revelations, she alternately fumed at Isa, then wept for her, the woman who had purposely misled her, the worst hypocrite and her best friend on earth. Eventually Jessie saw that she'd been given the kindest explanation for things beyond a child's comprehension. She would remain grateful to Isa, regardless of her sins. Poor Maw, how frequently had she said that worse things than a bairn could come to your door? With ten of her own, she made room for another. *Nobody* could have shown greater kindness or loved her better than Isa did. And despite failing to publicly acknowledge his paternity, Charlie had done well by her. Jessie's rage would forever focus on the one who had borne her. If Bella Turner cared, she would not have sent Charlie packing with his bastard, the outcast, while seven others were kept.

Toxic thoughts careered through Jessie's brain until she could stand it no more. She had to think of the future, not the past. She would not dwell on the despicable Bella Pattie. She would follow Davie's advice to forgive and forget, though there was precious little to forgive, since indifference amounted to less than nothing. The forgetting part would be easy. For as long as she lived, Jessie would not utter that woman's name.

It was with good reason that Maw described Bella Turner as *a bad woman.*

40
Finale

'The truth is rarely pure and never simple.' – Oscar Wilde

BRIDGETON, 1912

'JUST LET ME TALK to her for a few minutes, that's all I ask,' Bella begged, but the faceless person at the door refused to let her in. She stood shivering on the threshold, out in the cold. Inside the house, a warm fire burned in the hearth, and she sensed the girl was there. Distressed, she called Jessie's name out loud, into the silence of the kitchen.

'What's wrong, Mammy, are you all right?' Jeanie said loudly, coming to stand by the box bed.

Confused, blind and befuddled from sleep, Bella said, '*Jessie? Is that you?*'

So vivid was the dream that she imagined she'd found her lost child.

'You're getting mixed up. Come on, Mammy, it's Jeanie, you know my voice when you hear it.'

'Aye, of course,' lied Bella. 'I'm sorry.'

She would not admit that dreams and reality, like the past and the present, were so entangled that she could scarcely distinguish one from the other. Her early years remained clear, up till the gloom that descended in Coatbridge with Will's death ... then there was Charlie, though she could not envisage his face any more, just kept seeing a baby being carried off by a dark-haired young man who resembled Tam. She was in purgatory: the harder she tried to hack through the thicket of jumbled memories, the more bewildering it all became.

Kindly Jeanie patted the old woman's hand. 'Let me read you something from the paper. Everybody's talking about the *Titanic*, the ship that sank last week.'

The words 'iceberg ... the Atlantic ... few survivors ...' was all Bella made out. Yet odd snippets of the story struck a chord, and she pictured her older brother, Johnny, who had set sail for America. But surely that disaster took place a long time ago ... or did it? In her confusion, fragmented ideas popped into her head, like random pieces from a jigsaw. She no longer knew Jeanie or Aggie. They too were parts of the puzzle she could not link together into a coherent pattern.

'I wonder what's disturbing her so much, making her cry out for strangers?' Jeanie whispered to Aggie.

No response came.

Bella had never revealed what happened when Charlie departed with the baby. Aggie had her suspicions, but the secret would stay buried in the dark labyrinths of her mother's mind.

* * * * *

BROXBURN

Less than forty miles from Bridgeton, Jessie had also read of the sinking of the *Titanic*, but she was beset by other woes. With the disclosure of Isa's letter, a coolness had crept into her relationship with certain family members. Far from being thankful for the loving care Isa received from Jessie, they seemed aggrieved. They felt they'd been cheated out of what was properly theirs, found it incomprehensible that their Maw had named *Jessie* as her sole beneficiary. It was bad that the cuckoo in the nest had enjoyed greater comforts than they had known as children, but now she was to inherit everything, would walk off with all of their mother's worldly possessions! Not that there was much, apart from a few nice mementos, and the small leather pouch of gold sovereigns Isa had managed to collect ... but nevertheless they grumbled among themselves that Jessie had pulled a fast one. Many hands reach forth after a death.

'It annoyed them that I regarded Isa as my Maw, when in a way *they* were closer to her,' she confided to Davie.

'Not close enough to devote much time to her, though. They were happy to let you take the heavy end of things!'

'Well, they had their own problems, I suppose. I was still living at home. It was natural I'd nurse her.'

'*Natural*? Apart from Charlie and young Peter, none of them looked near, how natural was that? She maybe didn't say it, but your Maw noticed how *you* stood by her and Peter, when they were ill. You earned all you got,' Davie reassured her. 'Pay no attention to them. We've got better things to think about, like our wedding!'

Jessie smiled and nodded. 'Aye, I suppose you're right – as usual!'

He laughed.

* * * * *

When the twenty-sixth of April arrived, few of Isa's offspring attended Jessie and Davie's marriage ceremony. Charlie's daughter, Isabella, was bridesmaid and Peter Barclay was the best man. At the wedding in the house at Church Street, barely a dozen people stood huddled as the minister spoke, Charlie and Ellen among them.

Uncomfortable in his suit and shiny dress shoes that pinched his toes, Charlie allowed himself to remember Bella and their brief spell together. That episode in Coatbridge would eternally shine as one of the highlights of his youth, his first taste of the autonomy to do as he chose, not as Maw dictated. Perhaps he should have married Bella ... they could have made a go of things. Maw had been dead set against her, because she and Bella were two of a kind ... strong women struck by tragedy, who did what they had to. They held their families together, and survived.

268

Similar they might have been, but for Charlie, Bella possessed an extra something. In her he saw a rare, exotic element that would constantly keep her alive in his dreams. Occasionally he even imagined it was not Ellen, but Bella beside him in bed at night, a thought that could still excite him. Never could he articulate the feelings only Bella had aroused in him ... he cherished his memories of her, guarding them as his private retreat from the harshness of the daily grind.

In a sense, he had failed Jessie, had been remiss in not praising Bella's courage and resourcefulness, her steely determination and willingness to tackle whatever needed done. He ought to have described her quick-wittedness, her nimble fingers that could magically transform a drab length of cloth into a gown fit for a queen, and how she laughed. But he'd blown his chance and now it was too late. Bella had a sparkle that defied definition, and would always occupy a unique place in his heart. She had been a *fine* woman, his first and best love.

His thoughts were far away when it came to the signing of the register. The minister requested the names of the bride's parents, and no one spoke. Staring across at Charlie, Jessie cocked one challenging eyebrow. On this of all days, she would not sully her lips by naming the '*bad woman*' as Maw had so aptly called her. Instead, with a tight little smile, Jessie gracefully extended a hand, palm upwards, towards the man who had fathered her, inviting him to speak. It was high time Charlie owned up publicly to what he'd got off with for over a quarter century.

Taken unawares, Charlie coughed and straightened up. 'Oh! Sorry, aye. I'm the bride's father, Charles Bartholomew ... and her mother was Isabella.'

The minister dipped his nib in a pot of ink, and bent his head to write. And as he wrote, with the most painstaking, meticulous precision imaginable, he muttered slowly and deliberately, 'Mother ... was ... Isabella ... Bartholomew.'

Charlie gave a slight start, curbing his impulse to speak up, to correct the error. But what did it matter? In any case, this sounded better! Gradually his breathing steadied. After this, they'd all be ready for a nip of whisky from the bottle that sat over on the sideboard. The hard part was done. Bella's name need not again be lifted. He could relax ...

... Or so he believed, till the minister asked, 'And the mother's maiden surname?'

Jessie closed her mouth in a determined line.

It was Charlie's call.

He struggled but his memory had gone blank. What *on earth* had been Bella's own name? And did anybody care, for goodness' sake? It was all ancient history, nobody's business!

'Och, now, give me a minute,' he stuttered.

He sighed and stroked his chin. For a few embarrassing seconds that felt like hours, with all eyes upon him, he stood thinking. *Of course* he'd heard Bella's own name – he'd watched her sign it on Jessie's birth certificate! As a last resort he mutely recited the alphabet, getting less than half-way through before giving up. It was hopeless. Bella's surname eluded him completely. All he could remember was *Turner*. He'd known her initially as 'Mrs Turner'.

'Eh, her maiden surname was Turner. She was Isabella Turner.'

Well ... what difference would it make?

As the minister began to write, Charlie winked at Jessie.

She glanced at Davie, and they smiled to each other.

* * * * *

After his mother's death, King Edward VII destroyed as many incriminating letters, statues and memorials relating to John Brown or the Munshi as he could lay hands on. In the grounds of Balmoral Castle, there still stands a statue of John Brown and a house called 'Karim Cottage'. No one knows how much was paid to silence the blackmailer, but Queen Victoria will forever be remembered as a paragon of moral rectitude.

Jessie and Davie were blessed with two daughters. True to her word, Jessie would reveal no detail to them about Bella, except that she had been *'a bad woman'*. Of Isa, only kind words were spoken. She was extolled as a model of saintliness and goodness. Peter Inglis was excised from the record. The myth was passed down through generations and stood unchallenged for a century.

Queen or commoner, good or bad: history plasters over the cracks between fact and fiction, but nothing is ever as it seems.

ACKNOWLEDGEMENTS

Sources of historical and genealogical information relied on while writing this book include:

Lytton Strachey (1921) *Queen Victoria*.

www.scotlandspeople.gov.uk.

www.buittle-and-kelton-churches.org.uk.

www.scottishmining.co.uk.

For their encouragement and advice I would like to thank Leela Tsai, Barbara Golland, Ligia Arias, Naida Forbes, Isabel Soffer and Ian Lisk. A special mention goes to the late Irene Lisk for her insightful editorial comments.

I owe a particular debt of gratitude to the entire editing, design and publishing team at Kinord Books, without whom this project would not have seen the light of day.

Elinor Hunter's latest novel
from Kinord Books:

Sharpster

It's the swinging sixties, and Kelton MacLeod is on a year's scholarship at Aberdeen University. When local girl Carol falls for his easy American charm, she abandons family, friends and her fiancé to run off with Kelton to St Louis, Missouri.

Smooth as silk, slippery as soap, he is driven by boundless ambition. But too late, Carol discovers she has sacrificed everything for a psychopathic womaniser. Astounding business acumen propels Kelton's career in corporate pharmaceuticals, while his lies and manipulation make him the husband – and the boss – from hell.

Yet what goes around comes around … so will the long memories of all those he has wronged prove to be his undoing?

www.kinordbooks.com

Also from Kinord Books:

Taran's Wheel by Jim Forbes
(*Incomers*: Book 1)

What has become of the ancient talisman known as *Taran's Wheel*? A riddle from beyond the grave sets Delia on a hunt. Her search, which takes her from Chicago to the 'Pleasant Vale' of Cromar in Scotland, reveals the dramatic story of the Vale and its people.

But can this story lead Delia to Taran's Wheel, or will sinister forces deny her the prize, even threaten her life?

Scotch and Water by Jim Forbes
(*Incomers*: Book 2)

The 2014 referendum is history, but it's a time of drama for Edinburgh and the ancient land of Lothian.

A metal detector hobbyist is murdered just as he strikes gold. The discovery of cryptic writings sheds new light on a celebrated 19th-century Edinburgh family. A ruthless businesswoman exploits council corruption. Controversially, huge volumes of water are to be pumped to southern England. A violent ultra-nationalist cell plots mayhem in the wake of Scotland's 'no' to independence.

Like *scotch and water*, these apparently unconnected goings-on make a potent mix: a web of political, criminal and terrorist intrigue linked to a mysterious relic of some of Lothian's earliest incomers.

www.kinordbooks.com